# Praise for *Two Cabins, One Lake*

Marlow writes an amazing story filled with hilarious and interesting characters, creative vengeance, and deliciously dirty scenes.

—Arec, Rainy Thursdays

This is definitely going in my "favorites" and "books I'll read again" shelves.

—Ginger Snaps, The Spank and Ginger Show

[Shaye] is witty, hilarious and knows how to write revenge...or foreplay, however you want to see it. ;)

—Carla, Celebrity Readers

I absolutely loved this book. Shaye told the story so well, I felt like I had transported to Alaska.

—Nan Marie Costner

Good freakin lord Shaye has a gift. Her language, her flow, her expressive illustrious filthy descriptions of hot carnal sex???! She's fucking gifted!!!!

—Lindsay Holland

This is the best book I have read in a long time. It's funny, serious, heart stopping, aggravating, suspenseful, and most of all sexy. There are no low points in this one.

—Sandy Madden

The whole book was absolutely amazing and the only reason why I can't quite decide whether to rate it with 4 or 5 stars is that I loved the second one in the series even more!

—Edith Salfinger

# Also by Shaye Marlow

**Alaskan Romance**
TWO CABINS, ONE LAKE
TWO CAPTAINS, ONE CHAIR
TWO BRUTES, ONE BARISTA
TWO CRAZY, ONE WILD

**Erotic Sci-fi**
EROTIC ADVENTURES OF AN ALIEN CAPTIVE
DREAMER AWAKENED

**Firefighters**
SERVICED BY FIREFIGHTERS
SHARED BY FIREFIGHTERS
SANDWICHED BY FIREFIGHTERS
SPANKED BY FIREFIGHTERS

# Two Cabins,
# **One Lake**

Shaye Marlow

# Two Cabins, One Lake
## Shaye Marlow

# Acknowledgements

Thank you to my sister, for being one of those precious few who doesn't give a damn what other people think, and for teaching me about persistence.

# Chapter One

'S he came.' No, I'd used that one about a thousand times already. 'Exploded' and 'climaxed' were out. 'Orgasmed' was too clinical. 'Peaked'? No, too soft-core vague. I needed something fresh, something new, something crazy-hot.

I was drawing a blank. There probably wasn't just one word for what I needed. Okay, so what about a simile or metaphor? 'Rapid decompression'? Too technical. 'A million fiery shards of pleasure lanced at her innards'… The phrase failed the wince-test, so, no; too painful.

'The earth shook.'

For a wistful moment, I thought I might actually be having an orgasm, because damned if the earth wasn't shaking. Wait, that was my chair.

I finally surfaced enough from my word processor to remember that earthquakes were the most common cause of shaking in Alaska. So I did what any good Alaskan would do: I sat, and waited to see if it was going to get bigger.

My pots and pans were rattling on the rack over my kitchen sink when I realized this 'earthquake' was accompanied by a thrumming, pounding roar. Or was that in my ears? *Hell, maybe I am having an orgasm. I'd been enjoying that scene, but…*

But then the noise and vibrations reached their peak and a helicopter came into view, having flown directly over my cabin. I leaned forward, watching out my picture window as the helicopter crossed the lake. It set down on my neighbor's front lawn, a couple hundred feet down the shore from mine.

Three people stepped out onto the grass, and then the helicopter lifted back into the sky. The wind of its passage rippled the glassy water, and as it roared by overhead, my pots rattled again. The people disappeared into the cabin.

When they came back out, I indulged my burning curiosity, and engaged my binoculars. I'd purchased this set for birdwatching, but as I looked through them, I confirmed they worked just as well on potential new neighbors. The three men looked innocuous enough—no hunchbacks or scissor-hands, at least—and I wondered if one of them was the new owner.

Or was my new neighbor the helicopter pilot? It hadn't looked like any flight-service aircraft that I was familiar with. Besides, who would pay to charter a helicopter at over a thousand dollars an hour, when a float plane was infinitely cheaper and could carry more?

No sooner had I finished that thought, than a plane on floats dropped below the treetops on final approach. The DeHavilland Beaver *was* sporting familiar flight-service colors, I saw as it skimmed across the water, kicking up waves until it settled into a slow glide. It drifted up to the neighbor's dock, and the pilot unloaded five passengers. And then, a bunch of stuff. Boxes, a cooler, a barbecue.

Four of the guys began carrying things up to the cabin as a fifth helped the pilot get the Beaver turned around. The pilot gunned it, and with an ear-splitting roar, the float plane charged across the lake. It lifted up out of the water, and then the aluminum contraption was thrumming away over the trees.

I frowned. That was eight people now. What was this, one of those families that had as many children as possible because each one meant another permanent fund dividend? The permanent fund dividend was an annual oil royalty payment that each resident in Alaska received, usually one to two thousand dollars. There were reports of homesteading families with over a dozen children for this reason, some of them very much resembling the Craster's Keep situation from Game of Thrones.

But, I confirmed with my binoculars, none of these were children. They looked to be all in their twenties and thirties, clean, well-dressed types. I watched them crack open the cooler and start passing around beers. After their initial flurry of movement, they just milled and drank, and I lost interest in spying on them. I had misgivings about the mass consumption of alcohol on my little lake, but watching them do it wouldn't change anything.

The fact was, I needed to write. I had a deadline for the juicy little story I was working on, and that deadline was tomorrow. I'd gotten started on it first thing this morning, and was hoping to get it done—or at least very close to done—by evening, so I could go to the neighborhood Fourth of July party.

Not that this was much of a traditional 'neighborhood'. There were no roads to speak of, the main thoroughfare being the Kuskana River, and my next closest 'neighbor' was a mile downstream.

A flash of orange next door caught my eye. Flames leapt three feet up out of the grill, and a couple guys were laughing and patting each other on the back.

*Aha!* 'Her nerve endings flared like they'd been drenched in lighter fluid.' 'Douched' with lighter fluid? No, bad. I fiddled with it a bit, and continued on with my scene. My sexy, ladies-first hero had his head buried between my main char's milky thighs, and he kept her fire burning for several decadent sentences.

I was just getting back into the flow of things when my pots announced the helicopter's return. Three more people jumped out onto the grass, and the helicopter took off and thundered overhead. Again.

I was starting to get a little annoyed. One would think, if you owned an aircraft that loud, you'd have the common courtesy not to fly directly over a building. In fact, I was pretty sure there were regulations to that effect.

The body count next door was up to eleven, and I picked my binoculars back up to see if I could figure out what was going on over there. As I gazed through my high-powered lenses at the people, and the beer, and the barbecue, I finally put it together. It was a party. Housewarming slash Fourth of July *party.*

Having solved the riddle didn't make the activity next door any less distracting. For the first time ever, I considered turning my writing desk away from the window. It was sunny and already getting hot, even a little bit before noon. Seeing bare male chests begin to emerge from beneath their shirts finally decided me. There was no way I could write with *that* as my view.

It was as I was turning my desk that the Beaver touched down again. Another five people emptied out onto the dock, along with another load of boxes and a big flat-screen TV. Same drill; to the cabin with the stuff, to the beer with the people.

I stared blankly at my screen for a few minutes, and decided I'd break for lunch. The plan was to eat, and hopefully my new neighbor would complete his friend-ferrying, and then I could write.

One of the things I loved most about living in the Alaskan bush was the quiet. I slept with my window open at night, listening to the sunset birdsong, the breeze rustling the leaves, the gentle lapping of the lake twenty feet below my window. There were no highway sounds, no neighbor dogs barking, no train crossings or lawn mowers or kids shrieking with glee.

There was just me, and the wilderness.

And now, apparently, there was my neighbor and his couple dozen friends, whom he continued to ferry, all afternoon. The helicopter flew in—*whomp whomp whomp*—and out, and in—*whomp whomp whomp*—and out, about a dozen times over the course of the day. With each new trip, he brought a handful more people.

So, as the summer sun meandered its way across the sky, the noise level got higher and higher. The sounds carried with crystalline clarity across the water—the *boom boom boom* of a quality speaker emitting heavy bass, the drunken laughter and shrieks as people splashed in the lake.

I stuttered through another couple hundred words—trash, all of it. In frustration, I went and sat on my deck, wondering if I should just go to my own Fourth of July party instead of being tormented by my neighbor's.

But how could I enjoy myself, with three thousand words hanging over my head? Three thousand words, and only the rest of tonight and two to three hours tomorrow to do it in. And that wasn't counting editing. No, I couldn't go.

As the evening wore into a deeper, louder evening, and I still couldn't concentrate, I contemplated the merits of shooting my neighbor. On the one hand, there'd be no more loud, drunken parties. On the other, I'd have to dispose of the body—dumping it in the river would probably be my best bet. That would likely be easy enough, but I was pretty sure my new neighbor was the helicopter pilot, so shooting him would mean I'd be stuck with his friends thrashing through my woods for the next day or so, looking for food or phone. And *that* was unacceptable, because I was absolutely sure the first thing they'd blunder through with their ignorant city feet was my blueberry patch.

I also thought, briefly, about going over to join them. It would be the neighborly thing to do—uncork the Baileys that'd been sitting in my pantry, and go introduce myself. I knew if I was drinking with them, I wouldn't mind their debauchery quite so much.

But the idea was repugnant to me. I was an introvert, and I was already half-way to spitting mad. I knew if I went over there, the first thing out of my mouth wouldn't be a Pleasantville "Hey neighbor, welcome to the neighborhood!", but rather a "Shut the fuck up, you inconsiderate asshole Outsider!"

Okay, and maybe I was PMSing just a wee bit.

I'd owned this land since I was seventeen. I built the cabin with my own two hands and the help of my brothers when I was twenty-one, and I'd been living here full-time ever since.

The cabin across the lake had been there before I ever built mine, but it had been owned by an elderly couple who only ever came out on the weekends, and then rarely. For the last four years, it'd basically been just me on my quiet, peaceful lake.

And now?

*Whomp whomp whomp.*

I watched as the shiny red fucking thing—I don't know a damn thing about helicopters, other than that they are expensive, and some of them moonlight as ambulances—landed for the umpteenth time that day.

This time, the pilot cut the engine. The doors swung open before the blades had even slowed, and another group of people belched out onto the once-carefully-manicured grass. I watched closely, trying to get a lock on my miserable neighbor—surely karma had made him a tiny, bald, pock-marked, pot-bellied lump of a man—but he must have exited the other side and quickly blended into the crowd. Watching so many people having so much fun while my writing suffered was only making me angry, so I slammed my way back inside. I breathed deep of the lingering plywood smell in my cabin's interior, and willed myself to calm down. Now that the helicopter was done, I'd take a few minutes, eat dinner, and then see if I could finish up my story.

I had lights, compliments of a generator and a small battery bank, so I turned them on. Compliments of a well, I had running water, so I ran some into a double boiler steamer and started dinner. I wasn't some Julia Child out in the woods, whipping up delicate French confections, but I had had a recent shipment of fresh vegetables, so I steamed some broccoli, and as it was steaming, I decided it would be even better with cheese melted over it. Because everything is better with cheese. *Life* is better with cheese.

It was as I was watching said cheddar melt that I began to hear the *boom boom boom* of those speakers from inside my cabin. My nails dug into my hand-planed birch countertops as I restrained myself. I didn't know what I'd do if I gave myself free rein, but I knew my retaliations tended toward poetic justice. So it'd be loud, and probably disturbing.

I alternated bites of broccoli with some long, slow breaths. I finished my meal, washed the dishes—which was not a natural inclination of mine, but I'd learned the hard way to keep things clean and put away so as not to attract bears—and I went back to my desk.

I stared at that cursor for over half an hour. The noise was still a problem, but even more than that, now, was my mood. A good word for me right at that moment would have been 'incensed'. And an expression? 'Fit to be tied' seemed accurate. Not nearly in the right frame of mind for generating pillow talk.

The blaring gaiety next door seemed to be reaching its peak, and I finally abandoned my laptop to see what shenanigans could possibly require such a decibel level.

I didn't see the answer to my question.

What I *did* see was two drunken assholes carrying my lightweight Kevlar canoe toward the water. The last time I'd let someone borrow my canoe, it had come back decorated with bullet holes, after I dredged it from the lake. And those guys hadn't even been drunk. Of course, 'those guys' had been my brothers, and they were in a category all their own.

"Ah, *hell* no." I ran back through the house, shoved my bare feet into a pair of boots, and clomped down the front steps. I flew across my little yard and down the three steps to the rocky beach. The light was dying outside as I ran up to the two men. They were just starting to shove the canoe into the water before climbing in.

"Stop!" I bellowed.

They jumped a bit and looked up with big, sloppy-drunk smiles on their faces. "What's up, pretty girl?" one of them slurred.

"That is *my* canoe, and I do *not* give you permission to use it," I said, stopping a few feet away with my hands on my hips. I was going to give intimidation a try before I got into an all-out tug-of-war with them. Two men against one woman, with my precious canoe as the rope—yeah, I didn't like them odds.

One of them—he had floppy blonde hair, and looked and sounded suspiciously like a surfer—glanced at the tree line, and then back at me. "It was on Gary's property," he said.

*So* that's *the Devil's name. Gary.* I turned it over in my mind, villainizing it.

"No," I said, drawing out the word, "it was on *my* property. See that tree over there? The one with the orange tape on it? That's the edge of *Gary's* property. So I'd appreciate it if you'd leave *my* canoe, which you found on *my* property, alone."

They looked a little stunned by my vehemence. Or maybe it was the alcohol—one lifted a fifth of whiskey and took a long chug as I watched. A hundred dollars said that bottle would either be left in my canoe, or at the bottom of the lake. Or—

I winced as it slipped from the blonde idiot's grasp and shattered on the rocky shore. "Whoops," he said with a chuckle.

"All right, no need to get upset," the darker one said. "You wanna come party with us, pretty girl?"

What I wanted was to beat the hell out of the blonde for littering on my beach, and then smite the brunette for calling me 'girl', when he looked barely old enough to drink. "No," I gritted, "I really don't. Now unhand my canoe, and get off my beach. And tell *Gary* to turn it down." I was proud of all the spots in those sentences I'd managed to omit the F-bomb.

They laughed—which didn't sound like consent—but then turned their sloppy-drunk selves around to wander back in the direction of my evil neighbor's cabin. They shot glances back at me as they walked and laughed, leaving me with an almost-launched canoe and a beach full of broken glass.

I grimaced as I felt my emotions tip toward self-consciousness. I cleaned up okay, but as a general rule, I wore whatever I wanted when I was at my cabin, the more comfortable the better. Today I was wearing a baggy, tie-dyed T-shirt without a bra, and fleece pajama pants dotted with purple hearts, the ragged hems of which gathered over my mud-stained leather boots. I wasn't a fashionista by any means, but I was aware enough to know my clothing couldn't have been less in style, or clashed harder, if I'd been trying.

As for the rest of me: My long blonde hair—undyed, un-highlighted, and most recently trimmed by yours truly—was up in a messy ponytail, and I had no makeup or jewelry on, not that I usually wore any. My nails were short, un-manicured, and unpainted, on fingers that no one would call graceful; damaged by water, burned by fishing lines, and ripped by hooks.

Of course, in the Alaskan bush, style didn't matter. The goal was simple functionality. Keep it covered, keep it warm, keep it dry. The old folks next door—even my neighbors downriver—hadn't made me feel self-conscious a day in my life. They understood the score. But these young dicks? They had no clue.

Cussing them for making me feel awkward, I pushed the canoe the rest of the way out into the water, and then pulled it along the shore toward my cabin. There, I walked out onto my little dock and looped the bow line around a mooring cleat.

When I straightened to cast one last glance at the neighbor's partying cabin—every light in the house was on, and judging by the off-key howling, I suspected someone had hooked up a karaoke machine—I saw the would-be canoe thieves talking to someone on the lawn. They turned and pointed at me.

I returned their regard across the couple hundred feet of water separating them from my ire. I couldn't see much in the way of detail, but everything female in me acknowledged that the third man was beautifully shaped. Besides being terminally drunk and stupid, the first two hadn't been bad-looking, but this one...

He was tall, with broad shoulders and an athletic, narrow waist perfectly complemented by jeans and a green T-shirt. He had black hair that ate the light, and a wide stance that said 'I own this land'.

My girly parts stood up and took notice. But every other part of me—and they definitely had the majority—really, really wanted to slap him.

That Devil personified had to be the infamous Gary, and if that was the case, I may as well go drown myself in the tub now. I turned around before my lady bits got any more excited, and climbed back up to my cabin.

I didn't want a hot fucking neighbor. Or a fucking hot neighbor, or fucking a hot neighbor. I didn't want it any which way. I didn't want or need a distraction, particularly in the form of a *man*.

What I *wanted* was a sweet old couple who called more than they visited, and were quiet as church mice when they did appear. What I *needed* was to write.

It was already past my bedtime, and I had to get up early in the morning. Luckily, I had earplugs. I'd just sleep with them in. They couldn't possibly keep this up more than a night or two.

Clinging to that thought, I let my dog, Mocha, in for the night and brushed my teeth. I climbed up into the loft, flopped down onto the queen-sized mattress lying on my unfinished plywood floor, and drifted into a fitful sleep.

I don't know how long I slept before I was awoken by a *boom* heard even through my ear plugs. I shot upright, blinking in the darkness as a loud crackling was followed by another explosive *boom*.

Were they *shooting*?

Groggily, I dragged myself out of bed. I stumbled down the ladder and burst out onto the deck.

This being the Land of the Midnight Sun, the sky was a dim blue even in the dead of night. Every light was on next door, rippling and reflecting across the surface of the dark water. Most of the drunken revelers were on the lawn looking up, while a couple hunkered down.

There was a high-pitched whistle, and then ker*blam*! The firework exploded overhead, sending a shower of golden sparks over the lake.

For a moment, just the barest moment as all those little golden lights reflected off the lake, I didn't mind having been woken up. For that tiny, perfect sliver of time, as I watched all those little lights sparkle and begin to fall to earth, I didn't even mind that I had a neighbor. As long as he brought sparkly things.

Then the next one went off in the trees halfway between our two cabins.

And a tiny flame licked to life.

My whole chest clenched with sudden terror. Fires were a huge problem in Alaska in the summer. They caught in dry grasses and leaves and brush and ate hundreds of thousands of acres of forest every year. Lightning was the number one culprit, followed by campfires and *fireworks*. I'd loved the cool shadows of the old, gnarled trees around my cabin, so I had made a conscious decision not to cut a firebreak around it.

And now, there was a flame in my side yard, growing into a small fire.

"Fire!" I yelled across the lake. Shouts rang out across the water as I dashed back through my sliding door. I stomped into my shitkickers and hurtled the three steps to the ground. From my generator shack, I grabbed two shovels and a stack of five-gallon buckets. Then I vaulted down to the shore, and ran along it as fast as my legs would take me.

Distantly I acknowledged my polar fleece pants weren't the best to wear into this kind of work—synthetics tended to melt onto the skin. But at the moment, I was weighing my cabin against my hide... and my cabin was winning.

A group of people met me along the lake shore, not far from the broken glass. Without a word, the green-shirted bastard took one of my shovels, and handed the buckets off to his friends. Then he was off through the woods, taking the slope up from the lake as though it were nothing. I was right on his heels, headed grimly toward the brightening glow, grateful for his help but absolutely determined that this would not be a bonding experience.

*Not no, but hell no,* I thought, realizing the spot he'd set on fire was my blueberry patch. Now, to someone from the Lower 48, this might not sound like much. Someone from the Lower 48 might even be thinking, 'what's the big deal, just grow some more'. But that wasn't an option.

These were wild Alaskan blueberries, blueberries so wild and so Alaskan, some of them weren't even technically blueberries. They were better, darker, more flavorful, and yet more elusive, defying every attempt to cultivate and farm them. They'd been growing in that spot when I bought the land, and over the years, I'd managed to encourage their growth. Every year my beloved blueberry patch grew just a bit larger, and every fall, I enjoyed rich, tart blueberry pies and muffins.

And now? They were on fire. My neighbor had set my blueberries on fire.

Thank God the fire was still relatively small—less than a dozen feet across. I ducked low to avoid the billowing smoke as I beat at the flaming forest floor with the flat of my shovel. I cringed with each delicate blueberry branch I stomped on, each blackened, charred stem that caught at my pants. My eyes teared up, and my throat grew tight, and I knew it was from more than just the smoke.

One of the Devil's minions splashed water on the fire ahead of me, and I jumped over the plume of steam to attack the other side. I continued slapping out the flames, vaguely seeing the shape of my nemesis beating and stomping on the other side of my blueberry patch. My lips curled into a snarl, and again, I was grateful—but at the same time, I wanted to kick his ass.

Trying to steal my canoe? Littering on my beach? Small potatoes compared to burning down my blueberries.

To keep from flinging myself across my dead bushes to show him the broad side of my shovel, I focused on my work. My arms ached, and I felt sweat running down my spine from the heat and terror and exercise. I coughed as another couple buckets of water sprayed out across the blackened patch.

We were winning. I didn't realize it, though, until a green shirt materialized directly ahead of me, breaking me out of my blueberry-bereft daze. He was hard to see in the smoke and the dark, but my stupid girl-senses seemed able to recognize him even when blinded by darkness and tears. Unwilling even to look at him, I veered aside to make sure the fire was entirely out.

A few minutes later, after splashing a last couple buckets onto the charred and steaming ground myself, I stumbled back out of the woods.

I'd been self-conscious earlier. Now, picture me in the same clothes, but covered with dirt and soot and reeking of smoke. My hair had come mostly down, and I'd singed a couple pretty good-sized hanks of it. I had a bucket in one hand, and a shovel in the other, and my eyes were full of crazy.

My furious gaze found my neighbor. I threw the shovel down—the temptation to hit him with it was too great—and made a beeline for the bastard in the green shirt.

"Gary?" I demanded.

He turned toward me. He had thick black hair, rugged good looks, and a nose that looked like it'd been punched one too many times—but not nearly enough. The low light worshiped the strong planes of his face, particularly that stupid, pussy-liquefying dent in his chin. *Damn him.*

"Yeah?" the Devil said.

I slammed the bucket against his chest, making him stumble back a step. "What the *fuck*?"

He grabbed the bucket, preventing me from repeating the move. "It was an accident," he said.

"It was *carelessness* and *stupidity*," I spat. "I've been living here four years, and do you know how many times I've set the woods on fire?" I slapped the bucket from between us, making it bounce across the rocks with a satisfying clatter, and I stabbed my finger into his chest. Which was very firm, I was very irritated to notice. But nothing could stop me from my tirade. Not even his gorgeous green eyes, which I spent a moment too long noticing were very, very green. Beer bottle green.

Deep breath. *Back on track.*

"Zero. None. That fire could have spread and taken both our cabins. Hell, it would have probably killed me in my sleep if I hadn't woken up when I did. I would have been *burned alive.*" I glared up at him, panting with wrath.

"It's the Fourth of July," he said. "We had fireworks. That's what *normal* people do," he said, running a judging gaze from my wild, knotted hair down my stained, shapeless T-shirt to my ridiculous night pants and my scarred, muddy boots, "on the Fourth of July."

*I bet he'd just be* shocked *if I showed him my granny panties. Not. Stupid man.*

"'Normal people' aren't the most annoying bastards I've ever met," I said. "'Normal people' don't buzz a person's cabin two dozen times in one day, or play music loud enough to be heard miles away in the middle of the fucking night, or let their drunk, stupid friends try to steal someone else's canoe, and then leave broken glass all over the beach. I wonder—when you leave in a couple days, how many beer cans will I find on the bottom of the lake?"

He hooked his thumbs in his belt loops and rocked back on his heels, looking way too unfazed by my yelling. "Actually," he said, "I'll be here all summer." He said it with a lazy grin that made me want to slap him all over again. I could practically feel that dark stubble burning my palm. And why did that thought bring a stab of lust along with it?

But pure, unadulterated horror quickly followed, and I groaned. All summer? I had a couple *months* of this to look forward to? I had a half-dozen more deadlines, which had seemed barely manageable with full-time fish guiding and then my brothers' visit here in a couple weeks. But with a human noisemaker right next door, constantly interrupting my train of thought?

*Impossible.* I started to hyperventilate.

"Your name's Helly, right?" he said. "The previous owners told me about you. I was wondering how someone got a name like Helly, but," he looked me up and down, "I think I've figured it out."

Aaand, the fucker had just called me an angry hoyden.

My anger was red-lining. I knew my limits. Another minute of this, and I'd either have a stroke, or I'd hurt somebody.

I took the third option, and stomped back to my cabin.

# Chapter Two

M y alarm went off two hours later. As I lay there, blinking into the bluish glow of predawn coming through the window, my desire to hurt somebody was strong as ever. *Ah, who was I kidding?* 'Somebody'? I knew exactly who I wanted to hurt.

My head ached, my eyes felt like they were being gouged with steak knives, and I wanted nothing more than to roll over and go back to sleep. But I couldn't. I had a job.

So I rolled the other direction, my feet met the cool floor, and I climbed out of bed. I managed not to die on my way down the ladder from my loft, and I lumbered into the bathroom with eyes only half-open and the rest of my vision obscured by hair.

My bathroom was minimalist, the fixtures basic and functional. The décor consisted of mismatched Amazon purchases—a theme repeated in the rest of my humble abode—in bright, clashing colors.

I didn't bother turning on a light. My eyes, and my throbbing head, couldn't handle the glare of a lightbulb at this juncture in time.

I made the mistake of glancing at myself in the mirror before I climbed into the shower. I didn't know why it always seemed to work this way, but seeing the misery on my face made it real. I had dark circles under my eyes, distinguishable even beneath the soot smears, and what looked like a semi-permanent crease carved between my brows. The whites of my eyes were reddened from smoke and tears, making my blue irises look almost green.

I made a face at myself, and then showered and dressed in what I liked to call Fisherwoman Chic. I had the brand names that seemed to make my customers happy, the water-resistant synthetic materials with the newest vents and snaps and zippers. I honestly only wore them because my clients took me a little more seriously when I showed up and introduced myself as their fishing guide for the day. Men usually didn't like taking advice from a woman, especially a young blonde, but if I tied my hair back in a severe braid and wore the uniform, it seemed to help.

I had breakfast, fed the dog, packed a lunch, and poured a healthy dose of coffee in my biggest mug; this morning I wished it was gallon-sized, but I was already making plans to finagle a refill at the lodge. I let Mocha out as I stepped out the front door. From a rack on the side of my cabin, I gathered up a huge tackle box and two handfuls of rods strapped neatly together. These, I fastened to my four-wheeler.

It was five in the morning at this point, and the sky was lightening toward dawn, though everything still had a dusky cast. All was silent and still; even the neighbor's cabin, where tents had sprung up like pimples across the yard. A light fog hung over the lake, and droplets of dew wet the toes of my hip waders. I let the moment stretch out, enjoying what I considered the last moments of peace before my hectic day began.

Then I fired up the four-wheeler.

My commute consisted of driving almost a mile through a birch and spruce forest to the main river. I did this on a dirt trail that'd been carved by time and multiple passings of my tires. I motored along at a sedate speed, unwilling to tangle my lines or spill my coffee.

Mocha ran ahead like she always did, sniffing out points of interest amongst the high-bush cranberry and devil's club. She was a husky-mix mutt that moved like a ghost in the near-darkness, disappearing into the woods ahead of me just to streak up from behind moments later. She was a good bear dog, always letting me know with a bone-chilling growl when a threat was near.

Bears and moose were always a possibility, especially since they were at their most active at dawn and dusk. For the most part, the large animals we shared the woods with would turn and run the other direction when they heard someone coming. But there were always the exceptions, the protective mamas, the surprise encounters. Bears and moose could kill people, mauling them or stomping them all to hell. It didn't happen often, but it *did* happen, and I wasn't willing for it to happen to me.

So I carried a shotgun, loaded with slugs, wherever I went.

This morning, I made it to the river, and my boat, without shooting anything. I kept my Sea Ark river boat pulled up to the beach in a slough, a slower tributary of the Kuskana River. This placement kept it from being hit and dragged downstream by passing logs or chunks of ice. As a bonus, it was a little harder to see by people passing on the main river, so my boat went mostly unmolested.

The population of the river, the couple dozen year-round residents, were an honest lot that would never touch my boat. Hell, if it were only them present, I could probably leave my shotgun in the boat, and it would be there every morning till the end of time. But in the summer, the population of our little river ballooned with tourists and fishermen, and *they*, well… they were known to do stupid, often illegal things.

I parked my four-wheeler next to the trailhead, and loaded in my tackle, rods, gas, and shotgun.

Mocha sat on the shore as I pushed off and started my outboard jet. She watched, unperturbed, as I started to motor away. Sometimes she waited for me there, but usually she didn't, instead choosing to roam and explore until she met me back at the cabin later that evening. She was an independent dog; she hung out with me when it pleased her, and she went where she wanted when it didn't.

I got my last glimpse of her as I rounded the corner into faster, siltier water. I turned right, nosing my boat upstream, and throttled the engine. The roar of the outboard filled my ears, shattering the relative quiet of the misty river. The damp and wind buffeted me as I skimmed along on step, but my layers of fancy clothes kept me warm and dry.

The river was a product of melting glaciers high up in the surrounding mountains. Being glacial-fed, it was both silty—swirling with ultra-fine grey grit that made it opaque—and icy-cold, hovering around 40 degrees in the dead of summer.

There were some stirrings at the dock when I pulled in. Other guides, all men, rustled around in the bobbing boats, gearing up for the day. I recognized them all—some veterans, and some college students out for their first or second season, making a little extra money during the summer—and waved my good mornings as I tied off my boat and trudged up to the main building, thermal coffee mug in hand.

The fishing lodge was a big A-frame built with local timbers, already bustling with the morning rush. The smell of cinnamon and butter and bacon hit me as I let myself in the front door.

It was with a sinking feeling that I greeted my clients for the day. Two men, both of them obviously laboring under the sexist women-can't-fish delusion, eyed me dubiously. One of them even came right out and said it: "Our guide's a *woman?*" Then he walked away, probably to talk with management.

So yeah, if it seems sometimes like I have a chip on my shoulder, that might be why. That and, this morning at least, I was grumpy from lack of sleep and still mourning my blueberries.

And I had three thousand words to write before 8 p.m. Which, *shit*, I'd forgotten about.

It was established that yes, I would be guiding them, and yes, I'd been doing this for several years, and yes, I knew what I was doing. Glad *some*body was capable of diplomacy this early in the morning, I sat back and watched the exchange between one of the owners, Nancy, and the chauvinist man.

The situation deteriorated just a little bit more when I saw the two kids. They weren't grotesque or misshapen or anything, they were just... *Kids.*

I groaned. I hated guiding kids.

It was the curse of having a vagina; my employers were forever giving me the women and children, thinking I'd know what to do with them. The other women, yeah, we got along fine as long as they were there to fish and not just to look pretty and keep their French manicures immaculate and go "eeewww!" at their first glimpse of slime.

But kids? They broke shit, they fell in the water, they asked about a million questions, and couldn't cast without tangling their lines every damn time. They were sometimes cute, and their excitement was infectious, but overall: They were a pain in my ass.

My charges were still running around, taking their sweet time gathering up the last of their dusty equipment. Usually I'd be irritated by this, but today it gave me time to fill my insulated coffee mug, drain it, and then fill it again. I sat waiting for them almost an hour before we finally got out on the water.

We went to one of my favorite spots and first tried fishing from the boat. I quickly tired of this, as the children just wouldn't fucking stay still. Following my three rapid-fire cups of coffee, I was also having a bit of a bowel emergency, so I talked the men into trying out a little shore fishing.

Once ejected from my boat, the children ran free. They quickly became distracted with getting muddy and making a fort out of driftwood, and I—after my potty break in the woods—was able to actually concentrate on helping the men catch salmon.

They weren't bad as fishermen went. They caught their bag limit of Reds before noon, and then turned their attention to helping the kids catch theirs. We had lunch on the shore, and then went back to it. The kids caught their last fish, a fat, glossy Silver Salmon, around two in the afternoon, and I was able to enjoy one of those rare days where I got off early.

Considering the way it started, it had actually been a pretty good day. The men tipped well, I was able to find some TP when I needed it, and the children had only broken my cheapest rod. Thank God, and at the same time, damn them.

I heard my neighbor's helicopter before I even got back to my cabin. It skimmed by overhead just as I was pulling into the slough. I'd gotten lost in my normal daily routine, and had actually sort of forgotten about the new resident noise-maker.

I slid in to the shore and threw my anchor out a little harder than was strictly necessary. Grumbling, I loaded all of my equipment onto my four-wheeler.

Then I found out my four-wheeler wouldn't start.

Now this sucked, sure, but my day wasn't ruined. Shit like this happens when you live in the bush. You just gotta roll with the punches. So I was rolling, as I gathered up my fishing gear. I definitely couldn't leave my stuff out along the river where anyone could take it, but there was no way I could carry it all in one trip, so I gathered what I could, and I rolled on up the trail.

Purely by chance, I decided I would carry the shotgun on my second trip.

I was walking along the trail, concentrating on keeping my rod tips up off the ground, when I became aware of a lighter spot of uniform brown against the dark soil ahead of me. I looked up—and froze.

It was a brown bear, a damn big one, and it was standing there in the middle of the trail, practically taking up the whole trail, staring at me.

Something a lot of people from the Lower 48—and hell, the rest of the world—don't understand, is that bears aren't cute, cuddly, harmless creatures. People go to the zoo, see that fuzzy, adorable animal snoozing in a sunbeam, and they get this impression that bears are sweet creatures whose greatest ambition in life is a good nap.

Well, newsflash: Real bears aren't teddy bears. People who try to hug them get eaten. Bears are at the top of the food chain for some damn good reasons. They're a half-ton of sheer muscle behind five-inch claws and killing teeth. They kill to survive… and also sometimes just because.

We Alaskans have whole books full of gruesome bear attack stories. We're talking detailed, gory maulings where faces and scalps and all sorts of deliciously horrible body parts are rent open or ripped off. There are accounts of bears being shot right through the heart—heart, destroyed—and they continue to kill and rampage for a full ten minutes after.

So now you know where I'm coming from, when I tell you, I was walking back to my cabin after work Sunday afternoon, and I came face-to-face with a bear. There was nothing between us; no fence, no plate armor, not even the thinnest veneer of civilization. And in that unguarded moment, staring into the bear's eyes, I realized something. Humans are just bags of blood walking around, and we're pretty darn easy to pop. Despite what my forward-facing eyes said, I could be hunted, and killed. Sometimes, people are prey.

My heart doubled its pace, and my vision narrowed as my fight or flight response kicked in. But I wouldn't win against this thing in a fight, and I couldn't run.

It's something drilled into Alaskan kids: Don't run. Absolutely *do not* run. Bears are predators, they will give chase, and they can run thirty-five miles per frickin' hour. And when they catch you, they will tear you apart...

I was frozen there, trying to figure out what to do. I could have put my hands over my head to make myself look bigger, but they were full. I could have yelled to try and scare it, but I felt barely capable of a squeak. I really, really wished I had my gun.

It was still staring at me. Not afraid. A really bad sign.

I began to back away. Slowly. Just one step. Two. Over the thunder of my heart, I became aware of another noise, the low, thrumming drone of an aircraft getting closer.

The bear took a step to follow me. Then another. Did it look hungry?

I looked around for a tree to climb. There was nothing close. I had my Leatherman, but that knife was only two or three inches long, and it'd take a precious few seconds to pry out.

I took another couple steps back.

The bear chuffed, and advanced, moving a little faster. He'd been about thirty feet away. Now it was twenty-five.

I finally decided to try shouting. I made some noise, waving my rod- and tackle box-laden hands above my head.

He kept on coming.

I stumbled backward, shouting louder, barely aware that I was now competing with the thundering approach of an aircraft.

The bear paused. Cocked its head.

A helicopter *roared* by directly overhead, low above the treetops. The sound was enormous, the blast of air snapping off dead branches high up in the trees.

The bear turned to its right, and scooted into the woods.

Now I know I said don't run, but this was my chance. That bear could have turned around at any moment and come back for me, and I didn't want to be anywhere nearby when he did.

I sprinted along the trail, my neck prickling, sure at any moment I'd feel his claws in my back. After a harrowing couple-minute run, I broke out of the woods. I dropped my fishing gear as I crossed my little drive. I flew up my three steps, smashed through the door, and then slammed it behind me.

*Safe.* My breath heaved as I leaned back against the cool metal door. That had been one of my closest calls yet, and of course it had happened during one of the very, very few times I was caught without my gun.

My gun, which was on a broken-down four-wheeler, along with a bunch of expensive fishing equipment, next to a tourist-infested river. I had a story deadline, but I also had *stuff.* And that *stuff* allowed me to make a decent living as a fishing guide, so I really needed to rescue it, and soon. My choices were: I could play pack-mule again, or I could get the four-wheeler running.

I'm capable of lots of things—I can fish, and drive a boat, and shoot a gun—but I am not the least bit mechanically inclined. My four-wheeler might as well run on magic, propelled by fairy wings, for all I know. Although, I do feed it gas every once in a while, and I am pretty sure that fumy clear fluid has something to do with its propulsion. I know for damn sure the thing won't move without it.

But anyway, I'd checked. The tank had been full. It wasn't the gas, and thus it was beyond me.

My brothers were coming to visit in a little over two weeks, and I knew they'd probably be able to trouble-shoot it (if they didn't somehow *actually* shoot it, blow it up, or sink it in the process) but two weeks was too long. I still had work; I had to make that commute from cabin to boat several more mornings before their visit, and the four-wheeler was the best way to transport my fishing gear.

Though I really, really didn't want to do it, I knew exactly who I had to call.

"Hello?" said a cheerful tenor on the second ring.

"Ed, hi," I said. "How are you?" I wasn't usually much for small talk, except when trying to disguise that I was calling to ask for a favor.

"Helly! I haven't heard from you in weeks! Good, I'm good. How are you?"

I could hear him smiling on the other end, and I winced. Ed was a nice guy, definitely not the grungiest-looking bush rat I'd ever seen, and he'd had a thing for me for years. Problem was, I felt absolutely nothing for him, and I suspected his 'thing' originated from the fact that I was one of only two females under the age of 45 that resided on the river year-round.

We did the verbal dance, and I finally got to it: "Ed, I was wondering...well, my four-wheeler died, and I was wondering if you could possibly come by and take a look at it."

"Sure! I'd love to," he said. "When? I'm free right now."

See, now I just felt bad. This sweet guy was willing to jump on any excuse to spend time with me, and I just wanted to use him for his mechanical skills. Was there a special place in hell for me? Or was this why women eventually married—so they could have that shit on tap?

"That'd be great," I said. "The four-wheeler died down at my boat. Meet you there in 15 minutes?" Hopefully the fix would be quick, and then I could get back to my cabin, and meet my deadline.

"Sounds great!"

I signed off, and picked up the shotgun propped next to my front door. There was still a bear out there. And yes, I owned more than one gun. More than a few, even. At last count, a dozen.

It is Alaska, after all. Gotta have your guns.

I rescued my gear from the dirt drive, treating it with a little more care as I hung the rods on their rack, and set the tackle box beneath.

Shotgun in hand, I started warily back down the trail. The birds were singing and flitting about in the shadows under the canopy as if a bear hadn't almost 'popped' me and painted the forest with my blood. As I walked, I noticed the echoing *tat-tat-tat* of a woodpecker becomes something eerie when you're freaked out.

I caught a flash of movement out of the corner of my eye. I jumped and swung my gun around—it was a squirrel.

To my relief, the bear didn't make another appearance, and I arrived at the river unscathed except by mosquitos. When Ed pulled up, I was sitting side-saddle on my four-wheeler, and I saw him glance at the shotgun resting in my lap.

"I had a close call with a bear," I said by way of explanation.

He'd climbed ashore, and he paused in tossing out his anchor. "Just now?"

"On the way to my cabin, maybe twenty minutes ago."

He gave me his serious, concerned look. "I've got my rifle. You want me to see if—"

*Crap.* I didn't want his concern. "No, it's fine. I got caught without my gun, but it won't happen again. Just know that there's a brown bear in the area, and he doesn't seem to be afraid of people."

"Are you sure? It'd be no problem…"

I shook my head. I didn't want to fill the role of Ed's damsel in distress. I could take care of myself. Really, I just wanted him to fix my four-wheeler.

We made awkward conversation as he unfastened the grill and peeled a couple pieces of red plastic off the front end. It was awkward because I wanted to be nice to him, but I didn't want to lead him on. I was trying to strike a balance, but that was hard to do when you were as socially inept as I was. I tried to stay on safe topics, asking him how his Fourth of July went, whether he'd been fishing lately, what he thought of the weather.

Despite my best efforts, he managed to slip in an indirect date invite. "Are you going to the Hindmans' anniversary barbecue?" he asked. He looked up at me, hazel eyes earnest in the gap between his dark brown hair and beard. The man had so much facial hair, that if I hadn't heard him speak, I wouldn't have been sure he owned a mouth—but that wasn't unusual around these parts.

"I…" had been planning on it, because I liked the old couple, and there was free food, and Suzy'd be there, but I didn't want it to be a *date*.

"I'm going," he said, wrenching on something, blissfully unaware of the thoughts screaming through my head. "And I'd love to see you there."

His eyes squinched up, telling me he was smiling, and I actually wondered for all of three seconds why I couldn't be attracted to a guy like him. He was nice-looking, hardworking and honest, and he was obviously compatible with the lifestyle. So why wasn't I attracted to him?

Then I came to my senses and realized it didn't matter why. I just wasn't.

"Um," I said noncommittally.

He didn't seem to notice. "There," he said. "That should do it."

*Thank God.*

He straightened up and wiped some grease from his hands, and then walked around and started the four-wheeler. He smiled as the engine roared to life. He let it rumble for a few moments, and then shut it down.

Then he spoke. Here's what I heard: "It was the—" *something, something* "—which had disconnected from the—" *something, something* "—and you were low on—" *something, something* "—oh, and your battery—" *something, something*. Yeah, that last part had sounded kinda important. Oh well.

I nodded as if I'd understood, and thanked him. He put the front of my four-wheeler back together, packed up his tools, and then looked at me. I stood by during that awkward pause while he tried to think up some last thing to say, some brilliant thing that he probably hoped would inspire me to show him gratitude the old-fashioned way.

"Well," he finally said, "I might see you at the barbecue."

I nodded again.

He got in his boat.

I got on my four-wheeler, and headed back to my cabin. I felt Ed's longing like a physical presence as he watched me drive away. I really, really needed to stop letting him help me.

Back at my cabin, I was shucking off my damp, fishy clothes, when I heard it again, *whomp whomp whomp*, and felt the vibration that made my pots rattle. I finished dressing, and then went downstairs to glare out my window. I watched the helicopter collect three people and take off again. *Good.* It looked like my evil neighbor was taxiing his hungover friends back to whatever hole they'd crawled out of, rather than keeping them till Monday. I hoped that would bring the decibel level down a bit, and let me actually get some sleep tonight. Knowing it was for a good cause made me feel a little more inclined to tolerate the noise.

I started up the generator—I needed to run it a couple hours each day if I wanted the lights and running water—and threw a quick casserole into the oven for dinner.

Then I went back up my ladder, fetched my ear plugs, and sat down to finish my story. I could still hear the helicopter in the background, but it was faint. An hour in, I switched over to my own music, turning it up loud to drown out everything else.

I don't know if it was just that I was in a slightly better mood today, or if the writing gods were smiling on me, but I managed to finish my story. I got it edited, and then emailed—yes, courtesy of satellite, I even had internet in my little corner of the woods—by my deadline.

It was 8 p.m., and I'd eaten, and now that my story was done, it felt like a weight had been lifted off my shoulders. I went out on my deck with a beer and the binoculars, determined to relax by watching the silly antics of stick-legged sandpipers.

Just a few minutes later, the Devil flew overhead again. The wind of his passing made my hair fly everywhere, and scared the birds I'd been watching. I lowered the binoculars to watch him pick up what looked like the last of his guests.

Having cooled off a bit from last night, I was starting to wonder what his deal was. Most cabin owners in these parts showed up occasionally on weekends, or for whatever week or two they could get off. My new neighbor had said he was staying the summer, which seemed an odd amount of time, unless he was a schoolteacher.

Somehow, I didn't think he was a schoolteacher.

So what did he do for a living that let him afford the cabin, and the helicopter, and huge parties, but at the same time, let him hide out in bumfuck for a couple months? *Was* he running from something? That seemed like it was often the case around these parts; people who lived out here were trying to avoid the law, or grow pot (see avoid the law), or just be alone. With Gary's party last night, he'd proven he wasn't a loner. And he didn't look like a stoner. Which left trouble with the law.

I mulled that over a bit, and finally decided I didn't know, and I wasn't going to ask. I wasn't going to talk to my neighbor at all, if I could help it. He was way too hot to have a normal relationship with any-which-way, and I was going to do my level best to avoid him.

# Chapter Three

"I'm gonna kill him," I growled into the phone. It had been five days since my neighbor moved in, and he hadn't failed to disturb my peace on a single damn one of them.

"Who're you gonna kill?" my friend Suzy asked. "Brett?"

"No, not Brett. My new neighbor!" I was pacing around, and the glares I cast through my big picture window should have set something on fire.

"Oh, so he moved in then?"

"You knew about this?" My voice was rising.

"Well, sure, he's the son of one of my dad's old friends. Dad actually was the one to pass along that the place was for sale." I could hear her smile through the phone. "Why do you want to kill him?"

I didn't even know where to begin, but the biggest thing: "He is *loud*. He's got a helicopter, and he's doing some construction over there, and Manny's drilling him a well. There's pounding going on day and night. He actually woke me up yesterday *and today* with his sawing and hammering. He comes and goes with his helicopter, he's decided the airspace above my cabin is an acceptable flight path, and he's had Rob with the flight service make several trips in carrying building materials, and it's just been non-stop *noise*."

Suzy was making all the right sympathetic sounds, so I continued.

"The day he moved in, that very first day, he made a dozen trips with the helicopter, he had a huge party that went well into the wee hours of the morning, blaring their speakers and *littering on my beach*. And a couple of his friends tried to steal my canoe, and then they woke me up with fireworks, and, Suzy...he set my blueberry patch on fire."

"What?! On fire?" *See? I knew she'd understand.*

"One of his damn fireworks landed in my blueberry patch, and the woods were burning, and we barely got it out. He could have burned my cabin." Next door, the repetitive *thump thump thump* of the well-drilling made me want to tear out my hair. "So I was out until two a.m. putting out the fire, and then I had to be up by 4:30 to go to work, and Suzy, he burnt my blueberries." I actually felt like crying even now.

"Aww, Hel, I'm sorry. We'll find you some more blueberries, it'll be okay."

"It's not okay! How am I supposed to write with all this racket?"

She was starting to make some more soothing noises, but I continued: "You know what else he did? I went to bed early that second night, trying to catch up on my sleep after he finished carting all his buddies back to town, and do you know what woke me up at 11 o'clock that night?"

"No..."

"Loud fucking sex. And it went on for *hours*." Okay, that might have been a *slight* exaggeration. The sounds that I'd originally thought came from a dying baby moose reached an earth-shaking climax of yodeling cries ten minutes till midnight. I'd lain there in the dark, torn between rage and a growing lust, wondering what the hell my new neighbor had to be doing to a woman for her to make sounds like that. *I'd* sure never made sounds like that.

"Reaaally?" Suzy said, and by the way she drew out the word, I knew she was getting ideas. Which made me want to kick something.

I growled into the phone. "And that's when he's not muddying the water with his fucking jet ski." Day three of the Gary Invasion, I'd come home and there'd been a brand new jet ski bobbing at his dock. "I mean, who owns a jet ski?" In these parts? No one. "And where does he think he's going with it? It's just this little lake. You'd think he could find something more entertaining to do."

She laughed. "Well, Helly hon, the noise will die down after a bit. That well's only a couple-day operation, and I'm sure after he's got everything he needs, he won't need to make many more trips."

"He starts hammering and sawing at six a.m.!" I cried. "Which isn't a big deal on the days I work, but I really like to sleep a bit past *six* on my days off!"

I was practically panting with wrath. The same day the jet ski appeared, I'd come back to find a brand new boat—his, I could only imagine, because it was expensive, shiny, new, and damned annoying—parked in my spot. He was invading my quiet, peaceful life, and I didn't like it. Not at all.

"Deep breaths, Hel. Deep breaths. Okay, you're not gonna kill him."

I started to argue, but she cut me off.

"What you *are* gonna do is go over there and ask him to *please* hold off on the noise until—what time would be good for you?"

"Nine," I growled. How could she sound so calm, so reasonable? She wasn't here, that's how. She wasn't here, where it sounded like they were throwing around metal roofing. I rubbed between my eyes, where that damn groove was making another appearance.

"And ask him nicely, Hel. You can't just go over and start shooting people."

*I can't?* I eyed the shotgun propped next to the door. I'd been fondling it a lot lately.

"You can't," she said firmly, as though she'd heard my thought.

I was starting to calm down a little bit—a *little* bit, mind you—but I wasn't quite done being mad. "I can't write like this," I said.

"Do you have noise-cancelling headphones?"

"No."

"Damn. Well...play your own music?"

I grumbled a bit, and she laughed.

"You could come visit me. I haven't seen you in a couple weeks."

I groaned. "I can't. I have another deadline coming up. And the reason you haven't seen me is I've been working upriver, for the Bransons." Suzy lived downstream from me, in a cabin on the river, about ten minutes away by boat. When I was working downriver, I often stopped by on my way home. We'd sit out on her little deck gossiping and eating burgers as we soaked in the evening sunshine and listened to the fine hiss of silt as the river rolled by. She was the only other female resident even close to my age—two years younger, in fact—and the only other woman on the river who'd chosen to live by herself in the Alaskan bush.

"Well... are you coming to the Hindmans' barbecue?"

"Maybe..." There was still the Ed issue. On the other hand, it was an opportunity to escape my neighbor's noise, and see my friend. "Yeah, I'll be at the barbecue," I said.

"You seem really bothered by your new neighbor," she said. "What's his name again?"

I hadn't told her it in the first place, and I didn't want to soil my tongue with the Devil's name, but I finally manned up and spat, "Gary."

"And Gary has a helicopter, hmmm?"

"Yeah," I said. Lots of people had small planes, and that was cool; everybody loved a pilot. But owning a helicopter? Instant godlike status. "But he's a dick."

"A rich dick, then. And a good-looking one."

"How do you know that?"

Suzy cackled. "I didn't. You just told me. So he's hot? Young? Tall? Gimme."

I groaned.

"Helly..." she warned, sounding like she was gonna crawl through the phone and rip the info outta me if I didn't dish.

"He's a real prick," I said, prefacing what I was about to let pass through my lips. "But yeah. Six-footish, maybe a couple years older, black hair, green eyes, built."

"Green eyes?" She moaned. "And he's living there, not just for the weekend?"

This line of questioning was getting old. I didn't wanna talk to my neighbor, and I certainly didn't wanna talk about him. "For the summer, is what he said."

"God, I would give anything to be in your place, right next door. Do you have any idea how lucky you are?"

"He's. An. Ass," I stressed. A loud-ass.

Suzy seemed to mull that over for a moment. "Your brothers are coming to visit, right?"

*Ugh.* "Yeah." In exactly thirteen days, I'd be overrun by three crazy blondes who never had the decency to grow up.

"Maybe they'll kill each other," Suzy said. "Them and the neighbor."

Maybe they would. "Maybe they will." I began to smile. My brothers weren't actually bad people. They were just rowdy as hell, and I kinda doubted they could be killed short of being staked, having their heads cut off, and their bodies burnt to ash. So, really, I was just hoping they'd kill the neighbor.

"You got a plan for hiding the booze?" she asked.

"I was thinking I'd bury it this time." In previous years, I'd sunken my stash in the lake, and hidden it in a tree almost a mile away. My brothers had found it both times. And both times, they'd cleaned me out.

She laughed, and then sighed. "Actually, even though they'll be drinking you out of house and home, I'm glad they'll be there with you. I've been hearing about some break-ins downriver."

I spun away from the window. "Break-ins?"

"It's just summer cabins, not a big deal. Just vandals," she said. "You know we get 'em every summer. Probably just some idiot out from town for the weekend."

I didn't say anything, but I was worried about her. I was thinking maybe she should go stay with her parents at their lodge.

I must have been thinking it pretty hard. She laughed, and then said, "I've got a gun. A really big one." She did. It was a .50-cal. revolver, and it looked ridiculous in her tiny hands. She had one of those builds that made it look like she'd blow away in the wind. But somehow, she made that five pound revolver her bitch. I wasn't into girls, but even I could admit it was hot as hell to watch her blow holes in things with it. "They try and vandalize my place, I'll let them know what I think about that," she continued.

"I'll come visit you sometime when I'm off," I said. Maybe even when my brothers were here; it would be an excellent excuse to escape them. Plus I wanted to catch up on neighborhood gossip—she always had the best stuff, it was almost like she had eyes in the trees—but I also figured if I was there, that'd be two guns and upward of a dozen bullets the vandals would have to go through. Maybe we could even do some target shooting. Nothing like the sound of gunshots to discourage trespassers.

"Good, you do that. Leave your brothers home," she said. "But your neighbor…"

"The only way he'd be safe to bring into the house is if he was muzzled and leashed, and you spread some newspaper around beforehand."

"Okaaaay, kinky, but I think I could get into it. Could he talk through this muzzle?"

"No."

"Excellent." I could practically hear her rubbing her hands together.

I wasn't going to be visiting her with my neighbor, though. That'd be a cold day in hell.

But Suzy was right. This noise couldn't go on forever.

I just needed to keep my cool, and curb my tendency to get even, at least for now. And in the meantime, if I got the opportunity, I'd ask him—nicely—to quiet the hell down.


I worked another three days, writing as best I could in the evenings, and then I got another day off. The day so far had been relatively quiet. I'd woken up naturally, and hadn't yet heard hide nor hair of my neighbor. His helicopter sat quiet on his chewed-up lawn. Maybe he was taking the day off, too.

I was sitting at my laptop, once more in front of my big picture window, working on a sex scene. *Shower sex. Mmm, everybody likes shower sex.* The wet slide of skin on skin, the bubbles sluicing over sinuous curves and bulging muscle, the cool, slick tile pressing against an overheated back. I'd actually never done it, but I'd read about it, and I had one hell of an imagination. The face and body in my fantasy belonged to my neighbor, but I didn't let that disturb me too much. He was freaking hot, and I knew, probably better than most, that fantasy was a far cry from reality. Just because I could practically feel his big, strong hand sliding up my thigh didn't mean I would actually do anything with him. Ever.

My fingers tapped over the keyboard, detailing the way his naked chest would feel pressed against me. The firm bar of his erection. His teeth on my ear, his deep groan as I wrapped my hand around him. The way the hot water beat down on us both, reddening our skin. The mounting urgency dragging our breaths in faster...

I pressed my thighs together as I dove into the steamy scene.

*Crack!*

I jumped, glancing out the window. The lake was still, and I saw no motion next door. I didn't know what that sound had been—it had sounded like a gunshot, a sound common enough in these parts—but I wasn't going to let it distract me. Firming my resolve, I focused back on my screen.

My hero had my heroine pinned to the shower wall, and I quickly made the bathroom handicap-accessible so she had something to rest her ass on. He crowded between her thighs, and she gripped him, dragging him closer. They were staring into each other's eyes, poised on the precipice of penetration—

*Crack!*

Holy *fuck*. I slammed my wrist-splinted fists down on the desk in frustration, glaring out the window past my computer screen. It was gorgeous out, the sun high in the sky dappling everything in light and shadow, a slight breeze giving the scene movement. A loon sat lonely on the lake, gliding quietly across the rippling surface.

Across the way, there was still no movement at the Devil's hidey-hole.

*Crack!* Yet another gunshot split the silence, the sound ricocheting off the water. It sounded small-bore, but it was still, unmistakably, a gunshot.

What—the holy hell—was my neighbor up to now?

Another shot.

Knowing I couldn't write with all that racket, I decided to take care of chores until he quieted the fuck down. I changed the oil on the generator—one of the only mechanical tasks I was capable of, and that only because I'd been shown how about five times—and then started it up for the daily charge. I split some wood, washed some dishes, and even did my laundry and hung my clothes out to dry.

I had grilled cheese for lunch, and as I ate, I tried not to wonder what my neighbor was shooting at. I doubted it was a target; the shots were too sporadic for that. No, I was guessing he was shooting squirrels.

Or, more likely, I thought, gritting my teeth, spruce hens. The chicken-sized birds were game fowl, and they were dumb as rocks. They'd let a person approach to within just a few feet before they scattered. And when they flew away, it was low and slow, and then usually into a nearby tree.

It felt like taking advantage to go out and shoot them. Their meat was gamey and flavored heavily with spruce needles, so I honestly didn't see the point anyway. And in the spring, their little chicks were so damn cute...

So yeah, the Law of Asshole Behavior said he was probably out shooting my baby spruce hens. The bastard.

Fast forward to dinner time.

The Rich Bastard had been shooting off and on all day. I'd gone back to my laptop mid-afternoon, but the noise kept jerking me out of my headspace, and when I did manage to claw my way back inside, I found out my heroine wanted to rip the hero's dick off, rather than ride it.

I tried going with it for a few hundred words, having them wrestle around the bathroom with some angry, increasingly violent sex. When the hero lay dead, his back broken over the lip of the tub, blood dribbling from his mouth, I was finally clued in that I needed to step away for a bit.

I was pissed off by this point, and no amount of lavender bubble bath was going to calm me down.

Just a little after the light had gone out of my hero's green eyes, I realized my dog was missing. This wasn't like the Lower 48, where dogs are confined to fenced yards or kept on leashes every moment of every day. No, here we just kick the dog out the door, and it comes back when it wants to eat.

Don't get me wrong, though. I love my dog. And I don't actually kick her. I keep pretty good tabs on her, and I feed her well. I buy her good dog food and supplement her diet frequently with actual wild salmon—believe me, in Alaska, it overflows our damn freezers.

Mocha loves to spend her days outside, and has been known to disappear for hours on end. Occasionally I hear reports from miles up or down the river—sometimes even across it—that she went visiting.

That said, I hadn't seen her since sometime before lunch. I'd been out in the yard for fifteen minutes, calling her name.

Coming around to the back of the cabin, still calling my missing mutt, I noticed the clothes were dry. Worried about my dog, but trying not to worry, I started pulling my clothes off the line.

That's when I noticed the hole in my underwear.

Now, I'm familiar with holes, especially the holes that develop at the seams and along the waistband when you've worn a pair of underwear for longer than you probably should have (over the life of the garment, not all in one sitting). This wasn't like those holes.

"What the…" I reached up, fingering the little hole in the coral-colored cotton. It was about pencil eraser-sized, and for all of three seconds I wondered if spruce beetles could or would put holes in cloth. But the hole penetrated both sides…

And then, realization came.

My neighbor had shot a hole in my underwear. Let me just say that again. My neighbor. Shot a hole. In my underwear. In my coral-colored boy shorts. My favorite pair, actually.

And even more horrifying: My neighbor had been shooting all day. My dog was missing. And she looked a bit like a wolf.

"Oh no. Oh no." I dropped the basket of clothes I'd had propped on my hip, not caring when the clothes tumbled to the ground, and spun to look out toward my neighbor's cabin.

*Had he shot my dog?*

Now, Mocha and I didn't have the most traditional dog/owner relationship, but I loved that dog. And somewhere deep in her tiny brain, I think she was maybe fond of me too.

With no real memory of my feet moving, I was already halfway down the bank, moving toward his cabin. The beach passed in a flash. I barreled up his lawn, stomped up the steps to his front porch, glanced in through the screen door—and froze.

He was seated on a big leather couch, presenting me with his profile as Fast and Furious revved across the big flat screen on my right. Just beyond him, along the far wall, I spotted the saws that had been plaguing me for the last few days.

And lying next to him on his leather couch? My dog, Mocha, the traitor. She looked supremely comfortable, her head in his lap, her feet dangling off the cushions. Which was all sorts of crazy because she was skittish as hell, she hated men, and she *never* cuddled. *And,* she wasn't allowed on the furniture.

As I stood there, trying to process this new development, Gary the blueberry murderer ate a potato chip, and then fed her one. He fed my healthy dog a potato chip.

But none of that was what *really* got my attention. No, what really got my attention was the bare expanse of his shoulders and the side view of his beautiful, naked chest. He was slouched on the sofa—*slouched!*—and his muscles were bulging. He had a Daniel Craig body, all broad-shouldered and ripped and tanned. His fantastic chest was decorated with the perfect amount of dark hair sprinkled down the center and trailing into the waistband of a pair of lounge pants. I say 'sprinkled' because he looked downright edible. He was a loud-ass, but I was having the crazy urge to run my tongue down his happy trail.

The thought came as I stood gawking in his doorway: *All I'd have to do is put a bag over his head and a gag in his mouth, and I could really enjoy that body.*

"Enjoying the show?" Gary asked.

I looked up into his smirk. He wasn't talking about the movie, I realized. He'd caught me ogling.

"I thought you shot my dog," I said.

He frowned at me is if *I* were the evil one. "Why would I do that?" he asked, feeding the dog in question another potato chip. She took it with pathetic gratitude, licking his hand, making it seem like I starved her. The sight put my teeth on edge.

"She's on a diet. And you put a bullet hole in my panties," I said.

He frowned at me again, obviously irritated I kept interrupting the longest car chase I'd ever seen. "Every diet includes potato chips. And—did you just say I put a hole in your panties?"

"A *bullet* hole," I stressed.

"In your panties."

"They were hanging on the line."

He gave me this masculine smirk that made me either want to smack him or fuck him. "How do you know it was me?" he asked.

Another potato chip. The future flashed before my eyes, a future in which my dog gained fifty pounds and never came when she was called, because she was always over at the neighbor's, being fed Barbecue Lays.

"You were out bumbling through the woods all day, randomly shooting at poor, defenseless animals. Of course it was you."

He squinted at me, probably trying to decide if I was a tree-hugger. My jeans and flannel button-down over a T-shirt said not. But I liked my neck of the woods just exactly as it was. *Not* pocked with bullet holes and divest of adorable feathered woodland creatures.

"I do not 'bumble'. And how do you know the hole wasn't already there?" he asked. "Or made some other way; holes can be made lots of ways."

I was trying to hold my temper. I really, really was. And for some reason I wasn't going to examine, my pussy was really, really wet. But that was neither here nor there.

What *was* there was him, looking like a human lollipop, having terrorized me with his decibels all frickin' *week*, stolen my muse, and beaten my sex scene literally to death. The mosquitos in the shade of his porch were starting to eat me alive—*of course* he had particularly ravenous mosquitos—and now he wanted to discuss the origin of

The Panty Hole.

"*You* made a hole. In my panties. With a tiny bullet from your puny gun," I added for good measure. The hole had looked and the report had sounded like a .22, and no man liked to be accused of having a small gun. Which is, of course, why I went there.

He stood up. "My gun is not puny," he said, crossing his arms and glaring through the screen at me. "And if I had made a hole in your panties, it wouldn't be tiny."

My eyes flicked to his package. I couldn't help myself. "That's not what it looks like from here," I said coolly, even though it was quite the frickin' opposite of what it looked like from where I was standing.

He started toward me, those delicious muscles flexing in a way that made me forget the mosquitos drilling my exposed flesh. Oooo, he looked kinda angry. Why did that turn me on?

My breath caught, and I felt my pussy clenching, the rush of heat and moisture. *Shit. Shit, shit.* Why was I so sick and twisted? Why couldn't I get this hot for someone who volunteered at a soup kitchen, someone who helped old ladies across the street? Or fixed my four-wheeler?

This man, coming toward me with that look in his eyes? I got the feeling he did none of those things.

My heart thumped faster. There was still the screen between us, but I honestly didn't know what I'd do if and when he got to me. Punch him in the mouth, or kiss it just as hard?

I really wanted to touch that chest...

*Now is my chance!* "I want you to stop waking me up in the mornings," I blurted.

He paused. "What?"

"Your sawing and hammering and flying, you start at six in the morning. You keep waking me up. I'd appreciate it if you stopped." There, that had actually been pretty polite. Especially compared to the stream of profanities I could have unleashed.

Maybe getting the full-frontal of his chest, all that smooth flesh wrapped around those delicious muscles, was mellowing me out. Even now, I was having trouble holding eye contact. There was just so damn much of him that wanted—no, *needed*—my attention. He frowned. "You're outta here in the mornings before I ever start hammering anything."

I felt a blush crawling up my cheeks from the double-entendre, but said, "On the days that I work, that's true. But I don't work every day, and on the days that I don't, I like to sleep in."

He crossed his arms, and one of his brows climbed upward. "Till?"

"Nine." And I immediately wanted to kick myself after I said it, because it sounded like a damn question. Apparently my decisive voice had gone out the same window my libido had come in.

He got a look like he was gonna argue or maybe laugh in my face, but then a half-naked blonde emerged from the back hall. "Gary," she sing-songed in a way that made *me* want to spank her, unknowingly interrupting whatever it was that was going on between me and my hot neighbor. She looked gorgeous and rumpled in nothing but a forest green button-down, and it shamed me to admit it, but in that moment, I wondered if he preferred blondes.

I didn't like my neighbor, but I was starting to realize I wanted to fuck him.

He half turned toward her, then flicked another look at me. It was a 'you just wait' look. "Take your dog," he said.

I hurriedly opened the screen, and was relieved when Mocha listened despite my lack of potato chips. We started down the porch, and behind me I heard, "Who was that, babe?"

"No one, gorgeous. Did I tell you you could get out of bed?"

"No..." Nauseating giggle, then a squeal. Five dollars said I'd be hearing dying-baby-animal sounds tonight.

*No one...* Fuck me. Here I was, hard-up with nothing but my imagination and a battery operated boyfriend, while my neighbor imported gorgeous model-types for each day of the week.

And he'd had the nerve to shoot a hole in my Wednesday underwear. Life wasn't fair.

# Chapter Four

T he *very next morning*, the sawing started at 0600 sharp. I knew, because I was off. And home. And trying to sleep.

I was livid. I lay in bed grinding my teeth, listening to him constructing things when I should have been catching up on my beauty rest.

That *man* had been in my life less than two weeks, and he'd shot my peace and quiet all to hell. He was the loudest individual I'd ever encountered, bar none.

And right then and there, I decided I wasn't going to take it lying down. Not anymore.

Suzy had advised using my words, communicating, and I'd tried that. Obviously, it wasn't working.

I was going to start doing things my way. I couldn't make him stop, short of duct-taping him to a wall, but I sure as hell could give as good as I got.

The next morning, I had to work, but I pried my sad-sack self out of bed a half hour earlier than I usually did, right at the barest butt crack of dawn. I got dressed in my usual duds, making sure my shirt was long-sleeved because the mosquitos were worst at this time of day.

Then I went and got my chainsaw.

But it wasn't what you're thinking. I wasn't gonna bust in wearing a ski mask, chainsaw roaring. I didn't have any meat hooks and

Visqueen in my generator shack.

No, I just wanted to make some noise, as loudly and as closely as possible, and wake *his* ass up for a change.

It just so happened there was a fallen tree right on our property line that I'd been eyeballing for a couple months. It had cracked from the cold and been blown over in a high wind, so it wasn't rotten. And I could definitely use some more firewood before winter.

So this morning, despite my jaw-cracking yawn and my bone-deep desire to crawl back into bed for another thirty minutes, I was murdering two birds with one really loud stone. I was gonna get me some firewood... and annoy me a neighbor.

Everything was silent as I crept over to the line dividing our property. It wasn't a line, really. Just a couple pieces of faded neon orange tape tied to the branches to mark it out.

With an evil laugh, I fired up the chainsaw. I revved it good, getting it nice and warm while I glared daggers at Gary's front door. Again, not what you're thinking. I may have an anger problem, but I'm not a murderer.

Of people.

Yet.

Ignoring the way the mosquitos tried to crawl into my brain through my ears, I started on the log, cutting it into nice, even chunks. I'd even brought my axe, so once I was done with this, I could make some more racket splitting it. I had a whole half hour to work with, and I planned on making the biggest damn ruckus I possibly could in the allotted time.

Out of the corner of my eye, I noticed Gary's door opening, and an angry, bare-chested individual spilled forth. I think he was yelling something, but I couldn't hear him. And I didn't care to. With a scoff, I continued cutting, the buzzing roar of the chainsaw drowning out everything else.

I figured I'd let the mosquitos do my work for me. The mosquitos around these parts are bad. Like other blood-suckers, they avoid bright sunshine like the plague, lurk in the shadows, and hunt and feed voraciously from sundown to sunrise. So right now, an hour before dawn? They were absolutely nasty. They were also insidious, finding every crack in your clothes, every unprotected inch.

Gary, with that bare chest of his, had a lot of unprotected inches. He wasn't even all the way to me when he was driven, cursing, back into the house. As I waited for him to reappear, I toyed with the notion of staking him out for the mosquitos to eat. Was there any way I could manage it without being charged with a crime? Did I care? I thought the more pertinent question was, how could I get him to hold still long enough to stake him out? He was a big guy, and I knew he wouldn't go willingly. Maybe I could lure him out, just put a beer in a bear trap. *Ha.* Sadly, it probably would have worked on my brothers.

Gary was back out, decently clad, in less than five minutes. He stormed back over to me, and I ignored him. He was yelling, but I hit the gas on the saw again, and kept cutting. He finally crowded so close, I either had to ease off the trigger or risk cutting through his leg. The man had balls, I'd give him that.

I looked up at him, not even pretending I hadn't known he was there. "Yes?" I asked.

"What the hell are you doing?" he asked. He was breathing hard, his eyes flashing, and his hair was sticking up in a way that made me want to run my fingers through it. Even though I was furious with him. *Dammit.*

"I'm making firewood, neighbor. What are *you* doing?"

"At 4:15 in the morning?" he demanded.

"Well, you've been working *loudly* at six in the morning, so I just figured—"

He crossed his arms. "*That's* what this is about? Me waking you up?" He had a *tone*, one that said I was a lazy-ass that didn't work for a living, because I'd been asleep at six in the morning.

My jaw clenched. I revved the saw, and made another cut down through the birch.

I moved to make the next, about 18 inches further along, but I found his foot in the way. I thought about it. Then I looked up at him.

"This is *my* log," he said. "Sweet of you to cut it up for me, but if you could just come back later…"

"Your log?"

"My log," he agreed, pointing at the colorful bits of tape. "It's more than halfway on my property."

"This log came from a tree growing on my land," I pointed out. "Thus, my tree."

"It might have been, before it fell on my land," he said. "But it crossed the line, sweet cheeks. Therefore, it's mine."

I propped my chainsaw on my hip, looking at him incredulously. "What do you need with a log? Can't you just burn bricks of cash if it comes right down to it?"

"It doesn't matter what I'm going to do with my log," he said. "Frankly, it's none of your business what I do with my log, *or* my bricks of cash."

"It's only halfway on your land," I pointed out. Why the hell was I having this argument with him? Was it because it was four in the morning?

He stepped over the log, put his heel to it, and rolled what was left the rest of the way onto his land. "There. Does that solve this? Can I go back to sleep now?"

"No," I said. "That doesn't remotely solve this. And by that logic, you're standing on my land, and you are now mine."

He looked at me. And then he did something I will never forget.

He unzipped, he pulled himself out, and he pissed on the ground. Right there in front of me, his morning wood in his hand, his yellow stream splashing onto my land. A couple drops even hit my boot.

I jumped back, absolutely aghast. The man. Was pissing. Right in front of me.

"There," he said. "Now it's mine."

The uncouth *bastard*.

I looked up into that smug face, and I revved my chainsaw.

He tucked himself away. "I don't think you can be trusted with that," he said. "Give it here." He took a step toward me, reaching for my saw.

I swear to God, the man had a death wish. But as much as I wanted to give as good as I got, I didn't want to splatter blood all over my woods, or have to explain his death. I just wanted him to be quiet in the mornings until a decent hour. Was that so much to ask? I stepped away again, still clutching the chainsaw. He'd have to pry it from my cold, dead fingers.

He lunged in, and yanked it out of my hands. Then he turned it off.

I bolted. Except I didn't bolt toward my cabin. I bolted toward his.

"Helly!" he yelled behind me.

I vaulted his steps, sprang across his porch, and yanked his screen open so hard it crashed against the wall. Then I was inside, and I slammed the deadbolt home behind me. I leaned against the door, my heart pounding, my breaths coming fast.

I'd done it. I was in his cabin.

I quickly searched the dim interior. A couple changes had happened in the last two days. All of the furniture was pushed and stacked in one corner of the main living area. He'd ripped out the sheetrock and insulation of the right-hand wall until only the exterior siding remained. The carpet, too, was gone, and the chop saw and table saw I'd noticed the other day sat in the middle of the plywood floor. Over next to the half-demolished wall, I spotted his hammer.

"Helly!" he yelled again. I heard him try the knob, and then he began to bang on the door. "Open this door!"

I darted across to the back door and made sure that was locked, too. Then I picked up his hammer. I glanced at his wood stove, and then over at his chop saw. I smiled.

I laid the haft of the hammer across the saw's platform, and I sawed the damn thing in half.

"What the hell are you *doing*?" his muffled voice demanded.

After a bit of fiddling, I got the blade out of the chop saw. Then I studied the table saw. I had some experience with saws, but disabling this one was beyond me. So I unplugged it, took a pair of heavy-duty clippers lying on top of his toolbox, and cut the cord.

Mission complete.

He was still banging away at the front door, so I ran down to the end of the hall, pushed a window up, and slid out onto the grass. I kept the building between us as I crossed over into the woods. Then his banging and cussing concealed most of my noise as I skirted around his yard, saw blade still clutched to my chest.

I made it back to my cabin, and heard my chainsaw fire up. I smiled, imagining him cutting his way back into his house at 4:30 in the morning.

Then I grabbed my stuff, let my dog out, and went to work.

That evening, even before I got back home and turned off my four-wheeler, I heard Gary's response. He had set up his speakers and was playing music loud enough to rattle my windows from across the lake.

I found my chainsaw sitting on my front step, but the chain was missing.

And when I stepped out onto my deck, I spotted Mocha over at his place, hanging out on his lawn. As I watched, he fed her the rest of his hot dog.

The next day, I was off. Gary didn't wake me up until 8 a.m., so I was glad for small favors. I lazed around, had a late breakfast, and then decided I was going to get some sun.

We have record amounts of sunshine in Alaska in the summer, but the truth of the matter is, there are only a couple months of good, soak-able rays. And only a couple days where it's warm enough to lie outside nearly naked.

This was one of those days. It dawned sunny, and as the day proceeded into afternoon, it just got warmer, and sunnier. The birds were singing, the bees were pollinating. I could practically smell the heat; the scent of warm dirt and green things made me long to be outside.

The scene I was working on could wait. I was going sunbathing.

And so it was that I put on a blue bikini and carted a towel and water bottle—and my shotgun, after the incident with the bear— down to my dock. The dock was a basic thing, no more than a few boards strapped together over a large block of foam, just wide and long enough for me and my beach towel.

The problem with sunning somewhere more private was that my yard was almost entirely shaded by those trees I love. And with the shade came clouds of bloodthirsty mosquitos. The little biting beasties didn't venture so much onto the water, so I only came away with a couple bites each time I sunbathed. Reasonable collateral damage, the way I figured it.

Anyway, so there I was, pale, less-than-svelte self in a less-than-stylish bikini, soaking in some rays, actually getting damn close to falling asleep...

When my gods-be-damned neighbor made his presence known.

I heard—something. It was a whirring buzz I couldn't identify. It got louder and louder, sounding like it was coming at me from across the lake.

I finally sat up to look, and came pretty much face-to-face with—something. It was white, about a foot across, and had four propellers causing a surprisingly strong breeze to chill my skin as it hovered in place. I'd never seen one in person before, but I'd seen pictures.

It was a drone. And the little dark eye of its camera was pointed at me.

I stared at it for a few seconds, completely floored. My neighbor was *spying* on me?

Without hesitation, I hefted my shotgun to my shoulder, and I shot the thing down. It whirred and spun, and landed in the lake with a satisfying splash.

Then I looked over at the neighbor's. When he didn't come out and start jumping up and down on his lawn like an enraged monkey, I set down my gun, and I lay back on my towel.

What might have been a half hour later, I heard the distinctive roar of his jet ski firing up—shattering the peaceful quiet yet again.

*Calm. I am calm.* I'd just lay over here and tune out his noise, and he'd get bored soon and go away. The lake was only so big. That's what I told myself as he moved back, and forth, back, and forth. Soon the little waves of his passing began to lap at the dock, making the wood shift and creak.

I turned over onto my stomach. Any minute now, he'd get

bored.

That roar was moving closer. Yeah, he'd probably seen the flash of my white ass from across the lake. My skin prickled as if under his stare.

Closer.

What was the fucker gonna do, run me over? I had started to lift up, to turn my head to look, when it happened.

Cool water sprayed across me as he whizzed by, and I swear to God I heard him laugh. Then his waves, originating from just a couple feet away, hit. They rocked the dock, causing my water bottle to topple and roll off the edge. And I couldn't retrieve it because I was spread-eagled and clinging to my dock as it bucked like a rodeo bull.

When it finally settled down, and it looked like I wasn't going to follow my Nalgene into the drink—but I was still feeling cool rivulets of water down my back and thighs—I made a resolution.

I was going to kill him. All right, maybe not kill him. Those were strong words for someone with a shotgun not six inches from her fingertips. I wouldn't be using that on him—not yet, anyway.

But I was going to make him pay. And I'd always been a fan of tit for tat, someone steals, cut off the hand, that kind of thing. Just look at what I'd done to his tools.

So as I climbed to my feet, peeling my drenched beach towel up after me, I glared across the lake at him and his shiny new jet ski. He'd splashed me, and he'd used that infernal machine to do it. The solution seemed obvious.


For Gary, the rich devil that lived next door, justice came swiftly. That evening, he took a trip in his helicopter, allowing me to set it up. When he got back, I waited a few minutes after he walked into his cabin.

Then his jet ski fired up without him.

According to plan, he blundered out his front door, looking confused. I don't know if he'd been changing, or about to lounge or shower, but he wasn't wearing a shirt. The sight of his naked chest again grabbed my gaze and wouldn't let it go. *Gorgeous, gorgeous,* acknowledged everything feminine in me.

And as my body tightened, my arm tightened, the fishing line attached to the jet ski's gas pulled, and the stupid jet ski revved. How embarrassing.

He frowned at the possessed machine, and started down the lawn.

I waited, my smile growing wider and wider as he approached the dock. When he stepped up onto it, I yanked. The line tightened to apply full gas, and then snapped perfectly according to plan. Like a racehorse launching from the starting gate, the watercraft actually gained a little air before it was flying, unmanned, across the lake.

The Devil ran across the dock with a yell. But it was too late. The jet ski was already halfway across the lake and headed for the opposite shore at breakneck speed.

Infernal machine, check.

But I wasn't done.

I rammed into his back at full speed, stiff-arming a surprised, extremely hot, and befuddled neighbor out over the water. He was heavy, so he didn't stay in the air long.

*Splash!!*

As I stood there, taking in my handiwork, my shit-eating grin grew to epic proportions. Got me wet, check.

As the jet ski thrust itself against the rocks on the opposite shore, I might have even laughed a little.

Then the Devil surfaced. He turned around and zeroed in on me and—did I mention those peepers were a mesmerizing shade of green?—his confusion only lasted a microsecond. Once that was over with, I swear those eyes flashed red.

I squeaked, frozen in place like a deer caught in the high beams.

Then he ripped his gaze from me and started to wade toward shore. His shoulders were tense, his movements jerky, telegraphing his intentions as if he had a big neon sign over his head that flashed 'Payback!'.

I was so fucked.

I ran. That's right. I fucking ran. Fast, too, as fast as my little feet could carry me. My heart was thundering, my feet crunching on the beach as I set a new land record. And I might have been laughing a little. All right, I admit, I was cackling with glee. That look on his *face...*

I was in such deep shit. I'd violated the terms of our little feud, upped the ante.

I'd laid on hands.

I catapulted myself up the steps from the beach because the very master of the hounds of hell was on my heels. I was on my own turf now, less than fifty feet from my front door. I focused on that door as I pumped my legs. It was steel-core, very sturdy and with very good locks. Surely not even the Devil himself could breach those deadbolts.

Thirty feet away now. I flew across my yard, heart leaping with hope.

I heard him behind me.

Just before he plowed into my back.

"Argh!" I flailed as we went down, his weight on my legs.

We landed in pretty much the only patch of grass I owned, so the impact was relatively soft. I immediately tried to drag myself out from under him, clawing at the earth as I struggled like a fish on a hook. His hands latched onto my shirt, straining the seams as his knee dug into my ankle. I imagined it looked rather like that scene from Terminator as he crawled up me.

I reached out, trying to summon my front door by force of will alone. Yeah, it didn't move. *Fuck!*

He was fully on top of me now, and with a rough yank, he rolled me over. I looked up into his eyes, felt the weight and shape of his body acutely along the length of mine, his wet clothes soaking through mine as he pinned me. *Double fuck.*

Let it never be said I give up easy. I fought some more, shoving at him, trying to get him back far enough to get a foot on his torso. I had some strength in my legs, and having scrapped and fought with my brothers, I knew that with my back to the ground, I could launch him off me, possibly giving me the time I needed to reach my door.

He slid his hips firmly between my squirming legs, and then pinned my wrists next to my head. If I'd been a little more calm, I might have noticed that the way he subdued me was truly masterful. In this position, I could kick to my heart's content and not make contact. And I couldn't move my arms even a fraction of an inch. His grip was that solid.

His face was just inches above mine. My chest heaved, pressing my breasts against his firm chest. His...something deliciously hard...was pressing squarely against my clit.

I think we both realized our situation at the exact same moment. A moment which came simultaneously with my stupid betrayer of a body tilting its hips up against him. I couldn't help it. He had fought me to the ground, and I was suddenly hot, and wet, and I wanted him.

I hated him, but I wanted him. I stared up at him, panting, trying to get *that* figured out in my head.

He returned my look—he appeared confused, too—but he ground his pelvis against mine in a way that made my neck arch, and my breath expel on a moan. Heat flared between us, spreading from everywhere we touched. My pussy felt like it was on fire, and not in some terrible STD-ish way. No, this was in a the-Devil's-hard-cock-pressed-against-me-through-my-pants-and-I-never-wanted-anything-more kind of way. Go figure.

He ground against me again, and that look on his face said he wanted me too, despite what I'd done to his jet ski. I lifted my knees along his sides, maneuvering that bulge down into the dent of my hungry pussy.

*Oh yes.* My hands clenched, nails digging into my palms as I writhed under him. And he was moving against me, that tight heat rubbing into me harder and harder.

I could barely think, certainly not enough to acknowledge that we were dry-humping on my lawn. And suddenly he was missing from my field of vision. He tugged at my pants, the nicest-looking pair of sweats that I owned. I was so stunned, I just lay there as he started to drag them down.

*Wait. What underwear was I wearing? Was it my period panties?* It might have been my period panties. Not that I had any other kind...

Apparently he didn't care, because he just ripped them the fuck off me. I suddenly had grass against my ass, but then he was back over me, and he must have dealt with his own pants at some point, at least to get them open. The incredibly hot, hard length of his shaft pressed directly against my throbbing clit. He dragged my thigh up along his side as he ground against me.

Then he shoved my shirt up, and suddenly his mouth was on my breast. I lost my breath on another telling cry. He'd discovered my kryptonite, zeroed in on it like some evil supervillain. His mouth was the Devil's work. It was on my nipple, on the soft flesh around it, sucking in decadent amounts of my breast on each hard draw.

He wasn't sweet, and he wasn't gentle. He was punishing me with his mouth, scraping me with his teeth, sucking like my previous lovers had never dared.

I'd never been wetter. I ground up against him, making helpless noises of pleasure. I tried to bite my lips, tried not to let him know I was enjoying it, but it was futile. I don't remember putting my hands in his hair, but they were there, tangled in that wet black silk, holding him to me as I shook and burned.

'Heat'...this was nothing so tepid. This was spontaneous combustion, fire and massive pressure like in a diesel engine. He was revving me faster and faster with nothing to govern my response. I tightened up like a spring as the stinging draw of his mouth pulled something deep in my belly.

And, *Oh god*, it was happening. I could feel it overtaking me, like icy fire spreading outward from my pelvis. On my damn—front lawn—with just—his mouth—on my—breast—my neighbor—my evil—neighbor—was making me—*God, the pressure*—cum!

I writhed and bucked, yanked at his hair, and made enough noise to wake the dead. I was pretty sure there wouldn't be a game animal within ten miles of this location for *weeks*. There was no way he missed that he'd just given me a screaming orgasm, and it was obvious by the growl-like noise that vibrated against me, and the throb of his bare cock against my sopping cleft, that he enjoyed it.

Then another couple things happened simultaneously. I hit that post-orgasm slump, that I-got-what-I-wanted moment of indifference where I could take or leave the incredibly hot, hard male body on top of me. Even one this good-looking; I was just like, 'meh'.

That was the same moment I felt his cock against me, not the shaft, but the big, broad, silky head. And it wasn't pressing against my clit. Oh no, it was pressing between my sodden pussy lips, looking for full-on admission.

But I wasn't a theater. And this was my *neighbor*. Who, I had to admit, was damn sexy and apparently mucho-talented in the sack. Er, grass.

But whom I *hated*.

I panicked. "Wait! I'm not on birth control!" Hey, it was true. There are some things you really don't need when you're at least six months and several miles from the nearest sperm that could attack your precious egg.

He paused, staring down at me with some strong cocktail of emotion making itself evident on his face. Lust, confusion, anger, focus, frustration. It was all there, and for one insane moment, I wanted to kiss the disbelieving part of his reddened lips. But the urge was nuts, and luckily, it passed.

I pushed at his shoulders, taking advantage of his preoccupation to shove him off me—*hope he stubs his cock*—and scramble out from under him. I left my pants, my torn panties, and probably the shreds of my pride back there on the ground with him. And for the second time that day, I ran away.

# <u>Chapter Five</u>

**"Y**oo-hoo!"

I groaned and tightened my arm around my body pillow. I was sleeping in, dammit. It was my last day off before my brothers arrived, and I wanted it, I needed it... A good orgasm really took it out of a gal.

My half-open eyes detected a shadow moving high on my wall, and I sat up abruptly. Wait, had that voice from a few seconds ago been *real*? And had it come from...*inside*?

I heard someone whistling and the unmistakable sizzle of eggs in a frying pan.

*What. The fuck?* I thought furiously. Could it be my brothers? But they weren't due for another five days. And it didn't sound like my brothers.

My breathing and heartrate accelerated.

Yanking on the pants I'd left in a puddle next to the bed, and pulling the .45 from my nightstand drawer, I crept forward and peered over the bannister from the loft. Black hair that ate the light. Broad shoulders. Strong, tanned forearms and hands.

I watched with fascination as he made the egg flip without use of a spatula.

He looked up and caught sight of me. "*There* you are," he drawled.

"What. Are you doing. In my *cabin*?"

He blinked—a slow, innocent, infuriating motion. It wasn't convincing, not nearly so on that devilishly handsome face. "Just making you breakfast," he said, indicating the eggs and bacon he'd just arranged on a plate. "Don't you think we should talk about what happened yesterday?"

Was he dense? Was he a stalker? Both? I thought I'd locked the door. How the hell had he gotten in? What made him think he had the *right*?! Just because we'd almost bumped uglies on my pitiful lawn...

I tossed the .45 on my bed, relatively certain I wasn't going to need it. Then I scrambled down the ladder, ready to yell some sense into him. Then I turned around, and—

And...

*There he was.*

I was stunned to momentary speechlessness as I stared across the bare few feet that separated us. He was... he was...

Stunning. I'd seen him in the dark beside my lake, I'd seen him from a distance, even twice without his shirt. But a few feet away, in the natural light coming through the windows, occupying my space—he was like a punch to the gut. And he was just standing there, looking at home with his feet bare and a glass of water in his hand.

He was gorgeous. Life was so unfair.

"Like what you see?" he drawled.

"No," I croaked automatically, defensively. I still had my morning voice, and—it was like he sucked all the air out of the room. Seriously.

His eyes narrowed on me in a way I found extremely ominous. "I don't believe you," he said. Then he started to move forward.

Just like that, we picked up where we'd left off when he'd borrowed my dog—who was lazing in front of the couch, having completely failed her guard dog duties, the traitor.

But this time, he was trespassing, and encroaching on my personal space. My pussy clenched—and my eyes flicked to the shotgun leaning next to my front door. It was there, about a dozen feet away. I didn't think he'd try anything, but if he did, I'd have to get around him to get my boomstick. If he did, I'd fight dirty, and then I'd make thunder.

Resolved to put a slug-sized hole through him if need be, I glared as he came closer. My back hit the wall before I even realized I'd moved. *Shit*. It was never good to show fear.

I lifted my chin, trying to remedy my blunder. "I want you to get out of my cabin. Now." A good almost-fucking didn't give him the right to invade my space.

"I will," he murmured, looming over me, "when you admit you want me."

I pressed back against the wall, shocked into laughter. "Admit I want you? On what planet—?"

I didn't get to finish my sentence, because he reached out, and trailed his knuckles lightly down my cheek. And I didn't flinch away. No, I actually leaned into the caress and made the first— quickly abbreviated by me—part of a moan. I was mortified. *Was I so sex-starved that—?*

I didn't get to finish that *thought*, because he crowded up against me. There was barely an inch of room between us, and my nipples strained toward his chest. He was so *warm*—and so frickin' tall, and he smelled so frickin' good, and... I closed my eyes briefly, overwhelmed by the sheer enormity of his physical presence. *I've been in the woods too long.*

"I know you do," he said, his voice dropping low, into this la-la land of heated sighs and soaked panties. His hand braced against the wall next to my head as he leaned even closer. "Just tell me," he breathed against my lips. "Tell me you want me."

I tried to look up at him mutinously, but shivered instead. Had I woken up in one of my stories? His eyes took up the whole of my vision, and the morning light turned them into glowing chips of sea-green. He smelled like clean, crisp man.

And the gentle waft of his breath against me, the knowledge that his lips were only inches away from mine, was turning my legs to pudding. Was I really so desperate?

My mouth opened. I was going to yell at him, but no sound came out.

He moved that last inch that separated us, letting the aching points of my sensitive nipples press into his chest. His nose brushed against mine.

My chin tilted up. I couldn't help myself. I wanted those shapely lips. I wanted to kiss him for breakfast.

"Say it," he whispered.

*I need to masturbate more.*

To my shame, rather than telling him off, rather than calling him all the dirty names that were right on the tip of my tongue—all I made was a needy little noise. My fingers curled in his shirt, trying to pull him closer. I felt the bulge of his cock straining against my lower belly and I tilted my pelvis, pressing more firmly against it. I pushed up on tiptoes, straining toward his lips, needing him.

His lips were right...there...

And then, I felt a trickle. But it wasn't between my thighs. It was on the top of my head, and it was cool, and more and more, until water was running down my startled face and wetting my shoulders and the front of my shirt, making my nipples harden to diamond points.

I stared up at him in shock, seeing him move the now-empty glass away from me in my periphery. He smiled that awful, sexy Devil's smile. The bastard even had *dimples*.

"I got you wet," he said, looking down at the way my wet T-shirt stuck to the upper slopes of my breasts.

I could dump his body in the river. I could do it.

He laughed. Then he pushed away from me, set the glass on my table, and collected his shoes from beside my partly-open sliding deck door—*that's* how he got in! His gaze drifted to the side and he shot me a sly glance over his shoulder.

I stood there, chest heaving with equal parts shock, arousal, and fury, as I watched him cross the floor in front of me, throw back the deadbolt, and let himself out of my cabin the traditional way.

I cast about, looking for the subject of that sly glance. *What had he done, what had he done?* Then I saw it. My laptop, centered in front of my big picture window, lay open. I never left it open.

The bastard had been reading my book. And it was open to a sex scene.

# Chapter Six

I n my assessment of people who lived in the woods, I fell under the Loner category.

Thus, I wasn't much for barbecues. But Suzy was supposed to be there, and I hadn't seen her in a while. And there'd be free food, and I don't think I'd ever turned down free food. I'd even eaten what Gary had made me that morning.

The barbecue was an anniversary party for two of our longest-standing residents, a sweet old couple that ran the local post office.

Clearwater Lodge, owned and operated by Suzy's parents, was hosting the party. It was a neat little operation with eight cabins scattered back in the woods. None of them had indoor plumbing, but there was a central bath house with nice toilet facilities. The main building was a large, two-story chalet with a wrap-around deck that ended less than twenty feet from the river's edge.

As I approached in my boat, I saw that the party was already well under-way. Several people milled about on the deck and the lawn. Smoke billowed from the gazebo fire pit, and a breeze plucked at checked tablecloths already spread with food.

The lodge had pretty extensive boat parking at their dock, but every slot was full, so I pulled in to the shore alongside three other boats that'd done the same. I threw my anchor up on the beach, and picked my way over the other anchor lines to the steps that led up from the dock.

It was pretty much just at the top of the steps that I realized this hadn't been a good idea.

My ex-boyfriend slash asshole-extraordinaire stood twenty feet away, bullshitting with his guide buddies. Most fishing guides were viewed by the locals with the deepest suspicion, and in Brett's case, it was warranted. He was a skeezy, schmoozing, low-life egotist who'd do anything for a buck. We'd been together almost a year, and I had no idea how it had taken me as long as it did to catch on to what a grasping, arrogant, self-centered asshole he was.

We'd broken up six months ago, and I'd managed only to see him from afar, in another boat on the river, since. I didn't want to see him up close, without an expanse of icy water between us, and I certainly didn't want to conversate with the fucker.

I turned around, intending to walk back down those steps and motor away. I had a chest freezer full of food—I could find something else to eat.

"Helly!"

I winced. *Oh, goddamn.* I turned around. "Hey, Ed." Over his shoulder, I saw that Brett had glanced up at my name, and his shit-brown eyes were on me. *Double damn.*

"Hey," Ed said, ending his eager trot in front of me. "How's the four-wheeler running?"

"Great, thank you," I said. "I'd really like to pay you for your help. How much—"

"Naaahhh," he said, waving off my offer. "We're friends, right? Consider it a favor," he said with a wink.

I clenched my teeth. He didn't understand. I didn't want to owe him a 'favor'.

He took me by the elbow, and guided me toward *his* group of buddies. I let him, because I was shamelessly using him as a shield against my ex-boyfriend.

I glanced around for Suzy, but didn't see her.

"Beer?" Ed asked.

"Please." I was going to need to be well-liquored to tolerate this evening, I just knew it.

He introduced me to his group of friends—there were two I

didn't know—and then dashed off to get me a drink.

"Helly," the new friend named Max said. "That's an unusual name. Is it after the clothing line?"

Helly Hansen was a fancy outerwear brand, and it was a fair question, but I found it funny that a man was asking it. I smiled. "My name's actually Haley, it's just my brothers started calling me Helly instead, and it stuck."

"And do you work at one of the lodges?" he asked.

"I'm a fishing guide," I said. "I've worked for all of the lodges at one time or another."

Ed's friends tittered, the locals making their usual subtly sniping comments and jokes about female guides, and women doing men's work. Sexism in the Alaskan bush is alive and rampant, but my response was tempered by the knowledge that men truly were better at a lot of tasks (not including fishing, of course) necessary for survival in the wilderness. They were quite simply bigger and stronger, and that made a heck of a difference in daily life out here on the ragged edge of civilization. Just try pull-starting a snowmachine sometime, and you'll see what I mean. So although their comments irritated me, they were nothing I hadn't heard before.

"Isn't it bad luck to have a woman on a boat?" asked the other newb whose name I'd already forgotten. Ed's friends laughed as if he were funny.

Just because I'd heard it before didn't mean I had to put up with it. "Excuse me," I said. I turned around, snatched the beer out of Ed's outstretched hand, and chugged it as I crossed the lawn toward the steps.

"Helly!" Suzy's high, sweet voice cut through the hubbub.

I turned toward her. She was adorable, as usual, somehow turning a plaid shirt into a fashion statement, a red handkerchief failing to contain her cloud of curly brown hair. She had bright eyes caught somewhere between green and brown, a mischievous smile on an elfin face, and the cutest freckles I'd ever seen.

"Oh thank God," I said. "Please save me. Ed thinks I owe him something because he fixed my four-wheeler, and his friends are sexist pricks, and Brett's over there waiting for his opportunity to strike. All I wanted was free food!"

"Aww," Suzy said, patting my arm. "I'll protect you from them. Come get a burger with me."

We wound over to the grills, stopping along the way to congratulate Dotty and Harv. They were an adorable couple, both in their 70s. Dotty asked how my writing was going, and gave me a wink from under her cloud of white hair.

We finally moved on with me shaking my head. I really didn't understand why I got along so much better with older folk than with the assholes my own age. Maybe I should have been looking for an older man…

Suzy and I went through the burger line, and then settled at the picnic table up on the deck so I could keep an eye on both Brett and Ed.

"So how's it going with your new neighbor?" she asked.

I almost choked. And then I turned red. It was just yesterday we'd almost had sex in my yard, and then just this morning that he'd made me look like an idiot and dumped a glass of water on my head.

She laughed. "That good, huh? My parents invited him, but I haven't seen him yet."

I shot to my feet, ready to abandon my burger and get the hell outta Dodge. Ed and Brett in the same space were one thing. I absolutely knew adding my neighbor to the mix would trigger Armageddon.

"Oh, quit being so melodramatic." Suzy grabbed the hem of my shirt and yanked me back down to my seat. "You can share airspace with your neighbor. I told you, I'll protect you. Here, have another beer."

I whimpered, feeling like a trapped animal, and chugged my second beer. About ten minutes after that, I was at the point where everything was a wee bit fuzzy around the edges, and the world was doing a gentle wobble.

Suzy waited until my wobble stage to ask me again. "So, seriously, how's it going with the neighbor? Did you take my advice?"

I nodded. "I did ask him to be quiet in the mornings—you would have been proud of me, I was damn polite, but it was wasted on him because—do you know what he did?"

She shook her head, looking entertained. "No idea."

"The very. Next. Morning. He woke me up again. Six a.m., his damn saw starts up." My hand clenched into a fist, crushing my red plastic cup.

I must have had a look in my eye, because she said, "Oh, Helly, what did you do?" She knew me so well.

"I woke him up, with my chainsaw. Practically under his window. At four a.m.," I added with a self-satisfied smirk.

Suzy looked like she didn't know whether to gasp or laugh. She covered her open, smiling mouth with a dainty hand—*why couldn't my hands be that cute?*

"And… I locked myself in his cabin, cut his hammer in half, and stole his saw blade," I continued.

"Helly!" I'd obviously shocked her, but she recovered fast. She leaned forward, her eyes dancing. "What did he do?" she asked.

"Stole the chain off *my* saw, started playing loud music when he works, and is even more blatant about having stolen my dog," I said bitterly.

"What do you mean, he stole your dog?"

"I found her on his couch the other day. She had her head in his lap and he was feeding her junk food. And now, I see her hanging out over there a lot. More than she ever hangs out with me," I muttered, and I knew I was pouting, but I couldn't seem to stop.

"Wait. Mocha likes him? Mocha, your spooky dog, had her head in some guy's lap?"

"Yeah." My tipsy mind was going a little wild with the head-in-Gary's-lap imagery.

I glanced over to see Suzy's brows had shot to her hairline. Even though I was getting on toward drunk, I had just enough control of myself not to tell her about the orgasm he'd given me. If she found my dog changing sides shocking, I could only imagine how she might react to *that* news. More importantly, I wasn't nearly ready to own up to my little transgression.

"You know," she said finally, "I've always thought dogs were good judges of character."

I scoffed. "By that logic, he's a better character than me."

She just looked at me with this irritating little smile on her face. I went and got another beer.

The neighborhood women found us and sat down, and soon the table was full of talk. I frowned, hearing the break-ins were still going on downriver. And moving up. Whoever the perpetrators were, they were armed. If the cabin they were 'visiting' was locked, they were just as likely to shoot it open as they were to break the window.

"But they aren't really taking anything," one of the women said. "It's so odd. Guns, things of value, just left behind."

"They're probably just vandals," Suzy pointed out. "Those miserable people that take joy out of destroying other people's stuff."

"Or else they're looking for something," someone suggested.

"Has anybody even seen these people? They've been here for a couple weeks now; surely someone has seen something suspicious."

The women all shook their heads. "With all these fishermen in for the summer, there are way too many strange faces. No one stands out."

"Well, my Mikey has started sleeping with his gun under his pillow. If anyone tries to break into *our* cabin, they'll be sorry."

The conversation drifted on to commiserations about husbands, with Suzy gleefully soaking up details of the latest marital strife.

I finally tuned out entirely. *Husbands. Who needs 'em? Er…people with broken four-wheelers, that's who.*

When all of the females at my table gasped in unison, I looked up. I followed their gazes, and what did I see? You guessed it. My neighbor. The one who'd chased me, tackled me, and made me scare the wildlife.

I drank my third beer as they talked about how good-looking he was, what nice hair he had, what broad shoulders. *What big eyes and teeth, more like.*

"And he's got a helicopter!"

"Oooo!" went the group.

*Just kill me now.*

Conversation moved on from there, and I tried not to think too hard about why I kept watching Gary. He showed no discomfort at all moving around and talking to dozens of people he didn't know. If I was being objective, I could say he had a nice strong handshake, a lovely smile, and shoulders and biceps that strained at his shirt. He appeared to be quite charming when he wanted to be, and the one or two women who weren't at our table threw themselves at him.

Make that the women at our table, too. Even the married ones eventually excused themselves to go make his acquaintance.

At one point, Brett slithered his way in through the circle of ladies. I snorted, watching him balefully. I couldn't hear him, but I could see that ingratiating smile on his face, and I knew exactly what my horrible-human-being ex was up to. He was trying to make a new rich buddy, because God knows, you can never have too many of those.

It was interesting to see that Gary seemed immune. He was friendly enough, but he didn't seem more interested in talking to Brett than he was anyone else. I wasn't sure, but toward the end of one of Brett's little speeches, I thought I caught the faintest hint of irritation on Gary's face. He finally managed to escape my ex and went to get some food.

I had to stop watching him when he looked up and caught my eye. His lip quirked, and a rush of lust so strong it ought to be illegal blasted through me. Damn him. I had a perfectly nice man pursuing me—one with mechanical skills!—and it was this damn loud-ass piece of work that apparently did it for me. It made absolutely no sense.

Those beers finally caught up with me, and I excused myself to make my way to the restrooms in the bath house. The evening was getting more advanced—I guessed it to be a little after nine p.m.— and the shadows were getting longer.

I'd rounded the corner of the lodge and was tottering along when somebody grabbed me. I had a bare second to recognize Brett's face before his mouth crashed down on mine. Then he stuck his tongue down my throat.

I was drunk, but I wasn't *that* drunk.

I tried to push him away. "Brett, get off me!" I mumbled, my elocution foiled by his slimy tongue. I almost gagged at the over-powering taste of polish sausage and sauerkraut. When had I ever enjoyed his nasty kisses?

I finally shoved him off me, and staggered back, wiping his spit off my mouth. I glared at him. "What the fuck, Brett?"

"You know you want me, babe," he said. "Give us another chance. You know how good we are together."

"Fuck you," I said. And for the record, we weren't good together. Not at all. What he wanted was a little fuck-doll cheerleader, and though I was blonde, I had a few more brain cells to rub together than your average sex toy. And I really didn't want to fill that role for him. Not anymore.

I thought what I'd said was a pretty solid 'no', but he swooped in at me again with his mouth open and honing in on mine. He also reached for my breast.

I punched him in the gut, and stepped back so he didn't head-butt me when he folded over. Then, because I really couldn't resist, I planted my boot on his shoulder, and shoved him on his ass.

"And another one bites the dust," a familiar voice said.

I spun around, a motion that made my head swim. When I'd established that I wasn't gonna fall over, I said, "You!"

"Me," Gary agreed. He stood before me, looking unperturbed as he eyed my handiwork. Brett was still on the ground, acting like a giant pussy. I hadn't punched him *that* hard. I was a girl, for god-sakes. One who didn't work out. A proper cheerleader probably could have hit him harder.

"Where'd you learn your moves?" he asked.

I put my hands on my hips. "I have brothers."

Gary nodded. "Fair 'nuff."

Brett groaned, and we both watched as he rolled to his feet. His hair was messed up, he had grass stains on his ass, and he looked enraged. "You *bitch!*" he hissed.

He lunged for me, and I was gonna drop-kick his nutsack, but Gary stopped my ex in his tracks. He didn't even hit him; he just stepped in, seized his hand in a move that looked deceptively casual but was snake-strike fast, and did...*something* to it. Brett went up on his toes, and he whooped for air as his eyes bulged.

"Now," Gary said. "I could break your hand, or you could apologize to the nice lady and walk away."

"I'm sorry," Brett squeaked. "I'm sorry, I'm sorry."

Gary released him, frowning as the giant pussy douche hurried away. "That was too easy," he said.

I agreed with his assessment, but my eyes narrowed on him. "Why are you here?" I asked.

"I was invited," he said. "I was told there was free food."

I crossed my arms and was trying to invent some reason to yell at him when Ed rounded the corner and saw us.

He jogged over. "Hey, Helly, is this guy bothering you?" Ed asked.

I slapped my hand over my eyes, massaged the ache in my temples, and tried manfully not to scream. My love life was a goddamn circus.

"You okay?" Ed asked. His sticky-sweet concern grated on my nerves.

He'd been hounding me for *years*, and finally I'd had enough. I rounded on him, and alcohol-lubed words spilled forth. "Ed, I've been using you for your mechanical skills. I don't want you. I'm not interested in you, I'm not attracted to you, and I don't want to go out with you. I don't want you to ask me how I am or bring me beers or do me favors. I just want you to leave me alone. Please," I said, trying to soften what I was just then realizing was a really harsh rejection.

Ed made a sound remarkably like a sob, and then turned and ran away.

God, I *was* a bitch.

"They're dropping like flies," Gary observed. "For his mechanical skills, eh?"

I growled. "I'm fucking out of here." I turned to storm away, thought better of it, and stormed to the bathroom instead. By the time I let myself out, Gary was gone, and I was just a wee bit calmer. Still leaving, though.

Suzy grabbed me just before I made the stairs down to the dock.

"Where are you going?" she asked. As if that weren't completely apparent.

"I'm leaving!"

"Helly, you can't drive your boat like this. You could lose your guiding license. You know that."

My shoulders slumped. I did know that.

"I can take her home," said that familiar voice from behind me. "Before she makes anyone else cry."

We both turned to look at Gary. I opened my mouth to give him the reaming he deserved, and Suzy slapped me right in the boob.

"Ow," I said, rubbing it.

"That would be wonderful," Suzy said, beaming up at him. Obviously she was among his conquests; looking at him all googly-eyed, trusting her drunken best friend to his protection, and tit-slapping me when I was about to verbally fillet him.

Hadn't I told her he murdered my blueberries? The man was a *killer*, and she was sending me alone into the dark of night with him. Just because my dog liked him? Oh wait, he was the son of a family friend, too.

And he was hot—that was probably the real reason, right there. I wanted to tell her that hotness did not good people make, as evidenced by Brett, but she was still grinning up at Gary like an idiot. She probably wouldn't even hear me. Or she might slap me again.

I dropped my hand away from my boob when I realized he was watching me rub it. I grimaced.

We haggled over whose boat we were going to take, and I finally stumped into his. He'd had to park over on the shore, too, and I grinned as my boots left big clods of silt and mud on his shiny silver decking. I dropped into the seat in the front farthest from him.

Suzy waved from the shore. "I'll drop your boat off later tonight," she called.

I raised a hand, hoping she'd understand it meant, *'I'm kinda miffed at you, but I love you even though you give my neighbor googly eyes. But don't do it again. And thank you for being awesome and dropping off my boat. Hussy.'*

I think she mighta understood. Or maybe it was just my wet-cat expression. Either way, she laughed.

Then Gary pushed us off, and moved past me to his console in the back. I was hoping his outboard wouldn't start—even though that wish made no sense, considering we were now free-floating and starting to drift downstream—but it roared smoothly to life with a turn of his key. Key-start ignition, steering wheel, cushy seats. Fancy.

I grunted, eyeing his steering wheel. I had a tiller myself, a handle connected directly to the engine and jet, which offered more responsive steering for going up rocky, winding creeks. But he was a newb, so he probably didn't know that. He'd learn. Or he'd die. Either would be acceptable, but I knew which one I preferred.

I was facing the stern to keep the wind and blowing grit out of my eyes, but I avoided making eye contact, and I didn't speak to him. The roar of the boat motor was such that conversation would have been difficult, and I really didn't want to talk to him anyway.

He had a ball cap pulled down low over his eyes, but I still saw them flick to me a few times. There was a good ten minutes of roaring silence as we skimmed along.

After I realized my initial grumpiness was unmaintainable, I found myself trying really, really hard not to think about what his naked body would feel like pressed against mine. I couldn't seem to pry my gaze from his hand, where it wrapped around his steering wheel. I could easily imagine it gripping my hip as he drove into me. Or cupping and teasing my breast. I shuddered. *God, that had been good.*

When he nosed into our little slough, there was an unfamiliar boat in the parking spot we'd been squabbling over the past week. Gary cut the engine, and we slid in beside it.

I was looking around for some clue as to who the boat belonged to and why it was there, when three men stepped out of the shadows of the trail. The light wasn't all it could have been, but it was enough to see they weren't from around here. Their clothes were too nice, too light-colored, and they had hair product and tattoos and the glint of jewelry—women barely wore jewelry around here, let alone men (and don't even get me started on hair product). One was even wearing a Hawaiian shirt, and *no one* around here would be caught dead in a Hawaiian shirt.

They were big guys, and as they started down the beach toward me, they looked menacing and thuggish.

Because I was drunk, I climbed out of the boat onto the beach anyway.

One elbowed the other, pointing at me. I didn't know what that meant because I didn't speak thug.

"That's her," the elbower said in English.

"It's me," I sang. "And who the hell are you?"

They came closer, fanning out and moving toward me with a casual slowness that I would have found suspicious if I'd been sober. But I wasn't, and every time I blinked, it seemed like they teleported a foot or two. Which I found kinda funny.

"You shot down our drone," the one in the middle said.

I frowned. *Ah yes,* I guess I had shot down a drone. I cast a glance back at Gary. I'd thought it was his. But I guess it had been theirs. So the way I saw it, I had two choices: I could apologize, or I could get belligerent.

I took a step toward them. "You were spying on me," I accused.

The one in the middle shrugged, looking unrepentant. He had an expression on his face that I instantly hated, one that said he knew I was a buzzed blonde, and he very much wanted to take advantage of that.

He raked his gaze down over me. "You looked real good in a bikini," he said. They closed in another step, pushing past the edge of my casual-acquaintance bubble. "But now we're missing a drone. How are you gonna make that up to us? Hmm?"

He was leering, I realized. They were all leering. This had somehow turned into a bad situation.

The one to my right reached for me, and Gary caught his wrist. I hadn't realized he'd come up behind me, and I don't think they'd really noticed him at all.

But now the one with a captured wrist peered up under the brim of Gary's ball cap. His dark eyes narrowed. "Hey," he said, "you're—"

As he was speaking, he reached for Gary. Gary took exception to this, and drove the heel of his hand up into the guy's face. The thug toppled.

The other two leaped forward, knocking me aside as they rushed past. I spun as I fell, and wound up doing a butt-plant in the sand. The spinning made me dizzy as hell, but I'd landed facing Gary and the thugs.

He was beating them up. My vision kept oozing sideways, but I was able to gather that much. Gary was just a blur of movement with quick, hard jabs of his hands and elbows. I heard grunts. Thuds. In just moments, Gary was the last man standing. At his feet, the men groaned.

He bent over them, starting to pat them down. He came up with a gun, and this was the part my alcohol-soaked brain couldn't quite comprehend. Like some magic trick, the dark metal sort of clicked and slid apart in his hands. Then he tossed the parts away and re- peated the performance on the next guy's gun, and the next.

I shook my head, sure I was seeing things. It didn't surprise me that they all had guns, but what Gary had done with them… Guns didn't just fall apart, and they certainly didn't fall apart in the hands of some millionaire city-slicker. 'Cuz that's what Gary was. *Right*?

He looked up and saw me sitting in the sand, and his lips twitched. "You think you can drive a four-wheeler in your condi- tion?" he asked.

I scoffed. I wasn't *that* drunk. "Sure," I said, crawling to my feet. I brushed off my damp ass and eyed the thugs. Gary'd only had a few moments with them, but they only looked half-conscious at best.

"Why don't you go ahead on up to the cabin," Gary suggested. "I wanna have a talk with these three."

I met his eyes. "I thought the drone was yours."

This time he outright smiled at me. "I thought as much." He jerked his chin toward the four-wheeler. "Go. We'll have a talk about you shooting my property later."

I grunted, and managed to swing a leg up over the seat. When had putting the four-wheeler in gear gotten so complicated? I got it rolling in the right direction, and steered it carefully up along the trail.

I'd made it maybe halfway to my place when realization hit me. My thumb slipped off the gas, and the four-wheeler puttered to a halt on the darkening trail.

My neighbor, Gary, had just taken down three armed men. With his bare hands. In seconds.

I was seriously, seriously beginning to doubt he was a school teacher.

A flash of movement caught my eye, and I looked up to see Mocha streaking up the trail toward me, a big doggie smile on her face. "Heya girl," I said. She butted her head against my leg, and I leaned down to pet her.

That's how I found out how surprisingly comfortable it was resting my cheek against the gas cap. I didn't really decide to take a nap. My eyes just sort of drifted shut, and things went dark for what felt like just a moment before a concerned voice woke me.

"You okay? Helly?"

I sat up, looking around bleary-eyed. Gary was jogging along the trail toward me, though he slowed when I straightened.

"I thought you were driving home," he said, his voice warm with bottled laughter.

The four-wheeler was still running. And in gear, I noticed with a thread of embarrassment. "I got distracted," I said.

"Scoot forward a bit," he said, stopping so he was standing next to my boot.

"I can drive," I grumbled.

"Uh-huh. You just fell asleep while driving. You are drunk. Now scoot forward; I'll drive you home."

I scooted. Stupid alcohol, making me all agreeable and shit. I made a note to blame it later.

He swung up to straddle the seat behind me. My nipples hardened, and my breath came a little bit shorter. I couldn't help it. The man was hot, and now I knew he was dangerous, which only made him hotter. I was sitting between his legs, and then his arms came up to either side of me, caging me in.

"So you talked to them?" I asked, trying to keep my mind off the feel of the man behind me.

His breath was warm against my hair as he answered. "Yes. They won't bother you again."

"That's good," I said. I could barely think past... him.

He didn't intentionally crowd me, but as we moved down the trail, bouncing over roots, his thighs brushed mine. The spots where we occasionally touched felt overly warm and hypersensitive, the air between us charged. The vibrations of the engine weren't helping at all, and I actually felt like whimpering as we rocked over a big rut. Heat radiated from his solid body, beckoning mine.

I finally leaned back against him with a sigh, giving in to it. I was drunk, right? I was allowed to have no self-control. I turned my head until my cheek pressed against his neck, and just breathed him in. He smelled like shaving cream or aftershave today, a spicy male scent that had my head doing a lazy spin.

The heat was growing, and sexy thoughts started to flash through my head. I was finally starting to admit it to myself; I wanted him. At this point, though, my pride was such that I wouldn't throw myself at him. But if *he* went after *me*....

We were alone, riding back to my cabin, where I had a bed. And I was drunk, and easy, and I realized I really, really wanted him to take advantage of that.

By the time he steered us into my little drive, I was breathless with anticipation. He killed the engine, and then swung down from behind me.

Pussy throbbing, feeling his eyes on me, I dismounted.

He followed me to the stairs. As I pushed through the door, he started up after me.

*This is it,* I thought, turning to look at him.

Gary was very close. Standing on that top step, he was a dark presence filling my doorway. His eyes were enigmatic, the planes of his face utterly masculine in the shadow of his hat. I got caught up in admiring his strong jaw, the generous curve of lips I hadn't yet tasted. My gaze drifted lower. I wanted to shove his jacket off his solid shoulders, peel that T-shirt off him like a candy wrapper.

One of his arms lifted, bracing him against the doorframe. Something about that move, the way he crowded me, made me tighten with aching, breathless desire. Helpless against it, wanting him to take me *now*, I swayed toward him.

"Good night," he said. And then he pulled the door shut in my face.

I was still blinking into the darkness when he rapped on it. My heart jumped in my chest. *Had he changed his mind?* I reached for the knob.

"Lock this," I heard.

*Well… fuck.*

# Chapter Seven

I'd had four days to stew. That's not all I did, of course. I went to work each morning, I got another story sent off, I had dinner with Suzy, and I even sent my brothers a grocery list.

But I found myself glancing frequently out my window toward the neighbor's cabin. I wondered what he did for a living. I wondered where he'd learned to fight. But most of all, I wondered where on earth this overpowering attraction to him had come from.

I couldn't even write the steamy scenes he'd so inspired. Instead, on this sunny day off, in the last hours I had to myself before my brothers crashed into my life, I sat there at my desk, staring across the lake at his stupid cabin.

For the last four days, I'd thought about retaliation for the water glass incident. I'd planned about a dozen different ways of getting him back. But I knew, after him letting himself into my house and watching him manhandle my attackers, that it was a bad idea. The man was dangerous, and it seemed like neither of us had brakes. The situation would surely escalate, like in those mob movies. People would die, and someone would find a bloody moose's head on their sheets.

I wouldn't put it past my diabolically good-looking neighbor to climb in through my second-story window to consummate some devious plot. Actually, most of my fantasies of him crawling in my window like Edward Cullen—a sex scene I'd written before he'd broken in and read my stuff, dammit—didn't involve the kind of moisture that came out of a glass. And, unlike Edward the sparkly vamp, my fantasy lover wasn't hesitant and full of teenage angst. No, he had pitch black hair and a sexy dent in his chin, and he jumped on my supine form, pinning me to the mattress, and latched directly onto my neck.

I gasped, hand rising to cover a phantom hickey. *See?!!* This was why I couldn't write, couldn't think, couldn't do much of anything, really. Pent-up sexual frustration at its worst. My pussy'd been burning for *days*.

Because of *him*. I gnawed on my lip, still staring across the water.

What was he *doing* over there? I'd heard hammering noises, had been hearing them all day. The faint rasp of a saw.... I closed my eyes, imagining him sprawled in a sunbeam swirling with motes of sawdust, lying back on his elbows on an unfinished floor in nothing but an old pair of Carhartts.

This situation couldn't continue. I was obsessed; absolutely, irrevocably *in lust* with my evil neighbor.

So what were my options?

1: I could kill him. It was an option I'd already explored at length. I had a foolproof plan for body disposal, but he was rich, and I knew he had friends. People would investigate, and I was the only suspect—they'd probably find blood spatters, powder burns on my fingers, footprints, and my gun. I'd watched CSI; I knew how this worked.

And then there was my conscience, the potential jail time, and the fact that I'd be robbing the world of a gorgeous specimen of masculinity. Albeit a loud one.

2: I could ignore him. Yeah, that wasn't working, not at all.

The only choice left to me was, 3: Have sex with him. Hopefully over, and over, and over again, wild, sweaty, screaming monkey sex that put the ramblings of my sex-starved mind and shaking, feverish, key-stabbing fingers to shame. Dirty, dirty shame up against a wall, on some stairs, in the mud, in a canoe, in a frickin' tree if we could manage it.

I shuddered, trying to find a more comfortable position in my chair. The problem was, there wasn't one that didn't apply pressure—but not nearly enough!—to my raging lady-boner.

So, sex. But how should I go about it? Having been born and raised in Alaska, and having spent the last four years of my life in the woods, I was socially awkward. I knew it, probably everyone I met knew it. So, option 3A: I could put on makeup and stick out my chest and made small talk and try to flirt like a normal person... but I'd probably just look and sound ridiculous.

Option 3B: Just walk over there, and grab him. Yeah, that seemed more my style. It would take guts, though. And I probably shouldn't bring my gun.

But what would I say? 'We should fuck'? 'Hey neighbor, I was feeling horny and decided to drop by with some cream...' or 'Your cock felt delicious against me. I want it inside me. Now.'

I cringed a little, knowing those words would never actually pass my lips. My heroine's, sure. But mine? Way, way too forward.

How about the simpler 'Let's be fuck buddies'? See, that felt pretty good. Fuck buddies, I could do. I'd just tell him not to talk to me unless he was growling dirty nothings in my ear. No conversation outside of sex. I didn't want to talk to him; I just wanted his body.

*It could work*, I thought. I could be an adult about this. Whether *he* could remained to be seen, but really, as long as he could stay hard, and keep his mouth shut, we'd be in business.

*It could work.* I pushed back from my desk, mulling over the logistics. I was gonna go over there, but...

What to wear? My clothes were all ratty and baggy and stained, except for my fisherwoman getup, but I certainly wasn't wearing *that*.

I had one casual flowy skirt that Suzy had given me and that I hardly ever wore because it was impractical. Mosquitos would bite the hell out of my legs in that skirt, and I just knew one day I'd get it caught in my generator belts. But it seemed like a good choice for seduction. And nothing underneath, I decided. All of my underwear were ugly, and bare would make for quicker access.

Speaking of bare...should I shave? *Shit*. He'd been rubbing up against me the other day and he hadn't complained. But he hadn't been down close to my legs. I didn't have a lot in the way of body hair, and what little I had was blonde, but if you looked really, really close... *Ugh.*

I hated this crap. This was why I didn't live in town, considerations like these. Chased down and tackled on the lawn was so much easier. Simpler. And fun, much more fun than this premeditated crap.

And now I was mad at him for making me stress out about this. My eyes narrowed as I dropped my skirt back around my calves.

He'd gotten me wet. Literally, wet. Twice. Not to mention my pussy, which had been soaked almost since the first time I'd seen him. I could give him a little payback. I *should* give him a little payback. After all, what was I afraid of? That he'd chase me down and tackle me and give me an orgasm?

...Yeah, now we're on the same page.

I put on my most flattering top, brushed my hair, and went and got a bucket. I picked it up, rubbing my fingers over the scratch marks on its side. I remembered this bucket. It was the one I'd smacked away from Gary's chest so I could get to him after he set fire to my blueberries. I was still sore about that. Maybe if I got my teeth on him, I'd bite extra hard.

Before I lost my nerve, I picked my way along the beach to his place. I scooped the bucket half-full of lake water, and then walked up his lawn. My heart was beating fast, my lower belly tight with anticipation.

The sound of a hammer got louder. It seemed like it was coming from around back.

I circled the porch, fingers tight on the bucket, my breath rasping in my chest.

And there he was. The whole back wall of the living room had been torn down, and he was on his knees facing away from me, prying at a stubborn baseboard.

I paused, taking him in. He wore another plain cotton T-shirt, and he actually *was* wearing a pair of Carhartts. The worn duck hugged the hard curves of his ass as he bent over, making my heart stutter. A rich city boy had no right to own a pair of Carhartts that well-used, let alone to look so damn good in them.

And he looked like he knew what he was doing, efficiently dismantling that wall. All of his tools were set out across the interior space that had been stripped down to the plywood floor. A neat stack of lumber lay off to one side under a tarp, and large new windows leaned against the building beyond him.

I hesitated. This was inappropriate. What person in their right mind just walked up onto someone else's property and threw water on them? Especially on someone they barely knew, while they were working. It would be so childish, so *rude...*

My lips curved. Gary had done it. My heroine would do it.

And why not? There was a streak of crazy about a mile wide running through my family, and on this particular afternoon, I was going to embrace my heritage. Life is short—poke the bear.

I threw the water on him. My aim was perfect, the brunt of it dead-on his back.

He yelled, and flipped over onto his ass. He glared up at me, breathing hard.

I was breathing hard, too, my shoulders trembling as I tried not to laugh.

He leaned forward and pushed slowly to his feet, never taking his eyes off of me.

I gulped, but stayed rooted. I wasn't gonna run. I wanted to be caught.

I squealed as he scooped me up into his arms. I flailed, terrified that he'd drop me. People didn't pick me up. People knew better than to pick me up. I was a scary Alaskan chick with a big gun. The height was sickening, and the loss of control—I had no idea what he was going to do, and it made me cling embarrassingly tight to his head.

He laughed as he peeled me off him—and then I screamed for real as he threw me.

*Splash!*

*Fuck!* Why hadn't I seen this coming?

I righted myself and pushed to my feet in the soft muck at the bottom of the lake. *Ewwww.* Squeegeeing water out of my eyes, I glared up at him.

He was staring down at me. "Did I just see a flash of bare ass?" he asked.

I hadn't thought anything could, but a plunge in the lake seemed to have cooled my ardor. "I guess you'll never know," I said, turning, intending to avoid him entirely and swim back to my place.

*Splash!*

Strong hands grabbed me and pulled me back against a hard body.

His forearm curled around my waist, while his hand slid down my side, gathering my wet skirt in his fingers, dragging it up. My nails dug into his arm, and I couldn't seem to catch my breath as his callused fingers slid up the inside of my thigh.

Then, he touched me.

My world imploded. I threw my head back against his shoulder as my body tightened like a bow, grinding my clit against his fingers, and my ass against his growing erection. I moaned, long and low.

"Fuck," he said, a man after my own heart.

His stubble scraped against my neck as his fingers slid between my plump, slick folds. His breath was on me, and then his hot mouth. He treated my neck like he had my breasts, latching on, sucking hard, scraping with his teeth. He wasn't gentle, and I loved it.

He drove me *wild*. I bucked against him, hyperaware of each delicious slide of those fingers. I reached back and grabbed his hips, dragging him even closer, grinding us together to the point of pain.

And he was with me. He gave me what I wanted and more, pushing against me, squeezing my breast, his breath rasping fast and hot in my ear. Two thick digits pushed into me with authority, thrusting and curling. I made crazed noises as I arched into his hand, squeezing his fingers with delight. *Yessss!*

And then I felt it. A stinging sensation on my ankle. And another. I gasped, eyes opening wide as realization struck like lightning.

My breath released on a shriek. "Leeches!" I thrashed free of his hold, and flailed to shore. I ran up out of the water and dropped to my ass in his grass, swiping at the thin black things clinging to my pale skin. Alaskan leeches were nothing compared to the fat abominations in the Lower 48, but still—they were *so* disgusting! I shuddered as I got the last of them, still searching between my toes and twisting my leg this way and that to make absolutely *sure*.

I finally looked up to realize my neighbor was sitting on his heels just a few feet away. He was wet up to his scrumptious shoulders, his brown shirt clinging to him like a layer of bittersweet chocolate icing. And he was staring at me.

"Are you doing this on purpose?" he asked.

I looked down at myself. Back at him. "What?"

"Starting, then stopping. Teasing me. Frustrating me. This crazy act of yours—"

My spine stiffened. See, *this* was why I hadn't wanted him to talk. "Crazy *act*?" I asked, voice dangerously low. I realized at the last moment I'd put the emphasis on the wrong word, but I powered on, hoping he wouldn't notice. "You're the one who set fire to my blueberries, then splashed me, then *trespassed*."

"Your—*blueberries*?!" He looked momentarily puzzled, but then slashed his hand down, dismissing my argument. "We don't like each other, I get it. But you want me," he said, his eyes glinting.

I gasped. "N—" Not real sure what I was going to say, probably some inane lie.

He grabbed my ankle and dragged me across the grass to him. My skirt slid up, giving me a microsecond of panic. But then his weight was pressing down on me, and he had trapped my head between his hands, and his mouth sank down onto mine.

"Uhhh-mmmm." The sound ended on a sigh. I melted under him. Completely.

His mouth was amazing. Drugging. Warm and gentle and skilled as hell.

I had thought about drawing the line at kissing—it was way too intimate for what I had planned—but it only took him about two seconds to change my mind. How could I ever deprive myself of this?

His lips, his tongue, the slide and smell of him, that perfect pressure. He was warm over me, and heavy, pressing me to the ground, and my body responded as if the leech incident had never happened. I felt myself growing wetter, and I opened my thighs, pulling him between them. The bulge of his fly pressed against me, making me shudder.

I couldn't breathe, and I couldn't move. I was pinned to the ground, and it was the best, hottest kiss I'd ever had in the whole of my life.

Our mouths tore apart only when an airplane engine buzzed loud and low overhead.

"You've gotta be fucking kidding me," he half-laughed, his hips rocking against me as if he couldn't help himself.

"Oh shit," I panted. "Oh shit, I forgot."

He leaned back enough so I could see his raised brow. "You're expecting somebody?"

"My brothers," I wheezed. My brothers were coming to visit. *Today.* How could I have forgotten? My mind had been addled, that's how. Addled by lust.

Oh, fuck. There went my plans for seduction. And my brothers wouldn't just chase that plan away. They'd take it outside and use it for bullet practice. Then they'd chain it to the back of the four-wheeler and drag it through the woods, making sure it hit every root, every devil's club, and every wild rosebush in a mile radius.

We could both hear the plane circling the lake, angling for a landing.

Gary cupped my jaw—and kissed me again. He kissed me like he was drowning, like the rest of the world didn't exist, like there wasn't an airplane full of my gun-toting siblings on final approach. There was just me, and him, my thighs around his hips, and my fingers tangled in his thick, silky hair.

I forgot everything else, and I kissed him back with everything I had. Our tongues tangled, and our breath mingled, and he was in me so deep...

He finally drew back, and his eyes looked into mine for an endless moment. His beautiful eyes.

My heart thudded.

*No.* This wasn't supposed to happen. Gary was my evil neighbor. My fuck buddy, at most. *Not* a guy that made my heart fucking *thud*.

I shoved him off me, and decided right then—I wasn't kissing him again. Never, ever, no way, no sir.

# <u>Chapter Eight</u>

My brothers' plane cleared the trees on final descent as I was running, sopping wet from head to toe, back to my cabin. I slammed in through my door just after the plane touched down in the water, flew up to my loft, and did the fastest clothing change ever. New shirt, pants from yesterday, comb hands through hair— *Shit! Not while on ladder!*—sandals and out the door.

I met them on my little dock just as the plane drifted up alongside. I bent to secure the float to the mooring cleats.

The pilot climbed out, and the first thing I saw was his smirk. I had a sinking sensation in the pit of my stomach. *He'd seen.*

Rob Fulk was a burly red-headed gentleman in his forties who owned and operated the local flight service. I knew him by name, I was friendly with him, he'd even slept on my couch once for two nights in a row when he'd gotten weathered in. He'd shown me pictures of his new granddaughter.

And now I'd shown him my naked white thighs.

But he didn't say anything. He just gave me his usual greeting, a subtle nod with a murmured, "Helly." And then he opened up the doors.

My eldest brother Zack poured out, and my body was no longer my own. "Hel!" he cried. He picked me up in a crushing bear hug and twirled me around, ignoring the way the dock tipped dangerously under our combined weight. I couldn't breathe and I kinda wanted to whack him, but he had my arms pinned to my sides. Probably a strategic move on his part.

He finally set me down, and I couldn't help but grin up at him. He was a big guy with messy white-blonde hair, scars on his face, and tattoos slathered liberally across his skin. He had played hockey for the Alaska Aces for several years, and my limited understanding of what he did included skating and hurting people. Actually sounded kinda like something I would have been good at. Of course, that had all changed with his knee injury last season. Lately, he'd been doing construction jobs with Rory.

I saw Rory start to climb out after him, and I pushed at Zack's arm. "Take your bag and getcher ass up to the cabin," I said. "This dock won't hold all of us."

"Yes, ma'am," he said, with a salute and a devilish grin. He slung a duffel over his shoulder, tucked a box of groceries under his other arm, and swaggered away. Or maybe that was a limp.

"Little sister!" Rory lifted me off my feet and squeezed me till my ribs creaked. He and Zack were about the same size — or would have been, if Rory hadn't let himself gain a few extra pounds. Being hugged by him was like being hugged by a tank.

"Ror," I croaked. I croaked again, a little more desperately this time, when I was suspended there for another couple seconds.

"I've missed you," Rory whispered in my ear.

"Get off me, you overgrown brute," I growled, trying to pry myself free. He let go suddenly, and I almost tipped back into the water.

He rescued me at the last possible second, righting me with an evil grin.

I kicked him.

He pushed me.

I grabbed his arm and bent his pinkie back until he yowled, and then kicked him again.

J.D. laughed from inside the plane, kicking his brother from the back seat. "Go, you wuss. Outta the way."

J.D. was the runt of the litter. Where the others were each a couple inches over six foot — both damn near a full foot taller than me — J.D. topped out at a slender 5'9". He swung out of the plane and landed with deadly grace.

The thing about J.D. was, being the youngest and the smallest, he'd still thought he ought to be able to kick his brothers' asses. So he learned karate. Now he was a third or eighth or twenty-second — yeah, I wasn't sure, *bad sister!* — level black belt. Not to mention the wrestling, and Muay Thai, and whatever the newest fighting trend was.

The other two might shoot my plan and drag it at the end of a chain, but J.D.? He'd beat it to death with his bare hands. And maybe his feet.

J.D. wrapped me up in a tight hug, though he alone seemed to understand I didn't appreciate being crushed. Then he nudged me to the side, scooped up the remaining bags, and ran after his brothers. "I call the couch!" he shouted.

The hostile takeover had begun.

I stood there for a few moments, staring after them. Then, like an idiot, I glanced toward the neighbor's cabin. Gary was there, standing on his porch, still soaked to his armpits. Our eyes met.

Rob had seen, but somehow — *somehow* — my brothers had missed the heated embrace on my neighbor's lawn.

Upon entering my cabin, I was immediately hit by the riot of noise and motion. J.D. was unpacking an Xbox, Zack was digging around in my tiny fridge, and Rory...

"He cupped her quivering breasts. 'Yes,' she cried. 'Yes, yes! Take me now, Alfred. I want your huge, throbbing cock!'"

"Ah!" I yelled. I crossed the cabin in a flash, and tried to shoulder Rory away from my computer. "I did *not* write that!"

He laughed, picking up the laptop and easily evading my grasping hands. He adopted a ridiculous falsetto. "Put it in my mouth! Please, Alfred, I want every inch of your huge sausage. I want to guzzle gallons of your cum! I need your hot splooge like I need air!"

"Put that down!" I yelled. "I haven't backed up my files and you're gonna break it!" I should have secured the damn thing with a passcode before they came. I usually did, and I would have, but then I'd gotten busy with my neighbor instead.

And now Rory was spouting shoddy drivel and passing it off as my writing.

His hero's voice was low, over-sexed. "That's right, suck my big dick, Tasha," he said. "And Amie, lick my balls. Yes, just like that. Mmm, twins."

J.D. was laughing. He threw a pillow at his brother. "You're an idiot," he said.

"Where's the beer?" Zack demanded. He was rummaging in the boxes they'd piled on the table, looking frenzied. "Did we forget the beer?"

"Give. It. Back," I growled at Rory, giving him my crazy eyes.

They worked. He suddenly handed the laptop to me.

I took it with a sigh, and turned to set it gently back where it belonged.

Rory shot up my ladder to the loft. "I wonder if there's a vibrator up here," he said.

"Goddammit!" I dumped the laptop on my desk and chased him upstairs.

He was bent over, pulling open the drawer of my nightstand. "Aha! What have we—"

I head-butted him. We crashed into the far wall.

Before he could recover, I grabbed his nuts, and then squeezed. He slid down the wall and folded onto his knees until we were almost at the same eye level. When I was sure I had his attention, I hissed, "Repeat after me."

Rory nodded.

"This is Helly's bedroom."

He repeated.

"The loft is Helly's personal space. I will respect Helly's personal space. I will not go into Helly's personal space, for any reason. I will stay the fuck downstairs."

"Does she have you by the balls again?" Zack yelled from the kitchen.

Rory squeaked an affirmative. I heard J.D. laughing, and then that distinctive Xbox logo sound as he fired it up.

"Sucks, dude. Shoulda stayed downstairs," Zack said.

"Do you understand?" I asked.

He nodded.

I released him. "Go."

Rory fled. "It's pink!" he announced as he slid down the ladder. "And it had those little bunny ears!"

*Fuuuuck.* I dragged my hand down my face.

"That's sick, man, looking at your sister's jackrabbit," J.D. said. It sounded like he was scrolling through a menu.

"Aha!" Zack crowed. "Crisis averted! Ladies and gentlemen, the beer. Has been. Found!" I heard a beer fizz, and the sound of a cap landing on my floor.

I strode across my loft, slid down my ladder like Rory had, and crossed to Zack, who was just lifting a long-neck to his lips. I stole it from his hands, tipped it up to my mouth, and chugged. And chugged. And chugged.

I drank until there was none left, then plopped down on my couch and grabbed a controller. "Diablo III," I growled, and then motioned at Zack to gimme another. I'd need it to cope with their visit. The trick was to be just tipsy enough that I'd roll with their punches, but not drunk enough that I told them about my crush on the neighbor.

And in the meantime, I was gonna thrash demons with a really big mace.

We woke up late the next morning. I actually woke up on top of a mound of snoring, farting human flesh, my nose pressed into a hairy thigh. Truth be told, I almost screamed when the first thing I saw, and smelled, was my brother's package.

Gagging, I dragged myself into a sitting position and surveyed the wreckage. Beer bottles littered the floor along with brightly-colored candy wrappers. Someone had brought sunflower seeds and had tried to spit the shells into a bowl, but most appeared to have missed. My furniture had been rearranged, my favorite lamp was lying on the floor at a drunken angle, and my whole living room smelled like potato chips and ass.

Day one, I thought with a sigh.

Then I noticed Rory wasn't part of the pileup of bodies I'd been sandwiched in. I looked around, wondering if he could be in the bathroom. Maybe he stumbled outside to pee...?

I finally became aware that some of the snoring I was hearing came from above.

"You son-of-a-bitch!" I clambered up the ladder and kicked his ass outta my bed. It was his favorite trick, stealing my bed, and I had no idea how he continually got away with it.

After the commotion upstairs, my other two brothers were awake, and I struggled to get my ritual morning bathroom time.

By the time we were all showered, dressed, and fed, it was noon. According to my normal plan for my days off, I should have already gotten at least two thousand words done and had my second cup of coffee. Instead, I was nursing a headache along with my first cup, and wondering what shenanigans my brothers were going to get up to during their visit. Would my cabin survive it?

"Let's go fishing!" Zack exclaimed.

I groaned.

"What? It's a gorgeous, sunny Thursday, and there are a bunch of pike out there eating baby rainbow trout as we speak. We should go kill them," he concluded.

The problem with fishing was that they did not clean fish. *I* cleaned fish. So yeah, fishing was fun, but it always resulted in slimy, bloody work. That was fine when it was just me, but with all three of my brothers along multiplying the slimy, bloody work... Yeah.

"What, fish from the shore?" Rory asked. His tongue stuck out the side of his mouth as he tinkered with something on the table, something with little wires sticking out of it. He'd always liked blowing stuff up, and then he'd been a weapons guy in his couple years in the army. I really hoped he hadn't brought explosives into my cabin.

"Or from the canoe," Zack said.

"Hel's only got the one canoe," J.D. pointed out. He was dressed all in black as per his usual, black T and loose black pants. It made him look sleek and dangerous, like a panther lounging on my second-hand couch.

He also made a good point. My canoe only had two seats, and we'd sometimes stretched it to a third person sitting on a cooler in the middle. But four adults, three of them grown men? Completely out of the question.

"Well..." Zack glanced out the window. "I see two canoes out there."

"That's the neighbor's," I informed him. I watched Rory over the rim of my mug, trying to figure out what the hell he was doing.

Zack shrugged. "We could ask to borrow it."

"No!" My chair legs squeaked as I leapt to my feet, betraying my vehement reaction to that idea. I didn't want my brothers anywhere near the neighbor, and I *especially* didn't want them communicating. It seemed like a recipe for disaster; like throwing gasoline on a fire, like waving a red flag in front of a bull, like using a plug-in vibrator in the bathtub.

Zack stared at me, his stupid blue eyes starting to gleam.

I wanted to say more, wanted to tell them my neighbor was a dick, wanted to tell them he'd killed my blueberries and littered on my beach and almost shot my dog, and he was a devil with green eyes, and I didn't want to owe him any favors, and I most definitely didn't want to borrow his dirty canoe. But I didn't say those things. Instead, I clamped my mouth shut.

Zack had always been able to read me. I'd just said the one word, but with my eyes, and with my tone and volume and posture, I'd said far too much.

"I think," Zack drawled, "the lady doth protest too much."

"I wonder why she doth," Rory said, looking up from his work to peer out across the lake. The neighbor's helicopter sat, shiny and expensive on his now scarred and overgrown lawn, the cherry-red toy almost as big as the cabin itself. "I don't remember your neighbors having a helicopter," he said.

I shifted, wishing desperately for cover. I knew my face was an open book, and I didn't want to talk about the neighbor, not even to say I had a new one, because I'd give myself away. They'd figure out how attractive I found him, how he'd touched me, and how we'd nearly done the deed on my lawn. They'd *know*.

Zack's eyes narrowed. "She's keeping something from us," he said.

My heart was racing as I returned his gaze.

Then I did it. I made The Mistake.

I bolted. I raced to the bathroom and locked myself inside. Panting, feeling my crazy rising, I backed up across the thick pink rug.

Zack banged his fist on the door, rattled the knob, and then banged some more. "Come out, Helly! Come out and tell us about your neighbor." He said it in his evil sing-song voice that gave me nasty flashbacks to childhood teasing.

*Oh no.* I'd shown weakness—and my brothers smelled blood in the water.

I looked around wildly. It occurred to me to climb out the window, and take shelter in my generator shack. I could live there for a week, eating high bush cranberries and peeing in the woods. For the rest of the visit, I'd just entirely avoid the three-headed mythical monster I occasionally called family.

Or, or…if Zack picked the lock, I could hit him upside the head with the plunger. Yeah, I liked that idea better. Way too many mosquitos in the shed.

I heard voices conferring outside the door, and my apprehension increased.

"Helly, we've reached a decision," Zack announced. "We won't ask to borrow the neighbor's canoe."

I heaved a huge sigh, shoulders folding forward with the depth of my relief.

"We're gonna invite him to come fishing with us, instead." I heard a mad laugh, and then feet pounding away.

"*No!*" I frickin' *shrieked* it, and threw the door open. But it was too late. They were already gone.

Through the picture window, I saw the three of them running along the beach toward the neighbor's cabin. And what else could I do? I took off after them, continuing to yell, "Noooooooo!"

Yeah, that silence I was telling you about in which birds sang and water lapped? Drowned, shot all to hell, and trampled to death.

Gary opened his door just as I ran up behind the abominable trio. I saw him look at me, and then I doubled over panting, trying to catch my breath after the mad dash from my cabin to his.

"Well *hello*, Helly's new neighbor," Zack said, his drawl telling me in no uncertain terms he'd noticed my lake-buddy's sex appeal. "We're her brothers, Rory, J.D., and I'm Zack. And we were *wondering* if you'd like to go fishing with us today."

I straightened up and shook my head vigorously, making big eyes at Gary, begging him to decline. He looked at me for a long moment, holding eye contact. I really thought I was making an impression on him, that he'd say no—I mean, really, there was no reason on this earth why he'd say 'yes'!—and he'd go back into his cabin, and I'd go back to my side of the lake, and everything would be right with the world.

But then Gary said, "Sure. I'm Gary."

*Nooooooooo.* It felt like that part in the movies where the camera angle implodes.

Zack shot me a triumphant look, then, "Sweet. We're getting ready to go now, gonna take the canoes. We'll probably be gone most of the day, so if you've got any snacks, or beer," he said hintingly.

I was so shocked, I actually stood there for several seconds after my brothers had turned and walked away. And Gary continued to stand in his doorway, looking down at me, his lips twitching. I just couldn't *believe*...

We met Gary down at the canoes fifteen minutes later. Zack climbed in with Gary, while Rory, J.D., and I distributed our weight in mine. They tried to make me take the center seat perched on a cooler, but I absolutely refused. It was *my* canoe, and *my* fishing equipment, and *I* was gonna wind up cleaning the fish, and *I* was the lightest so the front was mine by right anyway—I was taking the front, dammit.

And then, of course they didn't want to fish on *my* lake.

"That's too easy," Zack called from the other canoe as we pulled alongside. "Let's go over the beaver dam, then take a couple of those portages, get up to one of those lakes where no one ever fishes." He waggled his brows. "Catch the Big One, one even bigger than cousin Ronnie got."

Usually I was all for a marathon fishing trip, but Gary was in the other canoe. He was looking at me with his eyes glowing unnervingly bright as they caught the sunlight shining off the water, looking relaxed and competent, his biceps bulging with each smooth, strong stroke of his paddle. Gary who'd kissed me, who'd beat thugs up for me, whose fingers felt like heaven sliding between my legs. Gary, who'd been fueling all of my sexual fantasies since he'd first burned his way across my retinas.

I wanted to bounce up and down on his cock, but I still didn't like him. I also didn't want to get to know him. I didn't want emotional investment. I didn't want to confirm he was an ass, or find out my dog was right and he was really a good guy. I wanted him to stay over there on his shelf, and just take him down when I had an itch I needed scratched.

Going fishing with him, especially fishing all evening, wasn't part of the Shelf Plan.

"Are you sure Gary is up for such a long trip?" I asked. *Hint, hint.* I kinda desperately wished Zack were in range of my paddle. He'd been careful to steer clear of me since the fishing invitation, but I really wanted to wallop him one.

They all looked at Gary. Gary was looking at me.

I probably looked like hitting something.

"Sounds like fun," the fucker said. Damn him. Damn *them*.

We nosed into the beaver dam and climbed out onto shore. There was a mad shuffle as my canoe-buddies and I tried to keep our balance on wet, beaver-chewed sticks while carry-pushing the canoe with the rods and cooler up over the dam and climbing up ourselves.

Zack and Gary mirrored our actions on the other end of the dam. With less stuff and fewer people, they made it to the top at about the same time. Once my canoe was afloat above the dam, Rory and J.D. climbed back aboard.

Zack leaned in to help steady my canoe, and I stepped back so I wouldn't be knocked into the water. He nudged me, knocking me off balance. My foot caught on a stick and I wobbled, arms windmilling, a breath away from toppling over backward and plunging three feet down and into the lake.

A hand grabbed my arm, hauling me upright just in time to see Zack vault into my seat. With a cackle of glee, he pushed the canoe—*my* canoe—off into the narrow channel.

"Zack! What the fuck?"

There was crazed laughter as the three paddled quickly away. Leaving me with Gary.

Leaving me. With Gary.

I looked down, realizing there was a big, strong hand still on my arm. Beyond that hand, a bicep bulged before a firm shoulder, and above that sat a rugged, slightly confused face. Gary was also staring down at his hand.

He let me go.

We stared at each other for a long moment. I didn't know what he was thinking; I couldn't tell. He might have been undressing me with his eyes, or replaying the sounds I made when I came.

I wondered if he could see what I was thinking. I was thinking that from here, I could boonie-bust back to my cabin. It'd be a bit marshy and a bit muddy, and I was in shorts, so the wild roses would scratch the hell out of my lower legs. But it was doable. The urge to ditch was strong.

He looked away. "You getting in?" he asked.

I crossed my arms, glaring at him. "Why are you doing this?" I asked.

"Maybe I want to go fishing."

"What do you know about fishing? You didn't even have your own rod." I'd had to bring an extra for him.

He glanced back at me, looking relaxed. Lazy, even. "Nothing," he answered. "Maybe I want to learn."

I scoffed.

"Maybe I want to get to know my neighbor," he suggested.

This time, I could see it. I could see, from the glint in his eyes, he was thinking about me naked, what he'd seen of me. Felt of me. I shuddered, remembering the sweet slide of his fingers.

"They're getting away," he drawled, nodding toward my brothers.

I glared out over the water, trying to make my decision.

It was a gorgeous day, the sun high overhead in a bright blue sky. A slight breeze was keeping the few mosquitos that dared to venture out over the water off of us. I'd already spotted a half-dozen pike swimming away from the canoe in the clear, shallow water. It was a good day for fishing.

And what would I do if I decided not to go? Stay home, shut myself in my cabin? Play video games? Or write some more erotica featuring the man that stood three feet from me? A pathetic thought. The thought of using my pink, bunny-eared vibrator was even sadder. My vibrator couldn't climb in through my window, or pin me up against the shower wall.

The man standing next to me could. And already had, in my stories.

I just had to avoid getting attached. I could do that. I'd be sitting several feet away, and facing forward. I wouldn't have to touch him, and I didn't have to look at him. Hell, I didn't even have to *talk* to him.

It was a beautiful day, and I wouldn't let him ruin that for me.

I think he knew the moment I capitulated, because his mouth curved into a smile.

I ignored how sexy he looked with it, and I climbed into his damn canoe.

# <u>Chapter Nine</u>

"We're gonna catch a bigger fish than them," I said, breaking the silence. I knew I was breaking my own no-talking rule, one which Gary had been obeying without having to be told, but I didn't do silence well. I'd been not-talking to him for two whole lakes now.

We'd portaged twice, and were on the fourth lake in a chain, the one Zack had wanted to catch the Big One on. It was now later afternoon, probably verging on 4 p.m. and my brothers were already out casting into the water. In the middle of the lake. Idiots.

"Dunno," said Gary. "They're pretty big."

I whipped around and gave him a Look, breaking my no-looking rule while I was at it.

Gary chuckled. "Okay," he said, "a big fish." He stroked with his paddle, then lifted it, the dripping loud in the silence. "What are we fishing for again?"

"Ugh." It had been a mistake to look at him. I was *still* looking at him, and my disgust didn't seem to be making him ugly, like I wanted it to. In fact, had he somehow managed to get more attractive in the past couple hours I'd been ignoring him? It sure as shit seemed that way.

"Northern Pike," I informed him.

He looked confused. "But this is Alaska. Aren't you supposed to have record-setting Rainbow Trout and a half dozen kinds of wild salmon?"

"Not since the pike ate them," I said. It felt eerily like a normal conversation. Where was the monster I knew as Gary? This mild guy seated about eight feet behind me didn't jive at all with the image I'd created. Had he not had his cocaine today or something?

That was an uncomfortable thought. He was rich. Rich people had expensive habits, and I didn't know anything about this particular rich guy. For all I knew, he had a couple pounds of coke in his closet.

"That looks like a good spot," I said, and steered the canoe over to a nice little cove. I pulled out my rod, the one I'd grabbed for Zack. I glanced over at Gary to see he hadn't even touched his.

He was just sitting there, his forearms braced on his paddle, which he'd laid across the canoe. And he was staring at me. Specifically at my fingers, which were busy hooking the swivel through a bright green spinner.

I glanced down at his rod, and saw it didn't even have a swivel tied to the line. Back up at him. Raised my brow.

He shrugged. "I'm more a hunter than a fisher."

"Do you even have a fishing license?" I asked.

"Nope," he said.

I grunted. The truth of the matter was, the Alaska Board of Fish and Game had to actually catch you for that to be an issue, and the idea of them coming to the lake we'd just travelled to was laughable. Further muddying the waters of the law, the reality was that pike were a menace with no bag limit; Fish and Game actually *wanted* them caught. Really, my only hesitation was the fact that I had my guiding license, and this might be construed as me guiding someone without a license. Which was bad juju. If we were caught.

Eh.

Reel-first, I held the newly-rigged rod out to my clueless, illegal, smokin'-hot canoe buddy. "Here. I'll use the other."

He took it, and I was pleased to note he was careful to swing the treble hooks out away from my face. Then he cast, rocking the boat.

I held on and gritted my teeth. "You'll want to cast toward shore," I said patiently (not). "And reel in fast enough to stay off the weeds on the bottom, but slow enough so you're not skipping along the top."

His lure caught on something. The rod tip bent as he pulled back, and his end of the canoe started to drift that direction. He tugged and yanked, and whatever it was he'd hooked didn't move.

I hadn't even gotten the other line rigged out, and he was already snagged. I was starting to feel like yelling.

I spent the next five minutes getting the lure up off a sunken log.

"I think I got the hang of it now," Gary said.

And then, with his very next cast—his *very next cast*, mind you—he threw the lure into the bushes up on shore.

I stared at the shining cord disappearing into the brush, watched it wave back and forth as he tried to yank it out—but only managed to yank it deeper—and I felt my shoulders tightening up. Now, I had a lot of experience fishing with newbs. I mean, a lot. What do you think I do for a living? I untangle lines, bait hooks while people are trying to spear them through my fingers, pretend it's all right when they break my rod-tips, and generally keep myself from yelling at bumbling idiots for hours at a time.

But this was Gary. Gary, the Devil who practically set my panties on fire along with my blueberry patch. Gary, who I wanted to strangle every day of the week. Gary... who wasn't paying me to play nice.

"I'll get it," he said. Wedging the rod in the canoe, he started to pull his end closer to shore.

"No, I can get it," I said. I just knew he'd yank so hard the hook would come back and puncture my eyeball, or he'd tip the canoe entirely clambering out of it. Or a lightning strike would come down out of the clear blue sky and fry me where I sat. It was safer all the way around if I got it.

So I started paddling, trying to drag *my* end closer to the brush.

"I said I'd get it," he said, paddling harder.

I matched his glare, and his paddling. The canoe rocked as we scudded sideways. Deciding to change my tack, I started paddling the other direction, swinging us around.

He tried to adjust his stroke, failed, and slid on by his mark. Putting me in perfect position to retrieve his lure. I'd outmaneuvered him.

Feeling smug, I reached out.

With one hard pull of his paddle, he dragged us both out away from the shore. His bail sang as his line spooled out.

"What the hell?" I demanded, trying to pull us back in. We needed to get his lure so we could get some real fishing done, so we could catch the biggest fish, so we could humiliate my brothers.

Gary resisted.

I swung around in my seat to glare at him. As usual, his expression was inscrutable. In that moment, it drove me just a little bit further than nuts.

And then he did it. He pulled back his paddle, and he did it.

He splashed me.

I gasped as lake water spattered across my face and upper body. The lake water wasn't really that cold, so it was just with surprise that I was doused. I think it was the Alaskan, uncivilized part of me, but I honestly didn't mind being wet. I didn't have any makeup to smear, and there was no one to care that my clothes were soaked. In fact, the cool water felt kinda nice.

No, the problem was, *he'd splashed me.*

I was a responsible, reasonable adult, so I did the only thing I *could* do. I splashed him back.

I hauled back and let my paddle fly, hitting the surface broadside, with just enough angle to send water spraying at him. I got just a glimpse of his face, his startled, dripping expression. I laughed.

Then he splashed me again, and it was *on*. Facing forward already, he definitely had the advantage, but I had a wealth of experience to draw on. Water flew, sparkling in the bright sunshine as the canoe spun in drunken circles and his line spooled out.

I laughed and when I looked around again, I got a big, direct splash to the face.

"Had enough yet?" he asked.

I blinked the water out of my eyes to see his grin. Oh, I'd gotten him good. His hair was plastered to his skull, his nose and chin were dripping... and that damn T-shirt was clinging to every dip and bulge in his ripped chest and abdomen.

I realized that his gaze was similarly stuck to my chest, and followed it down to find that my white T-shirt had gone transparent over my flimsy bra.

I jerked around to face forward and pulled the shirt away from my breasts. My face burned.

He splashed me again. Cool water splattered over my back.

*The uncivilized, immature, crazy-ass...* I took some nice, deep breaths. Then I said fuck it, and I splashed the hell out of him.

We flailed around for several minutes as the canoe drifted. We splashed each other until there was at least an inch of water in the bottom of the boat, until my arms felt like lead and my face ached from grinning, and we'd proven beyond a shadow of a doubt that neither of us had even the thinnest shred of maturity.

"I give! I give!" he finally cried.

"Ha!" I shouted, holding my paddle overhead in victory.

He laughed, long and loud, the deep, infectious sound carrying out across the lake. Damn but he had a gorgeous laugh.

Still grinning, I picked a strand of lake weed out of my hair. I was facing forward again, being careful not to turn around.

He sighed, and we listened to the water lap against the boat. It really was a beautiful day.

"Truce?" he finally asked.

I looked out over the lake, considering. "I don't like you," I said.

"I don't particularly *like* you," he replied.

I frowned, wondering what that emphasis was about, but I finally nodded. "Fine. Truce. We still need to catch that fish."

"Kinda hard to do when I've caught the shore," he said.

"Yup."

"And I don't think 'that fish' is gonna be here anymore."

"Nope. Not anymore," I agreed.

We retrieved his lure and moved to a spot about fifty feet further along the shore. And we finally got to it.

"So you do this for a living?" he asked.

*Ugh.* This was the part where I told him what I did, and he told me what he did, and we communicated like normal people.

That is, it would have been that part. And we would have. If I was normal. And him; I was definitely starting to have doubts about his normalcy, as well. Not sure if that was a good thing, or if it made me even more hesitant to get to know him. I knew all about Alaskan crazies—practically wrote the book—but Lower 48 crazies were a complete unknown.

I cast out, and didn't answer.

Which was probably why he felt it would be okay to ask, "Or do you make your living writing erotica?"

Damn him for reading my stuff. *Invading my home*, and reading my stuff.

"I just make a little money on the side with the erotica," I said, knowing I had to give him a little or be subjected to increasingly rude questions. Not sure how I knew this—maybe I was getting to know Gary just a little. *Ick.*

"So you're a fishing guide?" he asked.

"I'm a fishing guide during the summer, yes, and I make enough with the writing to get me through the winter," I admitted. I cast out again, irritated that I could hear the boys crowing with excitement as they pulled in fish after fish—even improperly placed as they were—and I hadn't caught shit yet. Isn't that just how it worked? The bumbling newb caught the record-breaker, while the most experienced person, the most knowledgeable, the most *deserving*, got the shaft.

"What about you?" I asked after another unsuccessful cast. Pike weren't like other fish. Pike were aggressive. If they were there, within a couple casts they'd attack your lure. They'd follow it, even lunge several inches out of the water to bite it.

"I'm…into stocks," he said.

I cut my eyes back at him. That had sounded like a half-truth at best to my brother-tuned ears.

Gary was giving me an innocent look.

That *fucker*. In all my mental acrobatics on how I was going to avoid talking to him, avoid getting to know him and avoid giving him information, I'd never actually thought I'd have trouble getting information *out* of him. This was not normal. But then again, someone who didn't turn around and run away as fast as they absolutely could when faced with my three wild brothers wasn't normal. They'd actually been the ones to chase off all three of my boyfriends before Brett.

The first, back in high school, had lasted a couple months. We'd flirted in class, and made out vigorously in his truck every chance we got. It had all ended when I brought him home for the first time. He'd come away with a black eye, bruised ribs, and a diagnosis of PTSD.

The second one hadn't lasted even that long. Just days after Freddie and I had first slept together, Zack came across us in the college cafeteria, and had invited him out shooting. Despite my warnings, he'd gone. I'm not sure what Zack said to him, but Freddie had never talked to me again, even ran the other way when I approached him.

The third one, I'd tried to keep a secret as long as possible. It was actually pretty easy, because we'd met on the internet and only communicated by email, text, and phone. It had been while I'd been living out here. But then my brothers had come to visit, and after that, my internet boyfriend went silent. I'd sent out dozens of emails and texts, and never gotten anything back. It was almost as if they'd killed him…

I glanced at Gary again, almost feeling sorry for him. He wasn't my boyfriend, but the brothers knew I was interested in him, obviously. It was a miracle he wasn't maimed yet. But I just knew—it was coming. And I kinda hoped that when it did, they wouldn't mess up his face.

Gary yelped. "I have one!" he yelled, wrenching back on the rod. Miraculously, he didn't topple backward into the water, and neither line nor rod broke.

"Gently," I said, reeling in my own line so they didn't tangle. "Reel it in slowly, let him tire himself out." I glanced around the bottom of the canoe and realized we hadn't brought a net. No matter, it seemed like I always wound up out pike fishing without a net.

When he brought the fish up to the boat, I asked him to hold it steady, and then I reached down, grabbed the steel leader, and hauled the fish into the boat. Gary's first pike was medium-sized, about 18 inches long.

If Gary had been a client, I would have made noises about how big it was, what a fighter it had been, how shiny its scales were, or some other tip-inflating crap. But he wasn't, so I was all business as I asked him to let the tension off the line.

"So that's a Northern Pike?" he asked.

"Yup." I turned around in my seat and he watched with fascination as I got a grip on the slimy thing and used my Leatherman pliers to pry the hook out of its mouth. I released his lure away from my face, and he seemed conscientious enough to keep it there. He continued to watch as I pulled the knife out of the multi-tool and stabbed the fish through the brain and spinal column.

Pike were insidious creatures. You could hit them upside the head with a bonker—the traditional method of killing fish—until you were red in the face, and they'd still be flailing around trying to swim in the bottom of the boat an hour later. By stabbing them, you guaranteed that they were dead and paralyzed while avoiding scaring off all of the other fish in a hundred-foot radius with the racket.

I glanced up and realized that at some point Gary had transferred his gaze to my chest. *Yeah—not dry yet.* I gave him a dirty look.

He gave me a slow, sexy wink.

My body betrayed me, lower belly clenching with a sudden, unexpected twist of arousal. *Shit shit shit.* I turned back around in a hurry, trying to keep my breathing under control. Gary being an ass should come with a warning label. Gary being charming...well, there weren't really words.

And I couldn't help but think he was some sort of weirdo. Here he was flirting with me over a canoe full of stinky fish I'd just stabbed to death, as I clutched a bloody knife in my fish-slimed hands. And I was unfashionable, and unornamented, and I had a tongue as sharp as my knife. So *why* was he flirting with me?

We fished on into evening. As the shadows lengthened, we began pulling them in regularly. Gary and I each got upwards of half a dozen. The bottom of the boat filled up, and my sandaled feet got splashed with blood and slime and grit.

At one point, I stood up in the bow to look down into the clear water and spot the fish.

"You're not supposed to stand up in a canoe," Gary pointed out.

I shrugged, dragging my gaze over the weedy bottom. Pike were territorial—they liked to stake out an area and they'd just lie there in the water. They were colored and mottled to be camouflaged, but I had a lot of experience spotting their slightly darker shapes.

"You'll tip the boat," Gary continued.

I pushed down with one foot, then the other, intentionally rocking the canoe, and then glanced back at him. "Does it look like the boat is tipping?" I mean, really, I was more likely to fall out than the boat was to tip. And even if it did tip, the water here at the edge was just two or three feet deep, so it wasn't like we'd be sucked into a black hole or something. Tipped canoes sucked—mostly because people laughed at you and took pictures—but they weren't the end of the world.

His expression was somewhere between disgruntled and thoughtful. I half-expected him to splash me again. But he didn't.

Instead, Gary paddled us slowly, gently forward. I hadn't thought 'slowly, gently' was in his repertoire—he seemed more a hard-and-fast kinda guy—but there it was. Depraved creature that I was, I shivered.

"See anything?" he asked.

"Noooo—Ah!" I stumbled, nearly falling backward into the boat, and then scrambled back into place, peering cautiously over the bow.

"What? What is it?"

It was...The Big One. It was huge, so big I'd thought it was a log. My brain whirred, trying to calculate how much that thing must weigh. Thirty pounds? At least. *Holy hell...* This one was way, way bigger than Ronnie's. This one right here was the reason I didn't swim in the lake. That thing had a maw big enough to latch onto my calf. And rows of teeth big and sharp enough to shred it. My heart started to race.

"Cast," I whispered. "Keep us right here—no sudden movements—and cast forward and slightly to the left." I was frozen in place, terrified I'd scare it. I needed to keep an eye on it, needed to not let it out of my sight. We *needed* to catch it.

I didn't know if his lure was big enough, if his line would hold, if his rod would break. But it's what we had. We *had* to try.

"Cast!" My voice was a high, excited whisper-squeak.

He cast.

I held my breath as his lure arced through the air. Then it splashed down, and it was perfect. He began to reel, and his lure came into sight, in a perfect spin, headed right by the Beast. I held my breath, leaning forward. *Yes. Yessss.*

The monstrous fish struck. I watched it swallow the lure whole. For a moment there, I thought I might actually die of excitement.

Gary yanked on the rod, and then applied a constant pressure. We started to list toward the fish.

The fish didn't move. It just lay there in the water, its fins moving gently as it stabilized itself, completely unfazed. The fish didn't know yet. The fish hadn't started to fight.

"I think I got a log again," Gary said.

"Keep tension on the line," I instructed in a hushed tone. "And for the love of God, don't jerk it."

He chuckled. "That's what she said."

I glanced back at him with fascinated disbelief. I didn't think I'd ever seen this before. Both he *and* the fish were clueless. Neither knew the fish was hooked. Neither knew the Big One was on the line. Yet another example of the Newb catching the Honker. *Goddammit.*

"You have a fish on the line," I said, slowly. "It's the biggest pike I've ever seen."

"You're funnin' me."

"I am not *'funnin'* you!" The fish chose that moment to shake its head, yanking the line and proving my point.

Gary's mouth opened in a stunned, satisfying O. He let the rod dip.

"Tension!" I snapped. I sat up a little straighter, searching the bottom of the boat with my eyes. A fish this size was gonna require a net. I couldn't pull this one into the boat by hand, no way. But we didn't have a net.

It was the biggest pike I'd ever seen, and we didn't have a fucking net.

The massive fish took off, line *scree*ing out as it arrowed toward the middle of the lake. The canoe did an ominous spin, and we were dragged slowly but surely into deeper water.

"Shit," I whispered.

The only option I could see for us landing the monster was to paddle to shore and drag the fish up onto it. To this end, I started paddling, trying to drag us back toward shore even as the fish tried to pull us farther out.

Gary was laughing, hooting and hollering as the fish executed an aerial dive, flinging water with a heavy splash that would have done a beaver proud.

I paddled harder, trying to figure out how we were gonna get the beast ashore. The shore wasn't a nice, gentle slope, and it was lined with a tangle of thigh-high brush right up to the very edge.

The fish suddenly turned around, and I watched it swim lazily alongside the boat, allowing us to coast those last few feet. We were in three feet of water now, only a few feet from the shore.

That was when I glanced down, and realized the lure had come mostly out of its mouth. The treble was hanging on by one hook— and that hook was bending.

We were gonna lose it.

"Fuck!" I threw the paddle away from me and shoved to my feet.

And, with a battle cry, I jumped from the boat.

I bitch about fishing a lot, but you gotta understand—I became a guide for a reason. I love to fish. I love to throw a perfect cast, pull the lure through the water at the perfect speed and depth, feel that yank as the fish strikes, and then fight it, tire it out, drag it to the boat, and bonk it to death. I love to carry those slimy fuckers up from the boat at the end of the day; I have a big, shit-eating grin plastered across my face every time. Half of my ceiling upstairs is filled with pictures of other people with big shit-eating grins, holding their dead fish—fish I helped them catch. I have a soul-deep feeling of satisfaction when I cut the perfect fillet, and I even love to eat them (weird, I know).

So you've gotta understand, when I say I jumped into the lake after the biggest pike I've ever seen, it's not an exaggeration. And no, I didn't swan-dive, 'cuz I'm not an idiot.

I jumped in feet-first right next to the behemoth pike, and I scooped it up in my arms. I have no idea how I caught it before it darted away. It defies the laws of physics and fishing, but there it was. I scooped it up into my arms, held onto it for dear life as it started to thrash, and I waded toward the shore.

The weeds were thick, and the muck beneath them sucked at my feet, but I wasn't gonna let that stop me. I carried that slimy, slippery, flailing fucker to shore, and then clambered up somehow, while holding it, and high-stepped it several feet into the brush. Then I dumped the huge bastard onto the ground and threw myself over it, so it had absolutely no hope of flopping away.

It was only as I was lying atop its surprisingly strong body that I resurfaced from my trophy-inspired fugue. I glanced up, and Gary was sitting in the canoe, staring at me with the kind of shock a genteel person might reserve for a train wreck—if the rail cars had been full of dildos.

And I guess I knew what I looked like. I was soaked from the neck down, had body-slammed a fish, and could probably only have surprised my new neighbor more if I'd caught it with my teeth.

The fish flailed again, slapping me in the face with its tail. *Ow.*

"Could you throw me my Leatherman?" I asked. My voice was surprisingly level.

He complied.

When I finally had the monster slain, I hefted it up off the ground.

Gary's beautiful green eyes grew wide. He cleared his throat. "Does that count as your catch, or mine?" he asked.

It was a good question. All means short of poison and dynamite were legal when it came to pike. So was it Gary's lure or my arms that caught the fish? In my opinion, it was more a philosophical question than a practical one.

"It's yours." Never let it be said that I'm a selfish person.

He had pulled the canoe in to shore, and I watched him clamber out of the boat. I stood there, trying to figure out what he thought he was doing.

He moved to me through the thigh-high bushes. His eyes were on the fish. "Here, let me—"

"Mmph!" I said, because he lunged in, grabbed hold of my face, and kissed me. I was tight and stiff with shock, and I couldn't do a damn thing because I had a knife in one hand — *sooooo tempting* — and a prize-winning fish in the other.

I was breathing hard through my nose, my eyes still open as his lips seduced mine. And his tongue — he licked at me, probed, seeking entrance. I went even tighter, and stiffer, and my mouth finally opened on a gasp, as he put his hand between my legs.

He thrust his tongue into my mouth, and I heard his groan of triumph, one of utter masculine delight, and my stupid pussy actually gushed in response. My body was pulsing, and my nipples shot hard from the slow, delicious slide of his tongue against mine.

I wanted to hit him with his fish for wresting such a response from me. Stubbornly, I fought it.

I nipped his tongue, and squeaked, going up on my toes when he applied pressure on my clit. *Oh, God*, he didn't fight fair. My eyes rolled back as he rubbed me through my wet shorts.

His mouth left mine and traced a heated trail along my jaw. The man was probably gonna get beaver fever from licking the water droplets off my skin, but I tilted my head to the side, inviting him.

With his hands and mouth, he made ripples of pleasure echo through my body. I just stood there, dripping, and let it happen. Because it felt wonderful. Because he made me feel beautiful. Wanted. Fish slime and all.

With a final pinch of my nipple through my soaked shirt and bra, he slid his hands away, and stepped back. I caught myself as I swayed toward him. I looked up into his eyes, momentarily lost.

"Are all Alaskan women like you?" he asked.

"No one's like me."

"That, I can believe," he said. "I'm gonna have it stuffed."

I blinked.

"The fish."

I finally caught up with the conversation and sighed happily. Moneybags was gonna do something useful for a change.


Gary and I were pretty much done for the evening, and the terrible trio were out of beer, so we headed back. The shadows were deepening as the sun sank toward the horizon, the day just starting to cool off. On the first portage, it started to rain. It was a light sprinkle that got heavier as we made our way back.

I was already wet, so I just got a bit wetter. And everybody else, Gary and my three brothers, gradually got soaked right along with me. By the time we clambered back down over the beaver dam, we were all shivering.

The temperature was now in the 50s, a normal and tolerable Alaskan night, but the 50s got a whole helluva lot colder when you were soaked. My fingers were so cold, my grip on my paddle kept slipping, and I was having fantasies about my wood stove. I had a diesel stove that I usually used for heating, but there was just something about a fire. And hot chocolate. I shuddered, mentally zeroing in on the box of Swiss Miss on my shelf.

When we slid up to my dock, I pulled The Big One out of the bottom of the boat. At the moment, I didn't give a damn about anything else. I carried it up and flopped it, whole, into the chest freezer at the side of my cabin.

My brothers and I banged through my door, the mood subdued by borderline hypothermia.

I was about to shut the door behind us when I glanced out, and realized Gary was still standing out there on the beach, in the dark. Alone.

I watched as he shook his head and took a step toward his place.

I thought about asking him to come in, I really did. Rory was already starting a fire, Zack was raiding my linen closet for blankets, and J.D. was firing up his Xbox. After I made hot chocolate, I guessed we'd swaddle up in blankets, plant ourselves in front of the TV, and play video games until we warmed up and/or passed out.

But I didn't open my mouth, and instead of inviting Gary, I watched my canoe-buddy blend into the shadows on the other side of the lake.

# <u>Chapter Ten</u>

A big, strong hand over my mouth woke me up.
My eyes snapped open with a gasp I had to suck through my nose. Something was on top of me, trapping me under my blankets. That something was pinning my arms to my sides and my hips flat to the mattress. That something was big, and heavy, and…

The dark shape hovering over me sharpened into a face, and the dull moonlight coming through the window glinted in through a bottle-green iris. *Gary.*

The devil raised his brows as if to ask, 'You figured out who it is yet?'

I nodded slightly, still undecided as to whether or not I was going to scream if he took his hand away. My brothers were downstairs. If I screamed, they'd find him. Then they'd kill him. Yeah, it was tempting.

He must have seen it in my expression. He left his hand in place.

He leaned back a bit, and reached down and grabbed something with his free hand. He pulled it up into my field of vision and it produced a faint rattling sound as he shook it. It was a shiny box, maybe the size of your standard tea box. I squinted in the darkness, and finally made out the roman helmet symbol on the side. My eyes flared wide.

With that same hand, he reached over, pulled open my

nightstand drawer—the same one with my pink bunny-eared vibrator—and tucked the box inside.

*What the…?*

He sank his knuckles into the mattress next to my shoulder as he leaned down over me. I smelled his shampoo as his stubble brushed my cheek, and felt the tickle of his nose against the shell of my ear.

I wiggled under him, sucking air through my nose. My neighbor breaks into my cabin—I cut my eyes to my window, confirming it was wide open, the curtain rippling slightly in a night breeze—by climbing in through my second-story window, pins me to the bed so I can't move a fucking *inch*, covers my mouth so I couldn't scream if I wanted to, and then shows me a box of condoms—effectively telling me my excuse from the other day would no longer hold water.

What did it say about me that I was quickly becoming more aroused than I'd ever been in my life? Heat and moisture blossomed between my thighs. My nipples were hard as beach pebbles on breasts squashed flat under the blankets. I strained upward, chafing against them, wanting more. I wanted those blankets gone, and his strong hands on me, rough, squeezing my breasts, shoving my legs apart.

If Gary's hand hadn't been there, my moan would have been loud. He laughed softly against my ear, and tilted his hips so the bulge of his erection pressed down against my belly. I only strained up harder, turning my face to look at him, thinking about biting his hand.

His head was practically on the pillow with mine. His eyes were crinkled slightly with amusement, and yet the look in them was intense as they flicked back and forth between my own. His breath, when he spoke, wafted across my cheek. "Yes or no?" he asked, his voice somehow managing to be both deep and soft.

He was asking me to tell him I wanted him. Which I didn't want to do. Even though I totally did.

I was breathing faster now, straining to free my arms. Some deep part of me seriously objected to having him on top of me, holding me down. But this was easily the hottest thing I'd ever experienced, and I honestly wasn't sure if it was despite it, or because of it.

I bent my knees and thrust my hips up, trying to unseat him. Or press up against him. Maybe both.

My efforts barely moved him, and then his tongue and breath were on my ear, making a wet-and-cool trail that sent shivers from my scalp clear down to my toes. He played with my ear until I was gasping, my hips shifting hungrily beneath him, and my toes felt like they might never uncurl. He pinched my lobe between his teeth, gave it a sharp, delicious tug, and then released it on a shaky exhale.

"Yes," he grated, shifting his weight onto his elbow, free hand sliding along my side. "Or no?" He squeezed my hip through the blanket, his thumb rubbing downward.

I was practically panting. I couldn't believe this was happening. Him, in my bedroom, in the dark, asking for my consent. With my brothers downstairs!

If I said the word, I could have him, tonight, right now.

*What the hell was I waiting for?*

The word tore out of me, buoyed up on a sea of need. "Yes. Yes," I said into his hand. Though it was muffled, my words were unmistakable.

He rolled off me so fast, I didn't know what to do with myself. But apparently he did. Cool air wafted as he threw the blanket back. Still stunned and gasping like a fish, I lay there in my night shirt and nothing else, and waited to see what he would do.

There was a flurry of motion in the dark. And then he was on me again, pushing my legs open, wedging himself between them as if he had every right. I discovered the bare skin of his hip sliding against my inner thigh. His shaft pressed directly against my wet folds.

I pushed up against him automatically, wanting him inside me *now*. I reached for him, but he grabbed my wrists. As he leaned forward, pinning them beside my head, his cock ground against me.

My mouth opened on a moan, and he claimed that, too. He simply wedged his way in and plundered. He didn't ask; he took. And, as I'd noticed on my lawn, he wasn't sweet or gentle. Our teeth clashed. He drank my sounds as he ground his hips against me.

But I only wanted it harder. I sucked his tongue with a hint of teeth, enjoying his groan, the way he grew even harder in that hot, tight space we'd created between us. I hooked my legs around him, digging my heels into his bare ass, pulling him as close as he could get.

His hands tightened on my wrists as his hips rolled, making fireworks go off in my head. Our breath hissed and the slippery, aching heat at my center intensified until I wanted to scream. But I couldn't, because of my fucking brothers.

Gary pulled back suddenly, leaving me lying there cool and...unrestrained. *No...* Now that he was no longer holding me down, I lost the need to move my wrists—something which totally confused me, too—and so I kept them there, lying next to my head.

He pushed up and away, and I wondered if he'd changed his mind. Maybe he'd realized what he was doing, or he liked waxed girls, or he thought I made weird sounds...

I stared up at him, wanting him back with a desperation that surprised even me. If I'd been pretending he was someone else, I most definitely couldn't now. The moonlight coming in from the side gilded his torso, all those lovely muscles, the gorgeous chest that expanded with each quick breath. That silvery light glinted in his eyes, and then his black hair fell over his face as he looked down.

Foil tore. His hands moved along his shaft, unrolling a condom over the cock I was seeing for the first time.

*Oh my...*

His eyes lifted until they met mine.

Fire. It was in his eyes, and it was what swept through my body.

*This is gonna be so fun...* I almost laughed out loud as he came back down to me.

Any sound I'd been tempted to make was quickly aborted when he pushed inside of me. I was ready for him—so damn ready, so friggin' wet—but I was *ready for him,* pussy swollen with arousal, and I felt every inch of his thick cock as he pushed into me. Pushed, and pushed. And *pushed,* stretching me to my limit, leaving me trembling, and so very full.

He reclaimed my wrists. And then he latched onto my neck.

With one hard draw, I was cumming.

Remember how I said I didn't do silence well? …Yeah. A thin sort of wail left my lips before he shifted that big, strong hand back over them.

He thrust, pushing through my squeezing muscles. I balled up my fist and hit his shoulder. I was trembling under him, every single muscle straining, my knees riding his sides as he pushed into me again, and again. I was already cumming, and as his pelvis ground against my clit, the feeling intensified beyond any sort of reason or measure. He was making it worse, so I hit him again, and this time my hand stayed on his shoulder, pushing, my nails digging into him.

My neck arched on a scream he was forcing to be quiet.

"Shh-shh-shhhh," he said. I was honestly only partially aware of what he was saying as he continued to do what he was doing, and I rode out the longest orgasm of my life. I must have made some more sounds, probably a lot more sounds, because he was suddenly chuckling next to my ear, his chest pressed to mine through my shirt. "Are we going to have to get you a gag?" he whispered.

I was gasping through my nose, my vision going dark, and yet I'd never felt anything so divine as his thick cock spearing to the depths of me, his hard body pinning me to my sheets, his hand tight on my wrist and face.

My eyes must have rolled back in my head or I must have given some other clue I was about to pass out, because he removed his hand from my mouth. I gasped, my free hand worrying his shoulder, fingers digging into the thick muscle there. As I lay there gulping air, I realized he'd gone still. He was thick and hard inside me, still above me, but he wasn't moving. Instead, he was looking patiently down at me. Waiting for me to rejoin the party.

Looking up into his eyes, I melted just a little. *Maybe he isn't such a bad guy…*

Then an aftershock squeezed me around him, touching off a whole new round of shivers. His hips flexed, pushing harder into me, making my legs tighten to either side of him.

He groaned. "You good?" His voice was quiet, strained.

My lips formed the words 'holy fuck', but I had my shit mostly back together, so I nodded.

His mouth formed a wicked grin, and then he recaptured my wrist. He pressed them both back into the mattress and did that crazy hip-roll again, the move that stirred his length inside me and rubbed my clit in the most incredible way. He did it again, and again, and in that moment I absolutely knew he was no stranger to a woman's body. He was doing things to mine that I'd never even imagined.

I couldn't feel my lips.

But I wasn't taking this next orgasm lying down. I channeled all my strength into the right side of my body, digging my foot into the mattress even as I hip-checked him and strained upward against his left hand. And I managed it. I don't know if he let me or if I really, momentarily overpowered him, I wasn't gonna analyze it.

He rolled, and I rode him over. I straightened up on my knees, and realized I still wore my nightshirt. Intolerable. I grabbed the hem and ripped it off over my head, freeing my breasts in the moonlight.

I tightened my legs to either side of his hips, and finally got my hands on that chest. I intentionally squeezed him, enjoying the resulting catch in his breath. His dark chest hair was crisp as I sifted my fingers through it, and traced down to where we joined. Then I tripped my fingers back up his abs and stroked across the hard little nubs of his nipples.

I wanted to lean down to lick him, but I liked my height advantage too much. I liked having him under me. A lot.

The heat was rising again, and I started to move. I began with just a tilt and roll of my hips, doing what he'd done to me. But as I watched his expression deepen into a place of pure pleasure, my pace quickened. A hard, fast rhythm overtook me, driving me on him. I threw my head back, feeling my hair spill down my back and tickle the upper slope of my ass.

His hands found my breasts, squeezing just exactly the way I wanted him to. My rhythm faltered as this new source of pleasure blindsided me. His abs flexed as he sat up, and suddenly it was his mouth on me, not his hands. I gasped, hovering above him, shaking again. I pulled his hair, wanting to punish him for doing what he did to me. He just sucked harder, and his free hand yanked my hips into him, grinding us together.

Just like that, it was happening again, and there was nothing I could do to control it. My last act before I lost my shit again was to grab his hand, drag it off my breast and up over my mouth.

He laughed breathlessly, and then I was cumming, and his laugh choked off. I pulled his hair again, yanking his head back so he had to look up at me. His fingers dug hard into my ass, his hips grinding him up into me, his eyes flashing in the moonlight.

*Fuck. Fuck, fuck fuck. Fuck me!* That's what I would have been saying if his hand wasn't obligingly plastered over my mouth. Heat flushed up my body, raising a fine sweat in its wake. I rocked wildly on him, feeling like I might shake apart in his arms. It went on and on and on, squeezing me around him, dragging forth muffled cries as I writhed in his lap.

I saw the moment he came. His arm went hard around my waist, locking us together, and he kept his eyes locked to mine, letting me see. His abs tensed against my belly and his cock jerked where it was buried deep inside me. I could feel him cum even through my own whirlwind of sensation, and it left me feeling deeply, primitively satisfied.

The pleasure was colossally large and loud as the last of it crashed through me, making my ears ring. Left to my own devices, I would have added to my body's clamor by screaming down the rafters. But instead, we just sat in the middle of my bed in the darkness and near silence, shuddering.

Gary finally rolled me back underneath him, stilling my movements with his weight. He kissed me, pressed his lips to the tender spot right in front of my ear. Then his hand slid off my face. He lifted up, his hand went down between us to hold the condom in place, and he pulled out.

I shuddered again, feeling suddenly bereft. Cold and empty.

He fell onto the bed beside me. I could feel his eyes on me.

I stared up at the ceiling, trying to figure out what the hell had just happened. My *neighbor* had crawled through my *window* and had *held me down*—

It had been unreal. He was exactly my speed, not too gentle, not too rough. He asked first, but still managed to take. And yet he *gave*.

He leaned over me then, crowding the thoughts right out of my head. His finger touched my swollen lips. I licked his fingertip, and then pulled it into my mouth.

His eyes flared.

I held his gaze as I sucked him. I rolled the flat of my tongue over his sensitive fingertip. His muscles rippled when I scraped my teeth gently across the joint.

He dragged his wet fingertip from my mouth, and then leaned close. His hand closed on my jaw, doing that controlling thing that I found so damn sexy. He turned my head so his lips were against my ear.

"We did your fantasy," he whispered. "Next time, mine." Then he let me go, his gaze boring into mine for a breathless moment.

I stared after him as he climbed out of bed, wondering what the hell he was talking about. *My fantasy?*

He disposed of the condom, and quickly pulled his clothes on. With one last glance, he slipped out of my window, blending almost instantly into the darkness.

Realization came slowly to my sex-addled brain. *My fantasy.* He'd read what I wrote. He'd read the scene I'd written of him sneaking into my bedroom window. He'd *enacted* a scene I wrote. Intentionally.

I put a trembling hand over my bruised mouth.

And it had been—beyond incredible. I'd had the most fantastic sex of my entire life, with the man who'd burned my blueberries to the ground... and with my brothers asleep downstairs.

And he wanted to do it—do *me*—again! This time, it was *my* hand that muffled a squee of excitement.

# <u>Chapter Eleven</u>

T he next morning, I lay in bed for a good half hour, grinning up at the ceiling. I'd imagined what had occurred between us more times than I could count, but none of it compared to the real thing. Something about his attitude, the exact same thing that had rubbed me the wrong way since he'd exploded into my life, seemed to rub me perfectly right in bed. Being with him last night had been amazing—and yes, I'd already checked my nightstand to make sure I wasn't dreaming. The 36 count box of Ultra Thin Trojan condoms was still there. I felt my loins heating, just thinking about how much fun we could have with all those condoms.

When I finally crawled out of bed, I was actually feeling somewhat chipper. I got dressed and descended the ladder to find my brothers beginning to stir.

Zack was sitting at the table, still swaddled in last night's blanket, nursing a cup of coffee. He looked like I usually felt in the mornings, all dazed and ornery, his blonde hair sticking out every-which-way. He was peering at me from under it with suspicion. "You're very cheerful this morning," he observed.

I grinned at him, so cheerful I thought he actually looked kinda cute sitting there, all tattooed and grumpy, with a droopy blanket. Not so cheerful I couldn't rub it in, though. "It's because I caught such a huge fucking fish yesterday, and it was so damn much bigger than any of yours."

"I thought Gary caught that fish."

I shrugged. Then I pranced off to the bathroom.

The mirror reflected my crazy grin, along with more evidence that last night had been real. My hair was bedhead crossed with freshly fucked, and a couple red marks decorated my neck. My nipples were chafed pink, and my hips and thighs gave that tell-tale next-morning protest as I sat on the toilet.

I yelped and jumped right back up, because hot urine splashed back at me. "What the *fuck*?" Dripping, I turned to glare down at the yellow puddle I'd made in the middle of a sheet of translucent cellophane stretched over the bowl.

Through the door, I could hear my fucking brothers roaring with laughter.

"You sons-of-bitches!" I yelled. I was gonna get them back. It was just how I operated.

At the same time, I knew that if this was the worst they did to me during their visit, I was getting off easy. At least it hadn't been a cherry bomb.

I removed the plastic and finished my business. Then I took a shower.

I glared at them over breakfast.

"So what's the plan for today?" Rory asked, carefully avoiding my gaze.

"How about we build my shed," I suggested. I'd planned one out to cover the snowmachine in summer, and the four-wheeler in winter, and to hold non-burnable trash in one corner, with my tools and various necessities in a low loft above it. I'd had the materials freighted in last winter.

And that was the agreement: My brothers could come visit for a week—if they built me a shed. I knew it was only day two, but I also knew my brothers. If I didn't make them do it, they wouldn't.

On cue, Zack grumbled. "Couldn't we do it tomorrow?" he asked.

"But that's exactly what you're gonna say tomorrow," I said. "How about we just get out there, get our shit together, and build me a shed. Like you said you would."

They finally caved, and I rounded up everything they'd need. I showed them where I wanted it, and almost immediately began to feel superfluous.

I hung around for a couple hours, but as they started to get the frame up, I excused myself. "I gotta clean fish," I said.

Nobody objected, because they knew if they did, they'd be wrist-deep in fish guts, and we all knew they'd rather be pounding nails.

I moved down to the dock and kicked open the lid to the cooler. Then I flopped the first pike out onto my cleaning table.

As I sliced beautiful fillets, I let myself replay last night. The feel of Gary's hands on me. The feel of him inside me. His sparkling eyes. I almost made myself want to gag, thinking about his 'sparkling' eyes, but there it was. I'd noticed them, I'd appreciated them.

And most of all, I wondered when we could do that again.

Smiling, I glanced toward his cabin. There was no movement over there that I could see, and my brothers were making enough noise that I couldn't hear what Gary was up to.

The fish took me a while. After I got the fillets deboned, packaged into Ziplocs, and thrown in the freezer, I rejoined the construction crew.

I fetched them some drinks, and found nails, and held things…but mostly I supervised. Rory and Zack were the ones doing most of the work, with J.D. sort of half-assedly tagging along.

Around noon, I went inside and cobbled together a soup. I wasn't much of a cook, but I figured I could make them lunch. Since they were building me a shed and all.

Last in were the egg noodles. As they disappeared into the broth, I glanced out my window to make sure my brothers were still out there. Yup, I was alone.

I called Suzy. She picked up after a couple rings.

"I had sex with him," I confessed.

"Wait, Helly?"

"Yeah."

"Who'd you have sex with?"

I braced myself, took a nice deep breath, and said, "With Gary."

"Wait, your evil neighbor Gary? The Blueberry Butcher, Gary?"

"Yeah."

"You had sex with him?" she asked, her voice rising.

I cringed, knowing I was in trouble. "Yeah."

She squealed so loud I had to hold the phone away from my ear. "Oh my god, oh my God, ohmigawd, tell me. Gimme the details. *Nao!*"

I cringed some more. How did you tell someone a guy had crawled through your bedroom window, put a hand over your mouth, and then fucked you silly? It had been great at the time, but in the light of day...it sounded stalker-ish. And weird. Nobody climbed in second-story windows for nookie.

"Uh..."

"Helly J. Adderack. You will tell me what happened *right now!* Aren't your brothers visiting? How did you have sex with your neighbor when your brothers are there?" She gasped. "Or did it happen *before*? And how was it?" she demanded.

My shit-eating grin was so wide it hurt my face as memories from last night flashed through my head. "Amazing," I admitted.

More squeals. She finally caught her breath enough to ask, "How did this happen? Last time you called, you wanted to kill him. At the barbecue, you tried to run away when you saw him. And aren't your brothers there?"

"The brothers *are* here," I said. I hesitated. "Well...promise not to tell anyone?" I knew full well I was talking to the gossip-monger of the century. But she was also my friend, and I knew she wouldn't blather about my personal life—as long as I specifically told her not to.

"Cross my heart," she said. "Now tell me!"

"We've been feuding, sorta," I started.

"You told me you sabotaged his saw," she said, and I could hear her smile.

"Yeah. But there's more. The next day, I was sunning on my dock, and he splashed me with his jet ski. So...I might have crashed the jet ski, and then I might have pushed him in."

"Crashed—wait, you pushed him in? To the lake?!"

"Yeah," I admitted.

"Wait. That was the day before the barbecue, right? Why didn't you tell me about this?"

"I'm getting to that part. So, he chased me, and he tackled me on my lawn—" I glanced out to make sure my brothers were still busy on the shed, and not in earshot.

"He *tackled* you?!" Suzy sounded as aghast as I'd been when Gary had 'claimed' my land.

"And he gave me an orgasm," I finished.

The silence on the other end was long, and loud. "He gave you an orgasm. On your lawn."

"Yeah. There was some grinding, and he had his mouth on me, and…. Then, the morning of the barbecue, he might have trespassed and almost kissed me, and made me breakfast, and dumped water on me, and read my stories."

"Tress—made you—he read your *stories*?" Suzy sounded breathless with excitement.

"Anyway, you've seen how freaking hot he is. So after the barbecue I decided I still didn't like him, I didn't want to talk to him, but I wanted to fuck him."

Suzy was making these little laughing noises, which made me smile.

"So I went over to his place and threw five gallons of water on him."

She still seemingly had nothing to say.

I sighed. "It made sense at the time, I swear. After I threw the water on him, he picked me up and threw me in the lake. And then he jumped in after me, and there might have been almost-sex in the lake, and then—my brothers flew in."

"In the *lake*?" Suzy asked. She took a deep breath, and then said, "Tell me how you managed to have sex with him with your brothers there."

I cringed a little. What Gary had done sounded semi-reasonable in the dead of night, but it seemed so angsty-teenager in the light of day. And to admit it to my friend over the phone?

Ah well, I'd already told her about all the other crazy shit I'd done. "He climbed in my bedroom window," I admitted.

She was silent a long moment, probably trying to digest everything I'd just told her. Suzy knew I wasn't exactly conventional—she wasn't either—but I still found it difficult revealing details that betrayed the extent of my neurosis. Maybe it was just me not being the best with people, but I'd always had the niggling worry that she was finally going to decide 'This bitch is crazy!' and wash her hands of me. Not that I thought she was the type of person to do that. It was complicated. *I* was complicated. Obviously. Just look at my sex life. Or usual lack thereof.

"Helly, let me get this straight," Suzy said. "This is a man that chases you down to give you orgasms, jumps into a lake after you to—to—"

"Finger me," I supplied, shutting off the heat on the soup. The noodles were done.

"And he crawls in your second-story window to give you amazing sex."

"Yeah..."

"Helly, you're not gonna wanna hear this, but...he sounds perfect for you."

I yelped as I burned myself on the pot.

"I mean, how many men would understand your method of seduction by five gallon bucket? How many would dare climb in your window, with your three crazy brothers downstairs? How many would climb in a window, *period*?"

I'd been stunned speechless by her original statement, but she was starting to make a certain sort of sense. How many men would grab me and kiss the hell out of me when I was holding a dead fish and a sharp knife, and was covered from neck to knees with slime?

How many would tolerate the damage I'd done? I'd broken into his cabin and cut the cord to his saw; trespassing and vandalism, right there. And then I'd crashed his jet ski. He could have called the police, but instead, he'd played my game.

"I've never seen you go for a nice, normal guy. Not once. Some guy says hello, nice to meet you, and you yawn and walk away. If he's persistent, you might use him for sex—"

"Or his mechanical skills," I muttered.

" —but then he's outta your life forever," Suzy said.

"Now this guy, this Gary, he's living next door so there's no real way you can ditch him, and he's not nice, and you had a water fight, and he climbed in your window, and you had sex!" Damn, her voice was getting high again.

Suzy continued. "I think this guy may be on your wavelength, which is...well...have you considered keeping him?"

"What?! No! I hate him!"

"No you don't, quit being a dweeb. Ooooohhh, I'm so excited for you. Don't fuck this up, Helly. This guy's the one!"

Where the hell had this conversation gone?

"I...gotta go," I said. "Lunch is done."

After lunch, J.D. sidled up to me. "So Helly, you wanna learn a move or two?"

"Right now?" I asked, looking up at Zack and Rory climbing around on the growing structure. I loved it when J.D. showed me his self-defense tricks—which he did pretty much as often as I saw him—but I really wanted that shed, and if me 'working' alongside my brothers was what got it done, then...

"Oh go ahead," Zack growled from where he was sticking up behind a wobbling rafter. "You two are pretty well useless when it comes to building anyway. We've got this."

Practically clapping with excitement, J.D. tugged me over onto my patch of grass. My crazy younger brother loved to fight. And he loved to share his favorite hobby with others. Usually more gently with me, than with the others. Usually.

"What do you wanna learn first?" he asked.

"I have no effing clue," I said. "Show me something."

He'd already shown me how to throw a punch, and a kick. He observed me doing each of these, and then he tweaked my form. I did a few more, and then we reviewed where and what to punch and kick. Then I got to try a few on him, which was my favorite part.

The truth was, if you hadn't guessed yet, I had an angry streak about a mile wide. So I really got into it, attacking him like he'd been aggravating me for weeks. The nice thing about J.D. was, I couldn't break him; no matter what I threw at him, he'd block it, or dodge it, or bounce it off his rock-hard abs.

And then he'd turn it into a lesson. "You see what I did there?" he'd ask. Then I'd get the chance to try and brain him again, so he could show me what to do when someone tried to hit me like that. Or sometimes, instead, he'd point out that I passed up several vulnerable areas, and lost precious moments going for an out-of-the-way target.

We moved into escaping holds. He pretended to be my attacker, and grabbed my wrist. "Now you could opt to pull some girly move, and just twist your wrist around and out of it—" he showed me how to do that "—or you could turn your body just a bit, and strike my forearm. There's a pressure point in there that'll make my arm go numb." He very helpfully pointed right to it.

I struck his arm, and his hand fell away. He laughed as he shook it out. "Yep, exactly like that."

"Kick his ass, Helly!" Zack yelled from the roof.

"What are you guys up to?" a familiar voice asked.

# **Chapter Twelve**

I spun around, and there he was, taking the last step up from the beach. His green eyes were on me, causing me to flush with awareness.

I'd been under him last night. I'd been on top of him. I'd had him *inside* me. And as I watched his body move, all of those muscles in graceful concert, I wanted nothing more than to have him again.

Gary was also making me nervous as hell. He'd been careful not to tip my brothers off last night, but now, in the light of day? Would he expect to act like we were an item? Were we?

"Teaching Helly how to fight," J.D. said. He bounced on the balls of his feet, as always ready for more.

"We were working on getting out of holds," I said, hoping Gary wouldn't notice how breathless I sounded, or that he'd attribute it to the workout.

"We were gonna do a headlock next. Wanna watch?" J.D. asked.

The way Gary was looking at me made me shiver. "Sure," he said.

J.D. moved in behind me and hooked an arm around my throat. He pulled back with authority, but not quite hard enough to cut off my air. Used to his manhandling, I stayed loose and waited for the lesson.

It was hard to keep my mind *on* the lesson, though, with Gary standing a few feet away, watching me with all kinds of wickedness in his eyes. J.D. had started in on his spiel, but I couldn't hear him past the eye-lock Gary and I had going on. I swear, he was fucking me with that look. I felt myself getting hot, just holding his gaze.

"Well?" J.D. said. "Go."

My face flamed. "Uhm, could you say that again?"

He breathed a heavy sigh in my ear. "So that's how it is, huh? Would it help if I turned you the other way?"

I nodded vigorously, and he turned me so my view consisted of a skeleton of a shed and two oblivious brothers. Nothing interesting there.

Then we got down to it. I wormed my way around, twisted my head to get it out, and gained control of his arm. In a variation, I was encouraged to pound his balls before reaching a hand up over his back to drag him down by clawing at his eyes. I peeled out of his hold for the fifth time, and knocked him to the ground with a "Ha!" of triumph.

"And what do you do when you get out of his hold?" Gary asked.

"Either beat him up some more...or run," I said grudgingly.

Gary stepped up to us, looking me over critically. "What do you weigh? 120? 130?"

I kept my mouth shut. If he wanted to know my weight, he'd have to drag it from my cold, dead...*shit*, I'd seen how well that worked with the chainsaw.

He seemed unfazed by my reticence. "And—" he gently pinched my upper arm, where my bicep was supposed to be "—you don't work out, do you?"

I shook my head.

"You guys are practicing for a bigger attacker, right? A man? Who'd probably be a few inches taller than you, stronger, and at least fifty pounds heavier?"

"I suppose..."

"Then, you run," he said firmly. "You get them down, you find your opportunity, and you run. You might be able to take them down that first time, especially since you'll have the element of surprise and they'll underestimate you, but after that... Like Brett, they're gonna be angry, and they're not gonna pull their punches. So I know you wanna get in there and hurt somebody, but the smart thing would be to get the hell out."

J.D. nodded. "He's right. Anybody at all trained will quickly get the upper hand, and even if they're not.... You should escape when you get the chance."

I huffed. Here I'd been thinking I was doing well, that I was such a badass. And here *they* were telling me to run, because if I didn't, I'd get hurt. It was ego-deflating.

"There's one hold I think you could benefit from knowing how to escape," Gary said. "May I?" he asked. He directed the question at J.D., who waved him on while backing up a few steps. Then Gary looked at me, and raised a brow.

It felt like a challenge, and it made my pulse race. "All right," I said. I had no idea what I was getting myself into, but that'd never stopped me before.

"Lie down on the ground, face up."

I eyed him for a long moment, and then J.D. My brother shrugged, his mouth quirked in a little grin.

I lowered myself to sit, and finally I lay back in the grass. The sky overhead was brilliant blue—it had really cleared up from the overcast morning.

"Bend your knees, feet flat on the ground."

This was going to be awkward, I just knew it. But I bent my knees, and watched the man who'd smothered my orgasmic screams drop to his a couple inches from my toes.

"I think it's really useful," he said, "for a woman to be able to get out from under an attacker who's trying to assault her. So what I'm going to do is move up between your legs, and hold you down, and talk you through escaping me."

His long pause drew my eyes to his. "Spread your legs," he said.

*Zing* went my nerve endings. But my brain had different ideas: *Oh my god, oh my god, oh my god, this is not happening. Not in front of my brothers.*

I looked to J.D., but he just looked entertained.

"I have it on good authority that lots of women have trouble escaping a man between their legs, holding them down," Gary said. And of course the bastard was talking about me, on this same damn patch of grass the other day. He wanted to recreate that, and this time he wanted me to get away.

"You'll get to try to kick me," he coaxed.

*Aw, hell,* I was in. I spread my knees apart, and he wedged himself into the space between. He didn't keep a respectable distance. Oh no, not Gary. Instead, he hooked his hands under my knees and pulled me flush against his thighs in a proprietary move that made me burn.

Then he captured my wrists, and leaned over me, levering my forearms up until he had them pressed to either side of my head. He was blocking my light, my thighs were hooked open over his, his mouth was directly over my own, and I wanted so badly in that moment to misbehave. But my brothers were watching.

"This is a pretty common hold, or so I've heard," he said, obviously teasing me.

I squirmed a little bit, but quit when it just rubbed me against him.

"Okay, so how do you get out?" he asked.

"I'd like to just get to the part where I'm kicking you."

"That's coming," he said with a curve to his lips. 'Just like you did', said his eyes. "Did your brother show you how to get out of a wrist hold?"

I nodded, biting my lip as I watched his lips wrap around his words.

"So you squirm your way out of my grip," he said. "But what do you do with your legs?"

"Kick you?"

"Yes, but you need to give yourself some room to do that. So you need to dig in a heel, and push your butt back, curling to the side like a shrimp. Then do it with the other heel, to the other side. From there, you can get a foot on me to push me away, or if you get the room, kick the hell out of me."

He showed me what he meant by a 'shrimp', walking me

through the heel-push move. "The key to this is explosive motion," he said. "You want out of my hold, you throw yourself into the action. Fully commit. Fight fast and furious, and you kick your way free," he said.

Fast and furious, I thought I could handle.

"Ready?"

My heart-rate jumped as I stared up at him, my body tensing. I nodded.

"Go."

I did just like he said. I yanked and twisted at my arms to free them, while simultaneously shoving backward across the grass. He stayed with me at first, but then I got ahead of him, got a foot on him, and wrenched an arm free. Then I jammed my other foot against his chest, and made him fly back off me.

"Good! But that was your opportunity to run," he said, jumping on me again. "Fight dirty," he said, panting as he struggled to hold me down. "If you get a hand free, gouge at your attacker's eyes, try your best to tear off their ear, scratch them, slap them, bite them, whatever it takes. Slam your heel into their crotch; that'll disable them completely."

We wrestled across the ground again, and I pulled my punches at first, until I realized Gary seemed able to take—and deflect—just as much abuse as J.D. So we fought and rolled across the ground for real.

Did I try to gouge out those gorgeous peepers, or crush his man-berries? Hell no; I had plans for those. But I put everything I had into throwing him, pummeling him, and getting away from his fine ass.

Er, *trying* to get away. It seemed like the slipperier I got, the harder he tried. He clung to me like a booger, hanging on even when I'd writhed myself face-down and slammed my butt up into his belly. He just made an "Oof!" sound, and laughed breathlessly as he hung onto me like I'd hung onto his fish.

I didn't feel like laughing. My skin was raw from Gary's handling, but it just seemed to add to a growing fire. A tingling heat permeated my blood, my muscles. The adrenaline rushing through my veins demanded action. I felt like a volcano fit to erupt, the river of lust inside me slamming up against the dam of my brothers' observation. I wanted to jump my loud neighbor so bad, it wasn't even funny.

I finally squirmed free, and the contact between my knee and the side of Gary's head was more accidental than anything else. He fell sideways, and I lunged to my feet, more than ready for this practice session to end. My skin felt chafed and tingly, my breasts full and aching, and my panties were a mess. Any more of this sensual torture, and I would not be held responsible for my actions.

Gary shook it off as he had done at least a half-dozen times already, and climbed to his feet.

J.D. stepped forward to clap him on the back. "Where'd you learn to fight?" he asked.

Gary shrugged. "Here and there," he said. Then, catching me watching him, he admitted, "I was in the marines for nine years."

"Oorah!" Rory called from the shed.

Gary waved at him and looked over at me.

I was watching him with lust still pounding through my veins. It was rushing through me with such force, I could hear it, and taste it, and God, could I feel it. The hot ache between my thighs was verging on pain, and I didn't think I could tolerate even one more touch from him. Not unless he was going to finish what he started.

The way he looked at me said he maybe had some understanding of what I was going through.

I was mentally dragging Gary up to my loft when Zack yelled from the shed. Gary walked over, and tossed him up a tape measure that'd been left next to the chop saw. A few seconds later, Zack yelled down a request for a 2X4 cut a certain length. Gary cut one, and passed it up to my brothers. Then he did it again. Within a matter of minutes, someone had given him J.D.'s hammer and belt, and suddenly my loud neighbor was pounding nails into the frame of my shed.

I watched with bemusement as this happened, and then watched him surreptitiously for the rest of the afternoon. Gary seemed competent in his work, and absorbed in it, which made observing him a little easier.

Around 3:30, at the height of a hot day, his shirt came off, and I almost dropped the gallon jug of water I was holding. He was just so… eye-catching. He had muscles that I now recognized as having been chiseled by the military, highly functional without being overly bulky. He had a nice thickness to his shoulders. And a tan. And that happy trail…

Before that moment, I would have said there was nothing sexy about construction. But I guess I just hadn't seen the right people doing it. I was unable to look away.

The way that scarred leather belt slung low across his hips. The way he handled his hammer; the commanding way he sank a nail in two solid thumps. The sweaty muscles of his arms and shoulders flexing.

The way his eyes sparked when he caught me looking.

*Oh God*, that was the same look he'd had on his face last night, when he'd been watching me cum.

"You might wanna close your mouth," J.D. whispered to me as he passed, "before you catch flies."

I snapped it shut, and saw Gary's mouth curl as he turned away.

I was feeling overly warm by that point, but I managed to resist the impulse to take off my own shirt. And for the next couple hours, I tried my best to aid my brothers with such male perfection on display. More like, I tried not to run into things and stumble over flat ground.

Yeah, I wasn't very successful at either. By six o'clock, they were putting the last screws into the metal roof, and I was so hot and bothered, I couldn't see straight. I pretty much fled into the cabin to make the men dinner.

I wasn't much for sexist bush roles bullshit, but when men made me a shed, I made them dinner. As I simmered red sauce and boiled water for spaghetti, I longed for just five minutes alone with my vibrator. But I wasn't going to get five minutes alone; not so long as my brothers were here. Through the window, I glimpsed the muscles of Gary's back flexing, the amazing way he filled out the seat of his jeans, and I groaned.

They finished up with the shed about the same time I had the food ready to go. I watched as they filed in, my greedy gaze absorbing the sight of Gary all sweaty and streaked with dirt and sawdust. Was it weird that even in that state, *especially* in that state, I found myself wanting to lick every square inch of him?

He used my bathroom to clean up and replace his shirt—which made my eyes so very, very sad—and they all gathered around the counter where I'd set up the buffet line.

"Is this moose spaghetti?" Rory asked, having been the first to fill his plate and take a big bite.

"Yup."

Gary's eyebrows lifted a bit. "Did you do the hunting?" he asked.

I shook my head. "I'm as much a hunter as you are a fisher."

Rory snorted, but otherwise made no comment.

Gary filled his plate and sat down, and I was left with the seat directly across from him—after I scrounged up one more chair and shoved my way in between my brothers. The fit was tight, and Zack wasn't at all circumspect with his elbows. I wrestled the parmesan from him, and then dumped a quarter-inch over the top of my meal.

"So Gar," started Zack, "where'd you learn the carpentry?"

"My dad was a contractor," he said. "I did a lot of odd jobs for him as a teen."

My eyebrows drifted upward. In the couple questions they'd asked him, my brothers had found out more about Gary than I had in two weeks. *Maybe if you were to actually talk to him, and ask him questions,* my inner critic sniped. But why would I want to do that? This was physical attraction, and that was it.

But I still listened with interest as he told them he'd gone into the marines straight out of high school. "I was infantry," Gary said.

Rory grunted. "Deployed?"

"Four times."

"Afghanistan?" Rory asked.

"Yes." Gary gave the short answer without looking up from his food. His shoulders seemed tense, and he had a look on his face, a hard, slightly bitter, slightly sad expression. It wasn't one I'd seen on him yet, and it pulled at me. I found myself wanting to erase that look from his face. In entirely physical ways, of course.

J.D. maybe saw it, too, and he changed the subject. "You ever buy that old rifle you were talking about getting from Mike Effey?" he asked, turning to look at me. "And what was it again?"

I started to smile. "Yeah, I did. It's a Weatherby Mark V. A real pretty one."

Zack hooted and rubbed his hands together. "Shooting after dinner!"

I wasn't going to argue with that. It was tradition that, during their visits every summer, they put a healthy dent in my ammo supply. Plus, they'd built me a shed.

"You gonna join us Gar?" Zack asked.

Gary looked at me. "Sure," he said.

And that's how we wound up in my side yard with a table full of guns. I went and got earplugs while Zack raided my gun closet. He brought out the handguns first, and I helped him get them laid out while Rory and J.D. played gopher and set up a target. They went about fifty feet out, past the closest couple of trees, in a direction I knew I had no neighbors.

We started with my Glock 19, a 9mm semi-automatic. My brothers went first, each firing a couple rounds using their own targets. They gathered around, ribbing each other for missed shots, obviously feeling manly with a gun in their hands and having refused my sissy hearing protection. I watched with arms crossed and hearing muffled while they gave a decent showing.

Then Gary. His hands seemed as competent curled around the black steel of the pistol as they had been on his hammer. And as they had been on me last night. His actions were quick, efficient, his fingers deft as he loaded and slid in the clip.

Really and truly, he looked like he'd been born with a gun in his hands. And he made that target his bitch, firing a nice tight grouping around the bullseye. He was a better shot than my brothers, easy.

He reloaded for me, a task which each man had been doing for himself. Which meant he was either being courteous, or he didn't think I knew what I was doing.

He handed me the gun, muzzle-down, and I tried to ignore the way my body ignited at the barest brush of his fingers. "Don't hurt yourself now," he said as he stepped back.

*Ah.*

I held the gun out from me, handling it gingerly. I looked at it as if it baffled me. "Do I have to cock it?" I asked.

My brothers snickered.

Gary didn't know exactly what was going on, but of course he knew that something was up. When I just continued to give him my best dumb blonde look—and with practice, it'd become pretty damn good—he said, "You have to pull the slide back for the first shot. That there on top," he explained at my continued apparent cluelessness. "It'll load a round."

I did so, jumping a little when it clicked. I looked at him with big eyes. "And…does it have a safety? Is it off?"

My brothers elbowed each other.

Gary shook his head again. "No safety. Just point and shoot."

I gave him a wide-eyed, simpering smile. And then I spun around and emptied the clip into the target. It had a bit of a kick, but I handled it. One didn't grow up with three brothers without toughening up.

The slide locked open, signaling that I was outta ammo. Hooting, Rory jogged out to retrieve my target. He brought it back and slapped it down on the corner of the table.

Bullseye, every single shot.

I shot Gary my triumphant look, the one that said, 'Take that, sucka!'

He looked at my target for a long moment, and then he looked at me. And if his glances all day had been hot, this one ought to have been measured in Kelvin. That look said 'I wanna fuck you right where you stand'. The lust he communicated with that one glance made my whole body sizzle.

This wasn't what I'd planned. I'd kinda wanted to humiliate him, embarrass him, laugh in his face.

Gary didn't look embarrassed. He looked turned on.

We went through the rest of the handguns this way. My brothers would shoot, and then Gary would shoot better, and then I'd put them all to shame. And every time that target came back with the center shot out of it, Gary gave me that look, and I got just a little bit hotter.

Then the brothers carried the handguns inside, and came back out with my rifles.

That's when Gary's eyes flickered. I wouldn't have noticed this if we hadn't been engaged in a hot bout of eye-fucking, but we were, and I did. His shoulders regained just a little of their tension as Zack lifted the Remington Model 700 with scope.

They adjusted the target—I couldn't have told you exactly how far it was, a hundred yards maybe?—and then they repeated their performance with the rifle. Good shots, not great.

Then they handed the gun to Gary. His shoulders had looked tight, but the moment that rifle settled into his grip, it seemed like the tension drained right out of him. He looked ultimately comfortable with that gun in his hands. He knew exactly how to hold it; there was absolutely no awkwardness, no shifting about or hesitation.

He chambered a round with powerful efficiency even as he took up a solid stance that seemed to telegraph that he meant business. He lifted the rifle up to his shoulder in a smooth, practiced motion. He looked through the scope, his breath sighed out, and he fired. The recoil barely touched him, and what he *didn't* do next was what I found most interesting.

He didn't then drop the rifle to chamber the next round, fiddle with it a bit like the brothers had, and joke around as he visually confirmed that the next had gone in. No, instead he kept it right up to his cheek, and his hand did this crazy-quick motion with the bolt. He didn't look up and he didn't change his stance. He just chambered and fired, chambered and fired. I felt the muscles holding up my jaw loosening as he squeezed off five rounds faster than I've ever seen anybody shoot a rifle.

But when they brought his target back, I saw that he had missed, and missed, and missed again. He'd driven five bullets two, five, eight inches away from center-target. The last one didn't even hit the paper.

*What the hell?* I looked at him suspiciously, wondering what the heck was going on. That rifle had looked like poetry in his hands, and he *missed*? He didn't strike me as a man who *missed*.

My brothers ribbed him good-naturedly and he shrugged. He wouldn't meet my eyes, and then when he didn't give me another one of his steamy glances after I repeated my bullseye performance with the rifle, I absolutely knew something was going on.

What was this, PTSD from having been in the marines? The man said he had been deployed four times, to Afghanistan. That had to have been hard on the soul.

My brothers moved on to my .450 Marlin, each giving the painfully powerful rifle a go. Gary did it again, hitting a few inches off. Same for the Weatherby.

I had no idea what was going on with his shooting.

But I did know one thing: I wanted him to climb in my window tonight.

# <u>Chapter Thirteen</u>

"Hel!"

I groaned, rolling over to bury my head deeper in the pillows.

"Hel, we're going fishing! Wanna come?"

"Again?" I mumbled.

"Salmon this time. If you don't come, we'll just borrow your boat, no problem."

I didn't want to fish for salmon. Helping idiots fish for salmon was what I did for a living, so helping these three idiots do the same didn't appeal to me at all. The only reason I could see for going with them was to protect my boat.

But it just wasn't enough to pry me out of bed.

"You staying then?"

I groaned again.

A couple minutes later, the door shut with a bang. I heard my four-wheeler fire up—the idea of three grown men on it amused me—and then the engine sounds faded away into the woods.

Leaving me in peace. I sighed and snuggled into my pillows, drifting back to sleep with a smile at the idea of a day without my crazy siblings.

I didn't get up until 10 that morning. I experienced a momentary pang of regret that Gary hadn't visited me last night, but it didn't keep my mood down for long.

Free of my brothers, alone for the first time in three days, I felt like dancing.

I plunked my wireless speaker on the bathroom counter, and turned my Sing-Along list up high. It was populated with hits from the sixties all the way through to today, anything that was catchy and upbeat and ultimately singable.

First up: *I Kissed A Girl.*

I stomped around the bathroom, wagging my hips, singing about cherry chapstick. My shirt came off first. It was kinda hard to get the pants off to the beat, but I did my best. I turned on the water and climbed in, glad I'd turned the music high enough to hear over the spray.

Still wiggling, I began to soap up.

I squealed on the opening guitar riff of *Fat Bottomed Girls,* grinning from ear to ear.

I was just belting out the hook, which was the only part I really knew, when something touched me. I squealed and jumped, almost porpoising out of the shower.

That something wrapped around my arm, keeping me upright until I stopped flailing. I looked down, blinking through the soap suds sliding into my eyes, to find a big, strong hand. Even through stinging tears, perhaps especially through them, I knew that hand.

A cool breeze finally announced a disturbance in the shower curtain, and another big, strong hand slid along my other arm. Then a big, strong body brushed against the back of me. I gasped, blinking stupidly at my tile wall.

*Fat Bottomed Girls* did its ending drum roll, and I was left in silence with the rushing water, and my pounding heart. The silence was incredibly loud.

Trust Gary to fill it. "Is this what happens when I give you orgasms?" he asked.

I didn't have a witty comeback; honestly, I couldn't even speak. The feel of his naked body against my back was short-circuiting my brain.

His hands drifted along my wrists, encircling them momentarily.

The move brought me right back to the night before last, when he'd pinned them next to my head. I swayed back toward him, and our wet skin melded. He already had an erection, and it rode along the upper slopes of my ass. He ground it against me, and I pushed back against him as images of a hot, fast fuck popped like soap bubbles in my brain.

I was getting ready to turn around and jump him when I heard it.

The opening lyrics of *Unchained Melody*.

I groaned, and he laughed, and I knew he recognized that song too. The song from *Ghost*, from the classic scene where Patrick Swayze and Demi Moore stroked and shaped a hunk of clay that bore a striking resemblance to a dong. Arguably the most romantic scene in a movie, ever. He'd been behind her, kissing her neck, his fingers sliding through hers as he got her dirty.

Just exactly the way Gary's were suddenly sliding through mine.

I groaned again. "Are we really gonna do this?"

His lips were against my neck. "Why not?"

"Because that was romance, and this…" I lost the rest of my sentence as he moved both of our hands to my breasts.

"This?" he asked. Our hands plumped and squeezed and stroked me. He left my hands there while his slipped across my soapy skin. My belly, my sides, my upper thighs. He was touching me softly, exploring me. Enchanting me.

The melody soared. The shower steamed.

I panted. "This…" What the hell had I even been saying? Something about romance and how this was…not? He was scrambling my thought processes.

His nose or lips touched my ear. "Mmm," he said. "I like the smell of your shampoo. But." He dragged me back under the spray. The water sluiced over my head, driving the suds before it.

"I am forever getting you wet," he said, his voice all deep and rumbly as his lips tracked across my shoulder.

I opened my mouth to deny it, but then his lips and teeth met my neck. I panted, tilting my head to give him better access as he did things to me that were probably going to leave a mark. My nipples stabbed into my palms, and sharp echoes of pleasure burned their way straight to my pussy.

His voice stroked into my ear again. "Are you planning on breaking me over the edge of the tub?" he asked.

My brain spun. I had no idea what he was talking about. Break him? Why would I do that? I wanted all his upright parts upright. I wanted to climb him like a fireman's pole. Why would I...?

Oh. Suddenly I remembered my shower scene. The one I'd written when he'd been terrorizing me with his noise. The one that had morphed into a violent fight and ended with a green-eyed devil lying dead, broken over the edge of the tub.

My lips curved. Served him right for reading my stuff. "Does that thought excite you?" I asked.

He laughed softly against my ear. "After your shooting yesterday? Strangely, yes." He bit me, making me shudder in his arms. My mind was filled with thoughts of praying mantises and mate-eating spiders, and somehow, it worked.

I moaned, every part of me hot and throbbing. I was close, just from the combination of playing with my own nipples and him teasing his way up and down my neck while his voice growled in my ear. And now his hands were wandering downward.

*Pour Some Sugar On Me.*

"You like the old stuff, don't you?"

"Huh?" His voice was doing wonderful things to me, but trying to understand what he was saying was throwing off my Wa. I wanted him to stop working up to it and get to the main event.

"Quit talking and *Pour. Some. Sugar on me!*" I demanded with the chorus. I wiggled my butt against him, rubbing his cock.

He spun me around and pushed me against the cool, slick tile wall. The slope of the tub's edge kept me off balance, and I would have slid into a puddle in the bottom without his hot, hard body pinning me in place. My moans went up in volume as my hands slid down his firm sides. I grabbed his ass, dragging him even closer, grinding his erection into my belly.

He grabbed my chin, just exactly like he had that night. And he kissed me. It was amazing. Wonderful. All-consuming. The song, the steam, the hot and cold…

His lips clashed with mine, slick and then velvety as I opened for him. He thrust his tongue into my mouth as if he owned it. He did it with a groan, as if he was enjoying himself just as much as I was. I loved that sound, loved the knowledge of what I did to him, loved sucking him, and digging my nails into his skin.

His chest hair abraded my nipples, and my pussy gushed with need. I slid a leg up the outside of his and hooked it around his thigh, trying to get closer. He caught it in his big, strong hand, and tore his mouth away.

"There's no grab bar in here for you to sit on," he panted, his hips nudging against me.

"Then pick me up, you slacker. Or do me from behind, I don't care." I yanked his head back down to mine, muffling his sexy laugh with my lips.

He lifted me up into his arms. I just about burst with excitement as I felt his thick cock nudge between my folds. He started to press up into me—and then he paused.

"Fuck," he gasped, pulling his lips from mine. "I forgot a condom."

"Goddammit," I said, clawing at him, feeling almost frantic with need. "I don't care! Just—pull out or something."

He groaned, peering up at me through the steamy spray as his hands tightened on my ass. "You sure?" he asked.

"Yes. Yes!" I cried.

He slammed me down on him, and he was the most wonderful thing I'd ever felt. He filled me, stretched me, tested my confines even as he ground against my clit. And without the condom, he felt about ten times better, sliding perfectly into me. I threw my head back and he buried his face against my breasts as he lifted me a few inches, and brought me back down. He was nipping me, kissing and sucking on anything he could reach, supporting all of my weight as he fucked me.

I swiveled my hips, making him stagger, and I dragged his head back by his hair, kissing him without mercy. Our teeth clashed as I tried to pull him even deeper into me. The muscles in his arms and shoulders were flexing hard, lifting me. He slammed me down on his cock. I clawed at him. He growled into my mouth.

That's when he stumbled. Or slipped, I'm not sure which. We unbalanced, and for a second I thought we were gonna slam into the tile wall. But no, we did one better. We tipped toward the curtain.

We plummeted, and the shower curtain screeched, and I grabbed for a towel to try and slow our descent. The towel pulled free, and with a loud squeak, we hit the floor.

And somehow—I have no idea how—I was unhurt. And laughing.

He growled again, and lifted his head, and his eyes were doing their sparkling thing. "I take it you're okay?"

"Oh yes," I said, strangely unperturbed by having my wet back pressed to the cool linoleum. My head and shoulder were jammed against the wall, and I was lying about a foot away from a toilet my brothers had been aiming at for a few days now.

But I was happy as a clam. Because my brothers weren't here, my music was still playing, and somehow—*somehow*—Gary was still inside me.

He did some maneuvering and lifted me. He edged us forward and laid me back down on the plush pink rug in front of my sink. "Okay?" he asked. I nodded.

Then he lifted my hips and drove into me. His grip stung, and he was in me so deep, he stole my breath away. I moaned. Gasped. Arched my back and pulled my legs out of his way. His balls pressed against my clenching asshole as he delved even further into me.

Yeah, we were on the bathroom floor, and it was ridiculous, and unsanitary, and it was fucking *great*.

Awash in pleasure, I tried to find something to hold onto. I tugged on the surviving towel. It fell. I clawed at the sink cabinets. They rattled with Gary's thrusts. My shoulder blades slid across the rug, edging back onto the cool floor. I pushed my hands over my head, trying to brace myself, but it was no use. He drove me before him.

I felt myself melting before his strong thrusts, softening under him. My vision was growing hazy.

"Oh, fuck," I said softly. The toes I had jammed against the rim of the counter were going numb. My belly quivered.

"Fuck?" he panted.

"Fuck," I agreed. I made a low keening sound as all of the sensations echoing through my body seemed to find the same wavelength. The shock of my orgasm hit me like a high, pure note, jolting me on Gary's driving cock.

"Fuck!" I cried. My legs kicked.

Gary laughed as he caught them, leaning over me, watching avidly as I fell apart under him. I heaved and bucked, and the poor cabinet door creaked as I did my level best to tear it from its hinges. My foot caught against the toilet seat, making it slam. Something rattled as it fell over.

My eyes rolled back in my head as I was caught on a long, womb-clenching, back-arching spasm. Gary groaned, grinding his cock into me. I locked my legs around him, taking him with me.

"Fuck, yes," he gasped. At the last possible second, he remembered he was supposed to pull out. He pulled back, prying himself free of my legs, and his cum spurted across my belly. I could feel his cock jerking and throbbing against my clit, felt each heavy surge of his release.

I moaned, shuddered with the last tremors of orgasm, and went still under him. My hand released its death grip on the cabinet door and flopped next to my head.

He groaned, and then fell across me, unheeding of the mess he smeared between us. He was big and warm, his skin wet. He was also fucking heavy, but at the moment I couldn't bring myself to care.

I lay there throbbing all over, just trying to catch my breath, feeling his heart thump its fast rhythm against mine. I moaned again as my brain came back online. "You're...trespassing again," I gasped.

"Yeah," he agreed. "Want breakfast?"

"Maybe...in a while. I'm not sure I can...walk."

He lifted his head to grin at me, and damn if it wasn't the most charming expression I'd ever seen. His damp hair was curling against his forehead, his white teeth flashing in the naturally-lit room, his eyes crinkling with mirth. Damn his gorgeous eyes.

I'd just had sex with the devil again, I realized.

And... he'd poured his sugar on me.

# **<u>Chapter Fourteen</u>**

G ary pushed his way into the shower after me. Now that we'd done the deed, I found his naked company slightly awkward. I didn't really know what to say, so I kept my mouth shut.

I tried to finish soaping up. I say 'tried' because I kept finding him in my way.

My neighbor wasn't exactly a small man. And he didn't seem to be washing up himself; he was just hogging the spray and watching me. When I bent down for my soap, he shifted a bit, and his bare ass bumped against my cheek.

I came to the sudden, irrevocable conclusion that my shower wasn't big enough for the two of us. "Do you mind?" I asked, straightening back up with exasperation.

His brow rose in inquiry.

"You're fucking big—"

"Why, thank you."

"—and I'm actually trying to finish my shower," I said, rolling my eyes. "You're in my way."

He took a step closer, looking at me innocently, now entirely blocking the spray. "Oh, I am?" he asked, invading my personal space.

"Yes," I said, stepping back, "you are."

He nudged even closer, and I wound up in the very end of the tub. My heel found the edge, and I couldn't go any further. I put my hands on his chest, trying to hold him off.

He leaned into me, pressing me back against the cool tile. Earlier, I'd been too turned on to recognize an unpleasant sensation, but now I fully appreciated the contrast between my flushed skin and the chilly ceramic.

I shrieked and shoved at him. He leaned harder. Improbably, I found myself laughing. But I was miffed, too. Go ahead and explain *that*.

"Get off me, you bastard," I said. I struggled between him and the wall until I finally pushed him back far enough to squeak out the side. I slid out of the tub through the back end of the curtain, and picked my way along the narrow gap next to the toilet.

He started to sing along to the music, taunting me with how much he was enjoying my warm shower. I thought about climbing back in the other end of the tub and reengaging. But a naked fight with my neighbor wasn't one I could win. I needed a tactical advantage.

I needed a weapon.

I was still dripping as I leaned down to grab one of the towels off the floor. As he turned off the water, I started to twist it. When he slid the shower curtain aside, I let fly.

The end of the towel snapped against his upper thigh, leaving a red welt and making him jump. I grinned in triumph.

He stared at me. "You did not just—"

I did it again, this shot landing dangerously close to his balls.

"You little—" He scrambled out of the tub, leaning down to pick up the other towel. My next blow glanced harmlessly off his back.

He came up with vengeance in his eyes, and I had some thoughts about the better part of valor, and living to fight another day. But I squelched those wussy thoughts, and held my ground. I got another shot in as he wound up his own towel. It flapped harmlessly against his hip.

Then he flicked his towel at me, making a crisp, loud *crack!* and missing me by less than an inch. I backed up, realizing I was in trouble. He had the advantage in reach, and he apparently knew what he was doing. My heart pumped faster as he matched my retreat.

He tried for me again, and I dodged. He missed, but barely. Then my back hit the door.

"Uh-oh," he drawled. "You're trapped. Whatcha gonna do?"

I had to fix it. Immediately. I yanked the door open and turned, trying to scoot through the crack before it was even fully open.

He caught me square on the ass cheek as I scrambled out of the bathroom. I yelped, jumped a foot, and ran for the kitchen table chased by his laugh. Panting, I skidded around the other side.

This situation had somehow gotten out of control. I was naked and still wet from the shower, hiding from a madman behind my kitchen table.

I'd been half-hoping he'd show some maturity, put aside his towel, and get dressed. But obviously I expected too much of him.

He stalked out of the bathroom, naked as the day he was born. His eyes locked on me like heat-seeking missiles, and he readied his towel as he crossed the few feet to the table.

I bounced on the balls of my feet, ready to move. My hair dripped cool water down my back, and the air in my cabin wasn't as warm as it should have been for such activities. Thus, my nipples were almost painfully hard. And my ass was smarting.

He started circling the table. I moved to keep it between us.

Suddenly his wrist snapped out, and he got me over the table, right on my waist.

*Ouch.* I hissed, covering the burning spot with my hand, and glared at him. "You *bastard.*" He'd hit me. He'd actually *hit* me.

His eyebrows rose. And then his mouth curled.

In the background, I heard the opening riffs of *Thunderstruck* by AC/DC.

*Fuck it.* Tossing down my towel, I charged him. I hit him like a linebacker, and I was smaller, but I had surprise and a backlog of rage on my side. He laughed as we careened the few feet across the dining room and thumped up against the sliding glass door. We grappled, and he flipped us around so it was *my* bare back pressed to the cool glass.

I objected. Loudly. We lost our balance, and slid sideways, squeaking across the window. He caught us against the doorframe.

I was squirming like an SOB, trying to use my slick skin to slip free.

He was having none of it. He growled, and heaved me up into his arms. I was laughing and kicking, terrified that he'd drop me, and that only made my squirming worse. I shrieked as gravity claimed me, and then I landed with an *oof* on my couch.

Before I even knew which way was up, he was on me. He pinned me to the cushions, his mouth covering mine even as the firm bar of his erection got caught between us—when had *that* happened? I yanked at his hair, because I wasn't done fighting, and he nipped my lip. I nipped him back, feeling exhilarated by the sting.

Then his mouth was on my breasts and I didn't have any real firm memory of how he got there. But I wasn't pushing him away anymore. I was pulling his head closer and pushing up against him for more.

As the lead singer got stuck on a railroad track, he worked his way even further down. I cried out at the first long stroke of his tongue alongside my clit.

Shivers of sensation bounced through me, waves of pleasure that robbed me of speech. I writhed on the couch under him, shocked and ridiculously aroused at the same time. How had this happened? How had I gone from singing in the shower to this gorgeous man's mouth buried between my thighs?

Arousal twisted in my belly at the sight of him down there, nose-deep in my blonde curls while he peered up at me with his sparkling green eyes. As I'd observed the other night, this man was no stranger to a woman's body, and he seemed absolutely ravenous for mine. He dove in, swirling and fluttering his tongue against my clit, driving me wild. My hips rocked under his mouth. I found myself short of breath, and felt a crazed flush rising.

He slid two fingers into my sopping pussy, and I lost it. I arched up off the cushions with a wild yell. My whole body shuddered as lightning coursed through my veins. My vision was sparkling, my nerve endings sizzling, and it seemed like even my lungs had seized.

He pulled his mouth away. He gripped my hips, and yanked me back down the couch. The blunt tip of his cock prodded at my slick, swollen folds as he crowded between my thighs.

I gasped. "Condom!" I twisted in his grip, trying to push myself onto him even as my brain said he needed a— "Condom," I panted.

"Fuck," he said. He held for a few breaths, his chest heaving as he struggled for control. But then he peeled himself off of me. He stood over me, and the first thing I focused on was the tip of his finger, pointed at my chest. "You stay right there," he ordered. "Don't move." Then he rounded the corner and I heard him start up the ladder to my loft.

Did I stay? Fuck no, I didn't.

I stumbled to my feet on wobbly legs, and started toward the dining area. I didn't have a destination in mind, I just didn't want to follow his orders. Pleasure-drunk was a good word for me right then. I tottered over and caught myself on the table, staring stupidly at my towel lying on the floor, tangled around a chair leg.

"Guess what I found next to the condoms," Gary said as he climbed back down.

Next to the condoms... *Oh no.*

He turned around and spotted me, standing, not at all where he'd left me. "I thought I told you not to move," he said, starting toward me. "In fact, I'm pretty sure I did."

Most of his words were lost to me. My eyes were stuck to the pink vibrator held loosely in his big, strong hand, and a sort of wind-tunnel roaring had filled my ears. What—the holy hell—was he planning on doing with that?

He set it on the table near my hip. And then he lifted *me* and dumped me onto the table next to it. I struggled a little bit, but he lodged himself between my legs, and licked and sucked at my breasts until I quieted down and quit fighting him.

Oh, this was not good. He'd learned my weakness.

He was still sucking and kneading, the master-work of his mouth consuming my attention completely, so I was only vaguely aware that he'd shifted his hips back. Something nudged against me, and as it started to push inside, I realized it was cooler than his cock would have been, and it was ribbed, and it—

"Ohhhh God," I moaned as he turned it on. He'd pushed it fully into me, and those little rabbit ears were vibrating madly against my clit, and with him sucking hard on my breasts, I was absolutely beside myself. I arched and cussed and moaned and dug my nails into his scalp, pulling on him so hard I was probably threatening to smother him in my cleavage.

He didn't seem to mind. He just rumbled his deep, masculine laugh, and then groaned. I felt his cock, hot and throbbing against my thigh, but my leg beyond that had gone tingly-numb. My vision was sparkling again, and my body was tightening.

"That's it," he said, tilting his face so he could watch me. "Cum for me. I want to feel you gush on my hand." And he turned the stupid thing up.

I arched so high, I was probably in danger of snapping my spine. There was absolutely no turning back with that thing pressed against me, accompanied by the hot draw of his mouth on my sensitive nipple. And when I got to that highest point, and began to plunge down the other side, I'm pretty sure I rattled the windows with my screams.

By the end of it, I was almost sobbing, and I would have told you I'd seen God. I couldn't feel my face, I couldn't do *anything*. My body was one big, throbbing mass of nerves. I felt like I'd been put through a forge and spat out onto my dining room table at over four hundred degrees. I got the distinct feeling I'd just fried brain cells.

That's when he finally pulled the vibrator free.

I heard foil crinkle, and he dragged my hips to the very edge of the table. Then he pushed his cock into me instead. It was a pretty good-sized vibrator, but he was bigger. Even so, it was laughable how easily he slid into my soaked pussy.

He groaned. "You're so wet."

*Ya think? After you made me cum three times inside an hour?* I guess it was a good thing I was still incapable of speech.

And it seemed like he was trying to keep me that way. I can't even describe how good he felt, just the push and pull of him sliding into me, the slick drag of him against my engorged flesh. He wasn't moving fast, just slow and steady as if he were savoring every second, every single inch.

I finally blinked enough of the stars out of my eyes to actually focus on him. He was watching himself disappear into me, but he met my gaze when he caught me looking. I reached for him, and he obligingly bent down over me.

I kissed him. I kissed him like he was a hot fudge sundae and I didn't have a spoon. It was hot and wet and sloppy, but he was right there with me. I dug my nails into his shoulders and sucked his tongue as I felt him moving in me. He groaned into my mouth, his hips propelling his driving cock just a little harder. The muscles in his shoulders flexed under my fingers, and the angle was such that his pubic bone ground against my clit with each sweet thrust.

"Yes, yes, yes," I whispered into his mouth, finding my voice. He kissed me again, and I drank his groan.

He was breathing hard, his pupils wide, his face flushed. He looked like I felt; absolutely ransacked by pleasure, and addicted to the feeling.

I'd had three orgasms already, but did I want to stop? Hell no. I wanted more. I wanted him, and every single shred of pleasure he could give me. And I wanted it now.

I tightened around him, intentionally milking his cock. My legs had been riding his waist, and I wrapped them around him so my heels dug into his butt.

Gary got the hint, grabbing my hips so he could drive into me. The table creaked, and our flesh slapped, and each hard thrust felt exponentially better than the last.

He was driving out the feel of everything else. Cool tabletop? Didn't care. The fact that my vibrator shimmied and fell onto the floor? Didn't notice. The music in the background? Shit, that was still on?

I came with a whimper instead of a bang. My lower belly seized up, and my pussy squeezed around him.

I hadn't noticed if I'd gushed for that vibrator, but as I came this fourth time, I made a mess around his cock. And he loved it, thrusting harder, using those tight squeezes for his own pleasure.

"God yes, you feel so good," he muttered. His fingers tightened on me almost to the point of pain, and he came with a roar that put my own mewling sounds to shame.

I looked up at him, our eyes met, and I couldn't look away. Right there, on my dining room table, we had a moment. A long one, as he emptied himself into me. I realized I was pressed up flush to my neighbor, this man who'd perturbed me so in the past couple weeks. He was inside me, as close as another person could get, and I frickin' liked it.

Then he collapsed on top of me. We lay there for a long time, our combined weight testing the table's strength. I was completely drained, completely sated, and only half-conscious until he finally pulled free.

I continued to lie there as he disappeared from view. It was my cabin. My table. I could lie naked on it if I wanted to. I could, and I did.

I heard him moving around, water running. The next time he came into my field of vision, he was dressed. He smiled down at me as he passed.

Then he proceeded to make me breakfast as if I wasn't spread-eagled on the table.

Finally, I began to feel a bit chilled and ridiculous, so I gingerly sat up. Oh yeah. I was gonna feel *that* in the morning. He laughed at me as I slid off the table and nearly went the rest of the way down onto the floor. My legs were like room-temp butter, and I was having difficulty straightening up.

Feeling crippled, I went to clean up, and then hobbled to my ladder. Climbing up it was interesting, and I was sure I felt his gaze on my ass as I did so. I managed to get dressed, and just barely resisted the urge to collapse on my bed and not get back up.

It was the smell of coffee that finally lured me back downstairs. I slid down the ladder, and Gary put a cup of it in my hands. Looking up into his face, I felt like blushing. I couldn't quite believe that morning had just happened.

How the hell did I go from hating my neighbor's guts to banging him almost bloody against every surface in the house? *How?*

"I didn't know if you took cream or sugar."

"I'll take it any way I can get it," I replied, cradling the hot brew. I dropped into a chair with a wince.

Then I watched as the bastard, my neighbor, the noisy guy who kept getting me wet, cooked me breakfast. He moved around the kitchen like he knew what he was doing; not like a rich, helpless bachelor. He cracked the eggs with an economy of motion, and dug around to find some fruit in my fridge.

"Knife?" he asked.

I indicated the drawer to the right of the sink, and then watched him quickly dismember a honeydew I'd been meaning to eat. I found myself enthralled with his strong, capable hands. Rich men shouldn't have strong, capable hands. Nor should they handle a knife with such deadly precision. So...was he a rich guy?

Did it matter?

I tapped my nails on the table, staring at his butt as he cooked me some eggs.

"We're feuding," I informed him, trying to remind myself as much as him.

"Oh?" His lips quirked as he started to plate the food. "Is that what this is? A feud?"

"That's exactly what this freaking is," I said. "I cannot coexist peacefully with you and your noise, and your disregard for my property. This lake is not big enough for the two of us." Sadly, the statement lacked the kind of conviction it would have had a few days ago.

"Uh-huh." He set my breakfast down in front of me. "Ketchup?"

"Tabasco, please. It's on the shelf—yep. Thank you." I salted and peppered my eggs, and then liberally laced them with Tabasco, wishing I hadn't been quite so polite. I'd had some small amount of manners hammered into me, but I really didn't want to be using up what little I had on my neighbor. Even if he was making a habit of feeding me.

I also really didn't want to like him, but he made a perfect over-easy egg. And his bacon was to die for. And he gave me awesome orgasms. Damn it.

He sat down to watch me eat. He was staring at me, and I wasn't sure if it was with fascination, or because I had something in my teeth. He'd probably finally realized how weird I was. He was the new neighbor of an oddball, shut-in hermit with a foul mouth and perpetually tangled hair.

I picked at a splinter on the table, squinting at him. He was treating me like we were buddies now. Were we buddies now? He gave me great sex, but... I was still mad at him for his noise. Sorta.

"Well," he said, standing up several silent minutes later. "Guess I should probably get back to the hammering and the sawing." He winked at me.

"What are you building over there, anyway?" I asked.

"I put a new bathroom in, and I had to plumb the kitchen. I'm adding a sunroom onto the south side of the living room, where the wall is missing."

"And why are *you* working on it? Why not hire someone to come in and get it done?"

"I enjoy the work," Gary said.

And *that* didn't particularly sound like a rich guy. Rich guys in these parts typically bought a parcel of land and paid professionals to quickly build them a mansion on a hill that they could come out and visit once or twice a summer. They didn't even grace the operation with their presence until there was hot, running water.

Contrast that with Gary, who'd probably used the outhouse (and at least once, my property) for the first week of his stay, and was doing his own work. He didn't seem like a rich guy, despite the helicopter. And 'stocks', my ass.

Gary was an enigma, and the mystery was driving me a little bit nuts.

Enigma or not, this delicious, infuriating man was disrupting my life. Ever since he'd moved in, it had been one thing after another. I'd almost been eaten by a bear—if that wasn't a sign, I didn't know what was. And now there were my brothers, stirring things up.

I just wanted some time to myself, some quiet and routine to bring me back to sanity. At least, that's what I was telling myself as I watched him walk away.

# **Chapter Fifteen**

My brothers looked guilty as sin.

I'd come to the cabin door as I heard the four-wheeler approach. When my brothers emerged from the trees, the first thing I noticed was their peculiar expressions, their subdued mood. Then, as they jumped off the machine, I saw that they were muddy and damp up to their thighs.

"What did you do?" I asked.

None of them would meet my gaze; they looked everywhere but. And they were so very, ominously silent.

Oh, this was a bad sign.

"You tell her, Zack," Rory muttered.

"No, J.D. should do it; she likes him best."

"Tell me what?" I asked, trying not to fly off the handle. The four-wheeler looked fine, but…where was their fishing equipment? Rather, where was *my* fishing equipment?

J.D. finally manned up. "We lost the boat," he said.

"You *what*??!"

"We lost the boat."

"Wait. *My* boat? You lost my boat? How did you 'lose' my boat?!" If they'd sunk it, I swear to God…

"Well," Zack said, "Rory had to take a shit. So we pulled to the edge so he could shit in the woods, because he was too much of a ninny to just swing his ass over the side."

I put my hand over my eyes, imagining my brothers shitting off the side of my $15,000 boat.

"Well, Rory was back in there pinching one off, and he yells for us to come look at something. So I climb up onto the shore, leaving J.D. in charge. And Rory's all excited because he's squeezed out this turd that's almost two feet long, longest turd of his life, he says, and he wants me to take his picture with it, and another one for scale, and—"

"It was huge!" Rory gushed.

"—and he's talking about breaking the Guinness World Record, and—" Zack caught me glaring at him, and shut his mouth on the rest of that statement. "Next thing I know, I look over, and J.D.'s standing next to me. I didn't think too much of it, cuz I figured he would have tied off the boat."

"I *did* tie off the boat," J.D. muttered.

"By the time we pried Rory away from his stupid turd and went back to the boat, it was gone."

My hands curled into fists. I was going to kill somebody. My brothers had lost my boat, and not just that; they'd lost it because of a turd.

"All right," I said. I leaned over and picked up a walking stick I'd propped against the cabin a month or so ago. "Who wants to die first?"

"Helly, we didn't mean to," J.D. started. With a yelp, he jumped out of the way of my first swing.

The other two brothers scattered across my lawn, looking scared.

With a war cry, I gave chase.

"It was an accident!" Rory cried after I got a good crack in against his shin. Yeah, I meant business.

Zack held up his hands, backing rapidly away from me. If he thought his sad-sack expression was gonna save him, well, he had another thing coming. I advanced, my blood running hot as I backed him up to the edge of the three-foot bank above the beach.

Desperately, he tried to placate me: "We thought maybe your neighbor would—"

"Would what?" Gary asked. He stepped up the last of the steps from the beach, a bag of potato chips in his hand. His brows rose slightly as he took in the sight of me with walking stick cocked to swing, and my six foot brother cowering at the edge of the bank. Then he tossed another potato chip into his mouth.

I whacked Zack. He flinched, and my blow glanced off his arm.

"Ow!" he cried.

"Hold still!" I took another swing, but he ducked under it and scrambled away.

"What'd I miss?" Gary asked.

"These fuckers," I spat, "lost my boat."

"Lost it? What do you mean, lost it?"

Rory groaned.

"That fucker," I said, pointing my stick at him, "took a shit in the woods, and those fuckers," I said, indicating the other two, "went to check it out, and nobody thought to tie off the goddamn boat."

Gary made a snorting noise that sounded suspiciously like it wanted to be a laugh. He straightened his face when I gave him my death glare. "So... it got swept downstream?" he asked. "The boat, I mean."

"That's where boats usually go, when they're not under power," I said, praying for patience.

"Shouldn't you go get it? Every minute you're chasing them around with a stick, it's probably being swept further and further..."

I planted my fist on my hip. "And how do you propose I do that?" I asked. "When I no longer have a frickin' boat?"

"Well...I have a boat," Gary pointed out. He fished out another chip. "Or, better yet," he said, his lips getting that devil's curve, "I've got a helicopter. It'd probably only take a couple minutes to spot a runaway boat from the air."

I glared at all three of my stupid brothers, wanting to hit them so bad I could taste it. This was like my neighbor setting my blueberries on fire. Four years, and I'd never caused a wildfire. Four years, and I'd never lost my boat. But them, in one day...

But for the moment, I needed to bottle my rage, and swallow my pride long enough to accept my neighbor's help. If that's what he was truly offering. And if it was without too many strings attached.

"You'd fly me around and help me find my boat?" I asked. Yes, we were now having sex, but a couple days ago, I hadn't even wanted to *talk* to him. Fuck buddies didn't necessarily help each other, did they? Is that what we were? I didn't know.

"Well...yeah."

A little of my tension left on a sigh. "That would be great," I said. "Now?"

Gary nodded, threw the last handful of chips into his mouth, and turned to walk back to his place.

I pointed at my brothers. "You three, stay here, and do not touch anything. If, when I come back, anything is burned, or shot, or smashed, or otherwise destroyed, you are sleeping outside tonight. Also, if we cannot find my boat, you are sleeping outside until you leave, and I will never invite you back. Got it?"

They nodded.

I turned to follow Gary.

And that's how I found myself in his helicopter. He opened the door for me, and I clambered awkwardly up. I was completely unfamiliar with the layout of the controls, but I figured I just wouldn't touch anything, and that wouldn't be a problem. I violated my own rule on the seatbelt, but nothing exploded.

He climbed in beside me, handed me my headset, and powered the engine up.

"Can you hear me?" he asked, his voice tinny through my headphones.

"Yes," I said, letting him know my mic was working.

"Ever been in one of these before?"

"No. Plenty of small planes, though."

He grinned. "You get air sick at all?" he asked.

I looked over at him suspiciously. He looked way too damn cheerful. Downright peppy. *Oh, right.* Because it wasn't *his* boat that was missing. And I'd had to ask him for help. And he was doing me a favor.

"No," I said.

"Excellent." With that, we sprang upward. He didn't lift off gently; he gunned it, and we shot hundreds of feet upward in just a second or two.

I clutched at the door as it felt like I gained a hundred pounds, and the world fell away. The straight-up motion was eerie, and the expanse of window was different, making me feel like I was hanging unsupported out over the trees. His cabin got really small beneath us, and the wind of his blades chopped the still water along his beach.

He quit climbing abruptly, and my stomach tried to fly up my throat. I lifted in my seat, tugging against my belt, and I squealed with laughter.

Gary grinned over at me, his eyes bright in the golden evening light, and I couldn't help but grin back. I loved to fly, and he was playing with me. My brothers may have lost my boat, but we were going to get it back. It was a gorgeous day, and I was several hundred feet up in the air over a vibrant green landscape. And if I was completely honest with myself, the company wasn't too terrible, either.

Gary nudged us over toward the river. A couple-minute trip by winding trail on my four-wheeler became a couple-second dash through the sky. He quickly had us skimming downriver, just a couple tree-lengths above the silty, boiling, glimmering water.

It was a beautiful evening, and I was finding it impossible to stay mad. I was also finding it hard to take my eyes off the pilot, despite the view.

His eyes were busy scanning ahead of us, occasionally flickering over the controls. He had a stick in his right hand, and his left was busy on some sort of lever that looked like an emergency brake.

"So when'd you learn to fly?" I asked. He'd answered questions for my brothers; why not me?

"A couple years ago," he said.

"After the military?" I asked.

"Yeah."

"Is it just for fun, or...?"

"I have my commercial helicopter license," he said, nodding

back at a boat full of waving fishermen. "I'm going to be flying for the heli-skiing outfit upstream this winter."

"Hmm." I still hadn't figured Gary out, and what he'd just told me didn't exactly help. He'd said he'd made bricks of money on stocks, but he was planning on flying for work. He had been in the marines, but last I heard, infantry didn't make enough money to buy a helicopter. And there was something queer about the way he handled a rifle.

"Is that it?" he asked, nodding to something ahead of us.

I leaned forward, and saw my Sea Ark washed up on the leading edge of a sandbar. It was more island than sandbar, with a sturdy-looking shore and a swath of trees at least twenty feet deep running down the length of it. On all sides, cold and silty water drifted by.

My boat was wedged up on shore sideways, with the jet down in the silt, and the anchor still in the boat. And only a hundred feet or so from it lay another boat that looked to be in similar condition.

As Gary lowered us to land on the island, I studied the strange boat. A feeling of recognition niggled at me, and as we got down alongside it, I finally figured it out. "Hey…isn't that those thugs' boat?"

Gary shrugged. "I didn't really look at their boat."

I grinned. "Too busy dodging their fists?"

"Something like that."

He set us softly down onto the sand and cut the engine. I hopped out and jogged over to the boats. I confirmed mine wasn't going anywhere — and that my fishing gear looked to be all still there — and then walked the hundred feet over to inspect the other boat.

Nobody intentionally parked their boat with the propeller in the sand like this one's was. And no one would leave a boat just lying low on the beach without an anchor out or a rope tied. If the water went up a few inches, it would be swept right on downstream.

"Weird, how it looks like it just washed up here, same as mine." It looked abandoned.

"Maybe one of them had a really long turd," Gary suggested.

"Maybe." Unlikely. If it even *was* their boat. My memory of that night was a bit hazy. It'd been dark, and I'd been drunk.

I stood next to it for a few moments, trying to figure out what to do. I didn't know where they were—heck, I didn't want to see them again anyway—so I couldn't exactly deliver it to them. Maybe the thugs actually *had* just left it here planning to come back. They hadn't looked like they were from around here, so maybe they didn't know how to tie up a boat or treat a prop. There was a rental company logo on the side, so maybe they'd just left the prop down like that because they didn't respect equipment they didn't own.

There was a phone number for the rental company on the sticker. I mulled it over a bit, and finally figured I'd secure the boat so that it didn't drift all the way out to the Cook Inlet. Then I'd just swing by here in a week or two, and if the boat was still here, I'd call that number and let them know they needed to come retrieve their rental. Mind made up, I threw out the anchor.

Then I crossed back over to my own boat, which was slightly less beached. Gary had excavated my jet and tilted the engine up to keep it out of the way. It took us both horsing on the frame to shove the boat back into the water. It finally floated free of the sucking mud, and I hopped up on the bow, intending to move to the back, tilt the engine down, and get started on my way.

"Helly," Gary said. I wasn't sure if I'd heard him say my name since that first time we met, when he'd implied that I had an anger problem. Oh wait, no, he'd also yelled it when I'd locked myself in his cabin and taken his saw blade. He'd had a tone, both those times.

And he had a tone now, but it was entirely different. His voice wrapped around my name in a way that sent shivers along my spine.

I turned, still on my haunches on the bow, and found him very close. He was gripping the heavy aluminum rim of the boat, keeping me from floating away. His eyes and mouth were about level with, and less than a foot from mine.

"Yeah?" I asked.

"I enjoyed flying with you," he said.

I nodded. "Ditto."

He smiled slowly. "I wasn't aware people said that anymore."

"What, 'ditto'? I do a lot of things that are probably out of style.

My jeans came from a thrift store. My music is—"

"Ancient," he said.

"Classic," I corrected. "My vibrator's state-of-the-art though."

He laughed softly. "I did notice that. Works real good, too."

"It works better when you're holding it," I admitted.

The corners of his eyes crinkled. "Oh yeah?" He lifted a hand and touched my cheek. His fingers were still cool from being pressed against the cold metal, and the gentle brush of them made my breath catch. His green eyes were full of light, like the sun through a wine bottle.

And they were getting bigger, I realized. Because he was sucking me in. He hadn't moved; just summoned me with those magical eyes.

I put a hand on his shoulder as I leaned closer, feeling the warm, firm muscle under the thin cotton of his shirt. His hand slid up past my jaw, his fingers threading into my hair as he cupped my head.

I met his lips halfway. I couldn't seem to help myself. It was like he had a field of gravity, and when I got within a certain range, I had no choice but to be drawn in.

This entry was a little less meteoric than most. My lips brushed softly over his.

A kiss with Gary was more than just taste or texture, so much more; it was his smell, the warmth radiating from his skin, the tickle of his breath against my cheek. It was sheer closeness, an intimacy I'd never really experienced before. The muscles of his shoulder tightened under my hand as he took some of my weight, and I realized it was also a statement of trust.

I flicked my tongue out to wet his bottom lip. His breath caught, and my lips curved against his. I tilted my head, deepening the kiss. His fingers tightened in my hair, and he made this little growling noise as his tongue met mine. Now it was my breath that stuttered, my body that responded with a slow burn.

I was in the middle of a silty, freezing river, perched on the bow of a boat, and I wanted nothing more than to drag Gary down onto it with me. Where he was concerned, I just couldn't seem to get enough.

Next thing I knew, my breasts were flattened against his chest, my arms wrapped around his neck. The kiss was spinning out of control, his tongue thrusting hotly against mine. His hand skimmed down to squeeze my butt, and I groaned as he pulled me flush against the hard length of his erection. The metal of the boat pressed into my knees, but I didn't care.

I didn't even hear the boat engine until it was almost on top of us. I tore my mouth away and opened my bleary eyes to glimpse Brett as he shot by only a few feet away. He had been glaring, so I was sure he'd seen everything.

Only seconds after he passed, Brett's wake hit my boat, rocking it. I clutched Gary's shoulders for balance. With me hanging off him, he was stuck in place when the first foot-high wave soaked his feet and legs. He grimaced at the cold water, but he just stood, and steadied me.

"Wasn't that the guy you punched at the barbecue?" he asked, looking after Brett's boat.

I nodded. "Brett. Ex-boyfriend," I explained.

"Who's bitter about the 'ex' part."

"Oh yeah."

"You gonna tell me what happened?"

I shrugged. "I have bad taste in men."

"Ouch."

"I wasn't talking about *you*," I protested. But between his cold, wet feet, and me inadvertently dissing him, the mood had been broken. I sighed. "Thank you for helping me find my boat."

"You're welcome." He didn't seem to be in any big hurry to let go of me, though. He leaned forward suddenly and licked my lip, the action jump-starting my flagging arousal. Then he stepped back, leaving me panting on my knees. "I'll make sure you make it back safe," he said.

"Okay." Normally I would have argued, pointing out that driving this boat around was what I did for a living, and I even had a license for that shit, but... If you want something from Helly, kiss her stupid first.

# <u>Chapter Sixteen</u>

I was awoken the next morning by a commotion. Naturally, I thought it was Gary.

Until I realized those sounds weren't sawing, or hammering. Mocha was barking, and there were thumps and bangs coming from outside.

I shot groggily to a sitting position. *Crap*, had I not let her in last night? A particularly loud thump, followed by a bout of frantic barking, actually made the building shudder. *What the hell?*

I climbed to my feet and yanked on the shirt and pants I'd been wearing yesterday. From downstairs, I heard one of my brothers moan. They'd been drunk last night when I'd gotten back with my boat. I looked over the railing, and confirmed that all three were still sprawled out, dead asleep.

Outside, my dog yelped.

"Motherfuck," I said. I scrambled down the ladder and flung myself out the door. I got down my steps, turned to the right, and came to a sudden halt.

There was a brown bear next to my chest freezer. The bear's butt was in the air as it swiped at something under my cabin. Beside the bear, my freezer was askew, the lid's edge dented upward and torn.

The bear was pawing at my dog, I realized, as I saw a flash of grey under the cabin, and Mocha began to bark again. I didn't even think—if I'd been thinking, I would have brought my shotgun out with me in the first place—I just reacted. I picked up a length of 2X4 from the shed project, and I threw it at the bear. It thumped against its butt and clattered to the ground.

"Get away from her, you ass!" I yelled. "Git!" Funny me, I know. When I'm personally threatened by a bear, I clam up, but threaten my dog, and: I picked up another board, and heaved it at the brute.

The bear finally noticed something was batting at it. It turned around.

And, looking into its beady eyes, I realized something: This was the same damn bear that'd menaced me on the trail a couple weeks ago. The one that had been advancing on me. The one that wasn't afraid of people.

He still didn't look afraid. And he was even closer today than he had been then. I felt rooted, my blood running cold as he looked across the dozen feet separating us.

Just like before, he took a step toward me.

Mocha zipped out from underneath the cabin to put herself between us, barking wildly at the brown bear. The bear hesitated.

Taking my opportunity, I dashed up the steps. I don't know if the bear had some psychic knowledge that I was about to ruin his day, but he turned around and tore into the woods.

I snatched up the shotgun, and swung back outside—but he was already gone. Swearing, my heart thudding with the remnants of fear and now a growing anger, I stood there panting, glaring into the woods.

I refused to be threatened on my own land. I didn't feel safe with that bear around, and it was obvious he was here to stay. He now knew I had food, and I got the feeling he thought I possibly *was* food. Thus, something had to be done.

I stomped over to my brothers—still mostly asleep, damn them—and I thumped Zack in the shoulder with the toe of my boot. The heathen was sprawled out on the floor in front of the couch, looking none the worse for wear for not having a mattress of any kind.

"Hey," I growled. "Wake up! All of you. Wake up!"

"Hel-ly," Rory moaned.

"Don't give me that," I said. "A bear was just out front. It tore open my freezer and was trying to eat my dog. So *wake up!*"

"A bear?" J.D. asked, squinting as he sat up on the couch.

"Do you guys have hunting licenses?" I asked.

"I do," Zack said.

"Me too," said Rory.

"Well, then get the hell up, 'cuz I have a job for you. I want you to go hunt down that bear, and *bring me its heart.*"

My brothers sprang to their feet, obviously feeling motivated now that they had something to hunt, and shoot, and kill. I snorted. *Men.*

As they got dressed, I fetched three rifles from my closet, and armed them. "Brown bear," I said, "Pretty good-sized one." I showed them what the beast had done to my freezer, and then pointed out the trail of snapped branches it had left when it fled into the bushes.

Making macho noises, my three brothers hiked off into the woods after the bear that had dared menace their sister.

My dog tried to follow them, but I managed to call her back. She squirmed as I ran my hands over her, checking her for injury. She was fine, no blood anywhere, not favoring any of her paws.

"Good girl," I told her, rubbing behind her ears. She might not have been a cuddler, but she'd been willing to take on a bear for me. "Good girl."

I went to the freezer and assessed the damage. The lid was bent, but it still opened. It looked like the bear'd gotten its paw in there — a few of the bags were sliced and torn. Miracle of miracles, it looked like the giant pike had been shoved into the back corner, and was entirely intact.

I straightened the freezer lid as best I could. I took a hammer to it, trying to pound it back into place. I got it reasonably straight, and stacked some rocks on it to help keep the seal. It was temporary, of course; I'd be needing a new freezer.

Once that was done, I went back inside. I showered and made myself breakfast.

I had been intending to just wait for my brothers to come back, but as I finished the last slice of honeydew, my gaze caught on the neighbor's cabin. I'd heard him sawing things as I jerry-rigged the freezer.

He was over there. And my brothers were gone.

My heart started to beat a little faster as I considered. Making my decision in all of two seconds, I pulled off my underwear, and put on the skirt. I knew my time was limited—my brothers could come back at any minute. I slipped on a pair of shoes (which probably looked completely silly with a skirt and no socks, but just then I didn't care) and jogged over.

My heart was racing as I walked around his front porch, my pussy already growing heated and moist. Really, all I had to do was think about the man, and I was ready to go.

He was inside, cutting something with a chop saw when I rounded the corner. I stood for a moment, just watching him as the saw blade screamed. He was wearing those clothes again; a pair of canvas work pants and a plain T-shirt that stretched across his shoulders. His tanned forearms turned and flexed under a light dusting of sawdust, and I was enthralled by the easy grip of those strong fingers.

He turned, board in hand, and finally saw me. He stopped.

I didn't have to guess at what he saw; I knew. When loose, my hair reached down to my breasts. The breeze tugged at the drying strands, and the sun glowed off it, and I met his gaze boldly. My nipples tightened under his slow perusal, until they strained against the fabric of my shirt even through the restrictive layer of my bra. The skirt hugged my hips and swirled around my knees, and he followed the long curve of my calves down to my scuffed shoes.

My chest felt tight as I watched him take me in. He was just so damn fine, and though we couldn't seem to hold a civil conversation—or maybe because of it—the man made me feel things I'd never even imagined possible. Sex with him was like a bonfire compared to all the candle flames that came before it. I was so wet, moisture began to trickle down my thighs, just from holding his gaze.

I could tell from the look in his eyes, he knew I wasn't there to borrow a cup of sugar.

He set the board down. He took the pencil out from behind his ear, and set it atop the sawhorse.

Then he lifted an arm, and crooked his finger. A wave of awareness went through me, making my whole body feel tingly and alive.

Holding his gaze, I stepped up into his cabin through the open wall.

We hadn't even touched yet, we were still a few feet apart, and yet my heart was thumping, my face was flushed, and there was a hot, wet ache between my legs. His eyes were glued to me, and his chest was rising and falling faster with his breaths, giving me the strong suspicion I was having the same effect on him.

His voice, when he spoke, was deep and low, scratchy with arousal and pitched for my ears alone. "Is that the same skirt?"

"It is," I said, taking another step toward him. My knees wobbled, already weakened with lust.

His fingers twitched as though he wanted nothing more than to grab me. "And...what do you have on underneath?" he asked. He held his breath, and I knew exactly what he wanted to hear.

I was happy to tell him. "Nothing," I whispered.

He groaned, and he looked down at me, searching my face, eyes sweeping across my hair. "Do you have any clue how fucking gorgeous you are?" he asked.

I took another step toward him, a step that put us so close that our toes almost brushed. I lifted my head, staring up at him, feeling like I'd entered his atmosphere. It was warm here, the colors bright, the air thin. "No."

"I didn't think so." His hands lifted, and my skin prickled with expectation. Gooseflesh shivered along my arms as he gently shackled my wrist. He pulled my hand across the space between us, and laid it over his fly.

My breath caught in my throat as I felt his steel-hard length, straining beneath the stiff canvas. Arousal punched through me, tightening my grip on him.

"You do that to me. Everything about you—your wide blue eyes, your beautiful blonde hair, the way you look when I make you angry." He leaned in so he could whisper in my ear. "You're gorgeous."

I whimpered, wanting him so bad, it hurt. I took that last step separating us, and pressed myself against him. "Please," I said, sliding my fingers into his belt loops, pulling him closer.

"Please what?"

"Please fuck me," I said. With him looking at me like that, I was shameless. I would have told him anything, done anything for him, because I knew it would only bring me pleasure.

"Oh, is that what you want?" he teased. His thumbs traced my hip bones before he slid his hands around the small of my back. He molded me to him, making his fly press into the gentle curve of my belly.

Then his hands slid back down, and squeezed my buttocks. Hard.

I thrilled inside even as I gasped and pushed up on tiptoes. I loved his unpredictability, how he combined gentle and rough so perfectly. We'd be going along, everything feeling incredible, and then he'd go and do something like that — and I was lost.

"How do you want it?" he asked, beginning to gather up my skirt.

I clung to the front of his shirt, feeling each brush of his fingertips through the material, a cool breeze as my skirt rose. I pressed my cheek against his collar, breathing in the clean scent of his skin.

"How?" he asked again, and then his fingers were beneath the skirt. They were on the lower slope of my ass, and sliding inward, just around my upper thigh.

I couldn't speak. His hand had my complete and utter attention. I pushed up even higher against him as those fingers found me from behind. I gasped, my cheeks clenching as his fingertips brushed my anus.

He made a sound of impatience, and then he pulled my knee up around his hip. The canvas was rough against my inner thigh, and my shoe struggled to contain my flexing foot and curling toes as I felt the cool air on my naked flesh, the hot slide of his hand between my legs.

He leaned in closer, his mouth near my ear. "I love the feel of you, so smooth and soft. Always so fucking wet for me. The way you shake with need."

I wanted to argue with that one, but the truth was, I was trembling in his arms. My knee was practically knocking, and my breath stuttered as his fingers found me again. He only touched me lightly at first, barely tickling along my curls.

His breath rasped in my ear. It felt like he surrounded me; his arms around me, the hot length of him against my front. I could feel the thud of his heart, and the hard press of his erection, and all else faded in importance. I only wanted more of him, to have him closer.

His fingers delved in further, tickling my sensitive, swollen bud. Then he slid on by, finding the sopping entrance between my inner lips. He groaned as his fingertips dipped into me. I shuddered, tilting my hips for him, desperately wanting the full length of his fingers—but he didn't give them to me. He just traced, and tickled, and just barely dipped, and then did it again.

I made a sound of frustration. My leg tightened around him, and I pulled on his shirt.

"How do you want it?" he whispered, his lips brushing against my ear.

I groaned as he did it again, the barest brush and tickle. I lost my breath completely as his slick fingers wandered back and stroked my anus. I felt excitement bubbling up in me, a great rising pressure of it. He was touching me like he had every right, like he owned me, and... was it weird that I loved it?

His fingertip pressed in a little harder, and my nipples did their damnedest to stab him in the chest. I reached up and looped my arms around his neck. And then I lifted my other leg, and wrapped it, too, around his waist. I hitched myself higher, until I had the bulge of his erection exactly where I wanted it, and then I sealed my lips to his neck.

I made a helpless sound against his skin, and we both shuddered as my body finally eased and began to let him in. His fingertip slid in through the tight ring of muscle, the squeeze only emphasizing the aching emptiness of my pussy.

"Gary," I gasped against his neck.

"What?" he murmured. He'd wrapped his free arm around me, and he clasped me tight as his finger slid into me.

I tried to climb him, aware of the solidness of him, the burning heat and prickle of perspiration that moistened my skin. My breasts smashed into him with each of my heaving breaths. I pressed my cheek to his neck, closing my eyes as his hair tickled my hot face. "Gary," I murmured again.

"You gotta talk to me here," he said. "Otherwise I'm going to keep doing what I'm doing."

I was silent. The pulsing ache in my pussy had been overridden by what he was doing to my ass. The curious feel of it, the forbidden sensations, the slight pull and sting all felt...amazing.

"God, Helly...what you do to me."

What *I* did to *him*? Didn't he understand how he captivated me completely? How one look from him destroyed me so utterly? He commanded my body, and the jury was still out on my mind. He could do anything to me, and I'd let him.

I rocked my hips against him, pressing my clit into his fly. His finger was moving in me, pressing its way in, then sliding out, mimicking the hot thrust of sex. And I found I liked it. I writhed, working myself on him.

Words were rising up in me, finally, buoyed by a burning wave of desperation. "Hard and fast," I said in a hot exhalation against his neck.

"That's my girl." In two steps, he had my bare butt on the saw horse. His hands slid between us, unbuttoning and unzipping. Then he was out, hard and hot, and his big, strong hands scooped me up and lifted.

I claimed his mouth, kissing him with everything I had. It was hot, and wonderfully wet, and so intense his coordination of our parts faltered. But finally he was pressing into me, and his hands were on my hips, and I was sinking down on him. He was filling me up, and the feel of it was so goddamn intense —

"Fuck, we forgot the condom again," he gasped.

I growled into his mouth, pulling on his hair. I glared into his eyes. "Don't get me pregnant," I ordered.

He stalled, looking uncertain.

"But do fuck me. Now," I ordered, rotating my hips on him. The feel of him inside me left me breathless. I'd been so well-prepped, I fancied I could feel every inch of him pressing me open. He was heavy inside me, warm and throbbing, the fit so deliciously tight.

He lowered me back onto that sawhorse, and then his hips were pumping up into me.

"Yes. Yes!" I cried. I loved the hot slide, every naked inch of him as he pushed in. He reached new depths today, bumping hot and sensitive parts inside me. His balls were already drawn up tight, and they ground against me.

"Helly," he gasped. He pressed his lips to my forehead, to my hair. His hands clenched on me, but then he seemed to remember himself, and he loosened his grip.

I wasn't helping. I writhed in his hold, pushing myself into each of his thrusts, arching my back so he rode hard against my clit. I moaned as our flesh slapped. The pleasure roared, and the sawhorse creaked.

He bent down, and I gasped with loss as his thrusts became shallower. But then he nipped at my aching nipple through my shirt, and I saw stars. My whole body tensed and tightened, and the arch of my back became even more pronounced. As he continued to nip and pull at my tortured nipple, my mouth opened in the beginnings of a silent scream. My thighs trembled around him.

He chuckled against my quivering flesh, feeling me start to contract around the tip of his cock. My pussy felt like it was on fire, and even just the tiniest nudge—

Squeezing my breast in his hand, he sucked on my nipple, hard.

I bucked under him, completely losing it. My orgasm was a wild thing. I didn't ride it; it rode me.

He let my breast pop free, and then he was pounding in tight between my legs, again and again, plowing through my squeezing muscles.

He had his hands full, trying to hang onto me. My body jerked under the assault as the pleasure redoubled, and then redoubled again. I couldn't come down until he quit, until he'd finished, until he stopped.

But he didn't stop. The top of my head felt like it was gonna fly off. My cheeks were on fire, my eyes wide open but I saw nothing. My whole body was alive with electricity, grounded by the burning thrust of him into me. I was cussing in my head, every awful, dirty word I knew. But I seemed to have lost my voice, and my breath, again.

My orgasm was long, and violent, and very, very wet. At some point, it began to feel like it was happening to someone else, this endless thrashing of my nerve endings. My toes were numb, and the feeling was crawling ever upward.

"Gah," I said. And then things went dark.

# Chapter Seventeen

"Helly, honey." The voice sounded like it came from a long, long way away. "Come back to me. I love that I do that to you, but I don't want to fuck a rag doll. Come back, sweetheart."

I realized I was dangling from his arms, his erection still thick and throbbing inside me.

He smiled down at me, and then pulled me in against his chest. His hands gripped my thighs, and he boosted me up into his arms. I snuggled against him, feeling his hips moving and a slight breeze on the back of my neck as he walked.

He carried me down the hall, and then turned left, through a doorway. One of his arms came from around me, and I realized he'd been pulling up mosquito netting as he bent and eased me under it and onto his bed.

I moaned as he withdrew and left me lying there with my lower legs dangling over the edge. I watched through the netting as he started to disrobe. He peeled his shirt off, revealing that chest I was so in love with—in *lust* with, I corrected with a wince—the curves and planes and dips lovingly—shit, there I went again—shadowed by the natural light slanting in through the window. I licked my lips, my gaze roaming over him, feeling like there weren't enough hours in the day to worship all that.

His erection rose high and hard from his gaping fly, still slick with my juices. I was sure his legs were really nice, and would have admired them, too, as he pushed his pants down, but my eyes were stuck to his dick. He had a beautiful one, as penises go. It was thick and long and straight, and filled me perfectly.

The things I wanted to do to this man... I wanted to have sex with him, in every position. I wanted him to push that inside me — in every hole. I hadn't nearly had my fill of him. Not by a long shot. Maybe I was staring at him with a lusty, half-lidded gaze, because if anything, his cock just throbbed higher, and harder.

He moved to his nightstand and pulled a condom out of his own 36-count box—*My God, how many did the man need?* His warm fingers wrapped around my lower leg, and he slid my shoes off my feet one at a time.

Then he crawled in under the netting next to me. He lifted me further up the bed, and then sat me up and pulled my shirt off over my head, undressing me as if I were a child.

Er—not so much like a child. As soon as he revealed my breasts in their lacy cups, he was cupping me with his callused hands, his thumbs caressing the upper slopes. Then he bent and brushed his stubbled cheek along the same path, making me shiver. He dragged down one cup and laid a long, wet lick across my hardened nipple.

I could feel my womb tightening. I knew if I let him continue on this course, I'd be a blubbering, pleasure-drunk idiot within a matter of minutes. And that's not what I wanted. So I pushed him away.

He fell back onto his ass on the bed, leaning back on one hand, blinking at me in a way that said he'd been into what he'd been doing just as much as I had. "Wha—?" he started.

I pushed him again, leaning into it. He resisted at first—and I resolved to trace each and every one of those abs with my tongue, later—but he finally let me push him onto his back.

He started to speak again, and I held out a hand like a traffic cop. "Stay," I commanded.

His brows climbed, and he looked to be right on the edge of disobeying, but I think my reaching back for my bra clasp was the magic ingredient. He watched my breasts bob free with a hungry expression. When he reached for them, I slapped his hand, and I knew that'd done it. His eyes flared, and those abs tensed up—

But then I leaned down, and licked across the head of his cock. Yeah, he rethought fighting me real fast. Now, I could have played with him, could have teased him, but I'm not a real patient person. So after a few experimental licks in which I tasted myself and sampled the flavor of his precum, I jumped right in, feet-first, just like I do everything else.

I slid my mouth and tongue up and down on him, taking as much as I could handle. I tilted my head a bit to watch him as I did so, and if I'd been able to smile with a cock in my mouth, I would have.

He looked absolutely ragged, his face flushed, his eyes dark. His chest heaved, and he had two big handfuls of the comforter. His hips nudged upward to meet each of my mouth's downward slides. The sight of him being driven wild, and the taste of him—the combined taste of us, really—and the thick intrusion of him bumping my throat, made my pussy burn.

He reached for me again, and I didn't know what he was gonna do—play with my breasts or pull me around so he could do naughty things to my backside again, maybe—but I did know that if I let him, I'd be distracted from my course. Remember the pleasure-drunk idiot? Yeah, I didn't really multitask in bed.

My current 'task' was to make him cum. I wanted him to cum in my mouth, and I wanted to watch the expression on his face as he did so.

So I resisted as he wrapped a hand around my thigh and tugged. "Helly," he said.

I pulled up off him and said, "Just...let me." Then I licked my way down his shaft and sucked one of his balls into my mouth.

He grabbed the comforter again, his thighs flexing under my forearm. "Fuck," he gasped.

Cussing, though: Cussing was allowed.

His balls were drawing up fast, and the other refused to be coaxed into my mouth. I licked across his puckered flesh, and up his rampant cock to engulf the angry head again. I sucked him hard, sliding the flat of my tongue along the underside, watching him fall apart under me.

I'd always found it hard to study someone else's pleasure when they were driving me out of my mind—or, hell, maybe I just hadn't wanted to—but I loved watching Gary climb toward that peak. His erection got even thicker and heavier in my mouth, the little tastes of salty precum coming more frequently. His muscles were doing this breathtaking rippling thing, and he was watching my mouth on his dick with rapt attention.

I pulled back enough to show him a flash of pink tongue flicking around his head, and his low moan seemed to resonate somewhere deep inside me. I didn't really know what was going on. Honestly, sucking cock wasn't my favorite thing. It'd been a chore with my previous boyfriends, but with Gary? It seemed to be its own reward. Sucking him was making me hotter, and wetter, than my previous boyfriends ever had with their best efforts.

"Helly," he rasped. It was the same word, but the tone was different again. This one was warning, and desperation, hope, and maybe even a teensy bit of gentle fondness.

"Go ahead," I whispered, concentrating on the tip of his dick. I cupped his balls, stroking those, too.

"I'm gonna—"

"I know," I said, meeting his eyes so he knew that I knew exactly what he was saying. "Go ahead," I repeated. Then, still meeting his gaze, I plunged down on him, taking as much of him as I could, feeling him nudge into my throat.

"Fuck!" he said again.

I sucked him hard, loving the way he gasped. He was quivering—yeah, I'd reduced Gary to quivering—and he groaned as his hips bucked up, pushing him into me. His cock jerked, and I felt the first warm gush in the back of my mouth. I swallowed him down, and the next, and the next, watching him do the Gary version of the drooling idiot.

I loved it. I think I was finally ready to admit that to myself. I loved being with him, loved every moment of it. It was better than any of my sex scenes, by far. It was more even than the details; more than the salty taste of him on my tongue, more than his ragged little sounds of pleasure—which I also loved.

There was something that went beyond pure physical lust here. There was a warmth, a connection. Some *something* that felt light and bright and happy in my chest, a sense of utter completion when I looked into his gorgeous green eyes.

I was in so much trouble here.

Gary surged upward suddenly, and pulled me up off his cock. He bore me backward even as his mouth covered mine. His kiss was hard, passionate. I wrapped my arms around his neck, welcoming him, loving that he didn't seem to mind the taste of himself.

He was moving slightly in my hold, his shoulders flexing against my arms, and then he was yanking at my skirt. I wanted to laugh, because the stubborn thing had stayed on through two bouts of mind-numbing sex, but his tongue was a pretty effective gag. I moaned instead, and lifted my butt up to help him as much as I could. Then I bent my knees so he could slide it off without pulling away.

He pushed me flat again, and then nudged his way between my legs. His hips pushed down against mine, and he lowered his upper body until my breasts were squashed beneath his chest. Then, as if having me pinned beneath him soothed his urgency, his kiss gentled somewhat.

His tongue became playful, flicking against mine, tracing my lower lip. His hands roamed down my sides as if trying to memorize the feel of my ribcage, my waist. One tucked under me to squeeze my ass in a way that had me hooking my leg over his hip, whimpering into his mouth. He'd gotten me all hot and bothered with that blowjob, and now it looked like he was going to tease me.

But of course he was. This was *Gary*. The only way this could be more like him was if he teased me loudly.

He finally pulled his mouth away entirely, chuckling when I lifted up to try to recapture it. His eyes gleamed in the low light, his fingers doing a little dance across the side of my breast. "Where are your brothers?" he asked.

*Uggghh.* I didn't want to talk about my brothers. I had a hot, naked man on top of me, and who knew how much time we had left before the terrible trio got back from their macho mission. What I *wanted* was to start stuffing some of my empty holes… raunchy, I know.

But that hot, naked man wasn't giving in to my tugging, and he had a brow raised in question. He even took the hand that'd been toying with my breast away, telling me clear as day that if I didn't answer, I wouldn't be getting any more.

"They went hunting," I said. I sighed with pleasure when he started petting me again.

"Hunting?"

"They went after a bear. It got into my freezer this morning. And it sorta, kinda charged me the other day."

His hand stopped. "What?"

I explained about the damn bear as I wiggled under him. I would have even settled for a thigh to grind up against. I just needed…a little bit more. I massaged his shoulders, trying to disguise the fact that I was trying to push him downward.

"So you sent your brothers after a rogue bear, and took the opportunity to run over here and jump me, hmm?" He nudged his mouth in near my ear, kissing and nibbling in a way that made me shiver.

I'd never felt such a sustained burn of arousal with my few other lovers. All Gary had to do was look at me, just blow a warm gust of breath across my neck… If he'd been upright, I would have climbed him like a tree. But he still had me pinned, and I think he was being willfully oblivious to my plight.

It was almost painful, this teasing. All he had to do was slide his hand down; just a couple touches of his fingers against my clit, and my suffering would be ended. But of course he didn't.

"So tell me about you," he said as he kissed his way down my neck. When I didn't answer after a few moments, he stopped.

I groaned. I was finding out pleasure deprivation was a helluva interrogation technique.

"What do you want to know?" I managed to ask. My body was alive with tingles, making it hard to think.

"Are your parents still alive?"

He had me pinned under him and he wanted to talk about my

*parents*? This was even worse than talking about my brothers. But he stopped his kisses again—this time he was tracing them along my collarbones—and I was forced to answer.

"Yes," I gasped.

He still didn't kiss me. I assumed he was waiting for more. "They're alive and well, they live in Palmer," I said, tugging his head back down.

He laughed against my skin, and his hand found my breast again.

"Oh...*God*," I said, arching up into that wonderful touch.

"Is that where you grew up?" he asked between trailing kisses down my chest.

"Yessss," I hissed as his stubble brushed the inner curves of my breasts. My skin broke out in gooseflesh, and I pressed my heels into his lower back.

He pinched my nipple, increasing the pressure until I dug my nails into him. "Why'd they name you Helly?" he asked.

"They didn't. It's Haley." His thumb started to do these little nipple circles, side-tracking me. It was only when he quit and looked up at me expectantly that I realized he wanted more. "It got perverted when the brothers couldn't pronounce it," I said. *And it was fitting, so it stuck.*

"Middle name?"

I groaned. "I hate my middle name."

"Everybody hates their middle name," he said. "Spit it out."

"Jolene," I growled.

He chuckled. "Helly-Jo," he mused.

"Only if you want to die."

"Age?" he asked, somehow managing to get even nosier. He had licked a spot close to my areola and was blowing a cool stream of air across it.

"Twenty-five."

"Did you go to college?" he asked. I barely heard him past the shockwaves he was generating with his soft-then-hard touches. He kept smoothing his hand around, barely touching me, almost tickling, and then he'd deliver a firm squeeze or rub or pinch that told me exactly what he *could* be doing.

"Two years," I said. "I didn't want to leave state, and U of A didn't have a lot I was interested in."

"Because you're interested in fishing. And sex," he said.

*More or less.* The way that word sounded issuing from between his scrumptious lips made my eyes nearly roll back in my head.

He took my nipple in his mouth, and I almost came off the bed. He sucked it and licked it, and flicked with his hot, wet tongue, making me practically cry with need. I had big handfuls of his thick black hair, and my legs moved restlessly along the outsides of his. My pussy was dripping; I could feel myself making a wet spot on his blanket. I needed him inside me, pretty damn urgently.

"Please," I moaned.

His mouth popped free. "What's your favorite color?" he asked.

"Fucking hell!" I panted. "Red!" This man was going to drive me to an early grave.

"Favorite movie?"

I groaned. "What is this, a date?"

He pulled his mouth free again, and I glanced down to find him looking at me. His lips were wet and reddened, and he had one brow raised in a look that said 'What? You want me to stop?'

"Son-of-a-bitch." I hadn't been calling him one, but he nipped me anyway, making me jump. "Kill Bill," I said.

His laughter shook the bed. Which was irritating, because every moment he was laughing, his lips and tongue weren't at work. I wished I had a whip.

"How can you expect me to give you all this info when you won't give any yourself?" I groused.

"Hmm." His hand was drifting lower, making me oh-so-hopeful. "Parents are alive. Missoula, Montana. Thirty-one. Didn't go to college. Green—"

"Your middle name," I said. "You skipped your middle name, you cheat. And why don't you give me your last, while you're at it." Was it irresponsible of me not to have gathered the last name of my lover? *Probably.*

He grimaced. "Middle's Gabriel. First is actually Gareth. Last is," he sighed, "Sweet."

I waited for it, this sweet last name of his. I raised my brows.

"Sweet. My last name is Sweet. Gareth Gabriel Sweet."

Oh, this was good. This was better than Jolene. "Sweet? I bet that was a fun name to have in the military. 'Get down and gimme fifty, Sweet'," I mocked.

He nipped me again. "And for the movie," he said, "Full Metal Jacket."

I didn't know what that was, but it sounded like a guy flick.

His hand paused. "You haven't watched it?"

Was I really so transparent? I shook my head, desperately hoping he'd put his mouth to better use than talking about *movies*.

"You'll like it. There's lots of cussing. And you're gonna watch it with me someday; *that's* a date."

I swallowed hard, looking into his eyes. Did that mean this was more than just sex to him, too?

He put his mouth back on me, running his tongue over my hardened nipples until I was blowing hard, my hips undulating under him. "I wonder if I can make you cum just from this," he said. Yeah, he'd probably caught on to the fact that every time he put his mouth on my breasts, I detonated.

And yeah, that'd be fun...but I didn't want to go that way. I wanted him inside me, wanted him to relieve that empty ache that seemed to grow the longer he was away.

"I need you," I said, my voice pleading, trying to express this raging mountain of need in three little words, willing him to understand.

He was hard again; I felt him pressing into my thigh.

"You need me?" He sounded kinda surprised, kinda pleased, kinda amused.

I nodded. "Inside me. Please."

"'Please'? You must want it bad."

I was nodding hard before he even finished speaking.

"You know, that word sounds real pretty coming from you," he said. "Can I hear it one more time?"

He was doing it again, pulling that power play crap. And maybe usually I would have told him to eat shit and die. But not right now. Right now, he had me by the short hairs. I was so far gone, I didn't give a damn. I wanted what he could give me, and I'd beg, if that's what he wanted.

"Please," I repeated.

"Since you asked so nicely." He pushed up onto his knees, and groped around on the bed until he found the condom packet. My heart was thudding as I met his gaze, as I watched him tear it open, and roll the condom down over himself.

And the bastard knew exactly how much I wanted him—damn my transparent face—because he did it all so *slowly*. And smugly. Watching me spread my legs for him with half-lidded eyes. He was all suited up and ready to go—and then he paused.

"How do you want it?" he asked.

"Inside me," I said with deadly sweetness. My sass definitely came and went.

"I'll let you try that again," he said. "How do you want it? And say please."

I don't know why this poured out of my mouth. After all, what I wanted was for him to fuck the hell out of me until I didn't even know my own name. Maybe I thought it'd be a challenge for him; maybe I thought it was the opposite of what *he* wanted.

I don't know, but what I said was: "Slow. Please."

*Why* did I say that? Because do you know what he did?

The fucker made love to me.

# <u>Chapter Eighteen</u>

I don't think this had ever happened to me before. I had sex. I fucked. I even screwed and got laid and...well, you get the idea. But slow? Gentle? In a way I actually liked? As a man held my gaze, and held me so close I could tell he only wanted me closer, and kissed me softly, with a lingering sweetness I'd probably be grinning about for days?

That shit didn't happen to Helly. But today...this morning—or it might have been afternoon by now—it surely did.

Have you ever had one of those epiphanies that sort of redefines things for you? Of course you have. Like the moment you realize your own mortality, or that demand determines price; something big.

Well, this was like that, except what I realized was that maybe there was somebody out there for me; somebody that got me, somebody that spoke my language, somebody that jived with my particular brand of crazy. And maybe, just maybe, that somebody was my loud-ass neighbor.

Suddenly I was thinking really, really hard about Suzy's suggestion. *Keep him.*

It was in the aftermath of this colossal revelation, as I lay there under him wondering what the hell I was supposed to say after someone so totally rocked my world, that he lifted his head.

I talk about getting lost in Gary's eyes a lot, but that's exactly what happens. I get utterly sidetracked, I lose track of time. I forget to breathe.

His hand came up to cradle my cheek as his eyes searched mine. His mouth opened, and I knew he was about to say something earth-shattering.

But then something must have caught his eye, because he lifted his head further, turning it to peer out his bedroom window. "It looks like one of your brothers is back," he said. "The one who likes to fight."

"Oh shit." I sidled out from underneath him, rolled out from under the mosquito net, and scooped up my clothes.

He lay back on the bed, watching me from behind the netting. "Why are we sneaking around like teenagers?" he asked as I yanked my shirt into place.

I paused with one leg through my skirt. "I don't know." Shaking my head, I pulled my clothes the rest of the way on, and stomped into my shoes. I took two steps toward the door, and then stopped.

I turned, crossed to the bed, flipped the mosquito net up, and crawled up until I could kiss him. His hands came up to either side of my face, and he kissed me back.

I didn't want to leave. It was amazing; *he* was amazing. I'd only known him a couple weeks, I'd hated him for at least half that time, and yet… I was starting to have trouble imagining my lake without him.

But my brother was over there, noticing I was gone, probably wondering where I was. Maybe one of them had gotten hurt, or maybe they needed more ammo, or…

I had to go. But I didn't want to leave.

I moaned a protest, and Gary laughed. I couldn't quite kiss him with his mouth stretched open, so I kissed the dent in his chin instead. Stupid, kissable dent. God, I loved the feel of his stubble.

"Go," he said.

I firmed my resolve, and finally edged back off the bed. Then I ran out of his cabin, along the lake, and up to my place.

The door swung open as I reached the bottom of my steps. J.D. stopped short, his gaze traveling over me. Loose, totally mussed hair, check. Reddened cheeks, reddened lips, chafe marks on my neck? Check. Skirt, when I never wore skirts? Check. Guilty expression? Oh yeah.

His gaze flicked from me over to Gary's cabin. Of all my brothers, J.D. was the least clueless. He'd figured out there was something going on between Gary and I when we'd been practicing holds, and heck, maybe before. He knew exactly what I'd been doing.

The corner of his mouth kicked up, and he just said, "Having a good morning?"

"Yeah." My grin couldn't be stifled. But I'd noticed he had two dark, crusty streaks on his face that looked suspiciously like war paint. "Tell me that's not bear blood," I said.

"It's not," he said obligingly. *Liar.* "But we need a good knife, a saw, Ziplocs if you have them, and some backpacks or bags."

I hurried to get the requested items, changed into some sturdy clothes, and spent the rest of the afternoon dealing with a dead bear. We got it skinned and beheaded—the Board of Fish and Game would want to see those—and the legs detached. We carved the good stuff off of the rest of the carcass, and packed it all into bags for the trip back to my cabin. The bones and intestines, we dumped into the river.

We got the rest back to my cabin. Over the next couple hours, I carved meat and loaded it into my maimed freezer. Bear meat was gamy and tough, but I wasn't the pickiest eater.

We were finally done with the bear fiasco around seven in the evening. My brothers had pulled out the filet mignon pieces and were insisting on barbecued bear steaks for dinner. They wanted a fire, and they wanted to sit around it in camp chairs while they barbecued.

I sighed, but gracefully gave in. I stank of bear guts and blood, and wanted nothing more than to take a shower.

But first, I called Suzy and begged her to come. "Please, Suzy. Don't leave me alone with them," I said, after explaining the incidents with the bear. My brothers were moving in and out of the cabin, getting things set up, so they could probably hear most of what I said, but I didn't care.

"What are you having with these bear steaks?" she asked, wavering. She'd already confirmed she hadn't eaten, but dinner company included my *brothers*, whose mischief was the stuff of legend.

"What do you want?" I was ready to do some heavy-duty negotiating to get her here.

"Blueberry pie?"

I groaned as she reminded me that my blueberry patch was currently blackened and dead. But I still had a few quart bags of the good stuff in my freezer. "Deal," is what I said. "You come and I'll make you a blueberry pie."

"Gimme a few minutes and I'll be there," she said.

I did a fist pump. "I need to take a quick shower, and I'll come pick you up at the river." I'd pick her up in a sedan chair if it meant I'd have someone intelligent to talk to.

We signed off, and I jumped in the shower to scrub the blood off myself. Then I got dressed in fresh clothes—my skirt was still lying discarded across the foot of my bed, and the sight of it made me smile—and hopped on my four-wheeler.

"Don't burn anything down while I'm gone," I instructed. "I'm going to get Suzy."

"Your friend, Suzy?" Zack asked.

"We haven't seen her in years," Rory added.

"I know." And there was a reason for that. Shaking my head, I went and picked up my friend.

When we got back, my brothers had a merry fire burning, and flames leapt from the barbecue.

"I've gotta throw in the pie," I told Suzy. "You can come if you want, or…" I gestured at my brothers, who were standing around the fire talking, their eyes on us. My mind painted in leather loincloths, war paint, and a writhing, wailing woman tied to a pole at the center.

Yeah, she came with me. We whipped that pie together in record time. It was gonna take an hour to bake, and then at least a few minutes to cool. Heathens that we were, my brothers and I had a habit of eating pies when they were still hot.

Suzy and I stepped back outside. When we moved to sit, J.D.

stepped in front of me. He jerked his chin toward Gary's place. "Wanna invite the neighbor?" he asked, face inscrutable.

I hesitated, unsure what to do. Yes, I had great sex with the neighbor. Yes, I'd decided I actually kinda liked him. But two thirds of the brothers still didn't know, and I wasn't sure if I could keep from giving myself away.

What's more, if Gary came, I might wind up neglecting my friend. I glanced down at Suzy to see what she thought. She'd parked herself in a camp chair and Rory had already handed her a beer. She had a little smile on her face, and she nodded, encouraging me. What a little matchmaker she was turning out to be.

So I walked my happy ass over to the neighbor's. I walked slowly, very aware of the noise and conversation behind me, and the silence ahead. I wasn't real sure what Gary was up to, but this would be a first, me inviting him to something—that didn't involve getting naked and sweaty.

I could have just walked around the back and stepped up into his cabin, but I decided to be polite, and I rapped at his door. He answered wearing the same clothes I'd so recently watched him shuck off. Just the sight of him standing in the shadows of his doorway made my tongue stick to the roof of my mouth.

I glanced back toward the fire, wondering if I could get away with pushing him back into the cabin and kissing the hell out of him. But at least two sets of eyes were on me. Dammit.

"We're having a fire and barbecue. Bear steaks and blueberry pie. You're invited," I said.

"You're inviting me?" he asked.

I nodded slowly. "I'm inviting you."

"Well, isn't that something."

I stepped back. "If you don't want to come…"

"No, I do. I'd love to," he added. And I could see in his eyes he really meant it.

Shit. Did *this* count as a date? Had I just invited my sexy-ass neighbor to dinner?

Feeling flustered, I stumbled sideways down his front steps. "Well…when you're ready. They'll be putting the steaks on soon."

"I'll be over in a few," he said.

Nodding, I fled back the way I'd come.

When I got back, the brothers had shifted to the other side of the fire and surrounded Suzy. Zack was sitting on one side, Rory on the other, and they were talking her ears off. But she was laughing, so I didn't know whether or not I should save her.

"She's fine," J.D. said, handing me a beer.

I wondered when he'd gotten so perceptive. Then I sat, and watched my two brothers charm the hell out of my friend. Which was crazy. My friend *hated* my brothers. But there she sat, seemingly enjoying their company. How could that be? They were rude, stinky idiots. Was it their looks?

I squinted at Zack and Rory, trying to look at them objectively. They were blonde like me. I guess their features were even enough, and they were in pretty good shape. Tallish... eh, I still didn't see it.

"What's that look for?" Gary asked, dropping into the chair next to me.

I jumped and glanced over at him with surprise. For such a loud man, he could be remarkably quiet.

"Them," I said, gesturing toward my friend and brothers with my beer. "Suzy hates my brothers."

"She doesn't look like she hates them," Gary offered.

"No." I snagged one of the last beers, and handed it to him.

"Why does she hate them?" he asked.

"Suzy's been my friend since the fourth grade," I said. "And my brothers have always been troublemakers. The last time she saw them—I think she was twelve, maybe—one of them stuck a frog down her shirt."

Gary smiled. "Sounds about right."

"They have quite a reputation for trouble," I said. "Especially shooting things and setting them on fire. Did you know they sank my last canoe?"

He shook his head.

"It was just last year. They came back from fishing with the bottom of my canoe looking like Swiss cheese, and some crazy story about a bear."

"Hey, we almost died that day," Rory called across the fire.

"Yeah, I almost killed you," I agreed.

"No, I mean for real. And it wasn't our fault. There was this bear, and...you want me to just tell you the story?" Rory asked. He looked at Gary, and then Suzy.

"Go ahead," Gary said.

Suzy nodded and blushed. Fascinating.

"So we were up a couple lakes, and we were fishing. And we had our guns, of course—I mean, this *is* bear country. So we were fishing, and we spotted this big-ass pike, much bigger than yours—"

I snorted.

"—and we thought, we didn't bring a lure big enough for that sucker, but we brought our guns. So Zack pulled his out, and he took aim, and he was about to shoot it, when a bear crashed out of the woods. It startled us, and he'd been standing up. He stumbled and almost tipped the canoe, and he sorta...squeezed one off...toward the bottom of the boat."

"Grazed my foot," Zack muttered.

Personally, I thought that was something he should never admit to anybody, but what did I know? I felt Gary's gaze on me, and I glanced over. He was looking at me with flames dancing in his eyes. Listening to the brothers, maybe, but looking at me. I shifted in my seat while I battled the urge to go sit in his lap.

"And then he fell out," J.D. said.

"And then he fell out of the canoe," Rory continued, "And I'm not real sure how it happened, but he shot the canoe again as he was going in."

"I was trying to find something to grab onto," Zack said.

"It was the most beautiful swan-dive I've ever seen," J.D. said wistfully.

"So now we've got two holes in the boat, a man overboard, and that bear climbed into the water and is swimming toward us."

"And we're taking on water," J.D. added.

"So I yell for Zack to grab the line trailing off the back, and I'm paddling like a mofo, and J.D.'s bailing the boat. We're skimming along at a pretty good clip, dragging Zack behind us. And he's hanging on with one arm and shooting at the bear with the other."

Mocha materialized out of the shadows and laid down between Gary's and my camp chairs. Her ears perked like she, too, were listening to the story. Gary reached under the arm of his chair and rubbed her head.

"But for some reason, he couldn't seem to hit a thousand pound animal," J.D. observed.

"Hey, you try hitting something that's only sticking a couple inches out of the water, while being chased by a bear, and dragged through the water, and trying not to drown," Zack groused. He looked a little embarrassed, and—I recognized it from my own experiences with the feeling—sorta like he wanted to punch something.

J.D. rolled his eyes.

"Or maybe he just made it mad," Rory said, ignoring them both. "Because the bear kept coming. He's still after us, going about the same speed as our canoe, and Zack's yelling that he's outta ammo. So J.D. pulls out *his* gun—"

"And we hit a bump," J.D. said.

"We didn't hit a bump, you idiot. There are no *bumps* on the water."

"There was a *bump* just another minute down the line."

"Yeah, but we're not there yet. Anyway, he pulls out his gun, and for no apparent reason—"

"It was an accident."

"—J.D. *accidentally* shoots another hole in the bottom of the boat. And then *he's* standing up, shooting at the bear over my head as I'm paddling. The water in the boat's like two inches deep now, and rising. And Zack's freaking out, shrieking like a little girl."

"Those were manly shouts of encouragement," Zack insisted, "because you were *paddling* like a little girl."

Rory took a deep breath. "And that's when we entered the rapids."

"There are rapids up there?" Gary whispered into my ear. The backs of his knuckles grazed mine, making shivers run through me despite the heat of the fire.

"Yeah, but they're just class one or two," I whispered back.

"We started down the rapids with J.D. standing up facing backward, and I'm yelling at him to sit the hell down—he usually spots for us, makes sure we don't hit nothin'—and he finally does, yelling about how the bear turned around. But it was too late. He had failed us."

"Heeey," J.D. protested.

Zack sniggered.

"We slammed into a big rock, nose-first, and I mean dead-on. And so the whole damn front end is crunched. And we're still dragging Zack. And we're sinking." Rory paused for dramatic effect.

"Oh, this is the good part," I said. "So tell them what you did then."

"So we made it the rest of the way down the rapids, but by the time we got down, I just figured, you know what, the bear turned around, so we're no longer in any immediate danger. And we're sinking. I mean, there's no helping it now; the canoe was fucked. Zack's already soaked. And these two jokers got to shoot the canoe. The damage was done, right?" Rory's eyes were twinkling.

"You didn't," Gary said.

"I sure as shit did. I emptied my clip into the fucker."

I groaned and covered my face with my hand.

"You could have at least waited until we got back to the bottom lake," Zack pointed out.

Rory shrugged. "So we sorta hiked and waded and swam home, but we did help Hel here buy a new canoe."

There was a long silence as everyone thought long and hard about the implications of shooting your canoe. In that silence, Zack got up and transferred the filet mignons from a bowl of marinade to the grill. Fat sizzled, and the smell of cooking meat began to fill the air.

J.D. spoke up next, his eyes glimmering as he looked from me to Gary. "Did you know Helly used to be a real girly girl?"

Gary's eyes traveled from my unmade face and carelessly ponytailed hair, over my plaid shirt, and down my faded jeans to my sturdy pair of hiking boots. He shook his head.

"Yeah, she played with Barbies, the whole nine yards," Zack said.

"Until they burned them," I muttered, trying to figure out whether I should blush over playing with Barbies, when it was pretty much the accepted thing for girls to do.

"Until we burnt 'em," Zack agreed. "She got even, but she's had a chip on her shoulder ever since."

"How'd you get even?" Gary asked.

"I burned their fort."

Gary laughed. "Of course you did. And you were how old?"

"Seven."

"Actually, that's pretty much how Helly became the woman she is today. She kept getting back at us for the pranks that we pulled, and the more she got back at us, the less I think she remembered she was a girl. Only a year or two after the Barbie incident, she was running around in the mud and getting into trouble with us."

"They still managed to pull pranks on me, though," I said. "This one time, they ripped off my dress — the last dress that I owned — in front of about thirty people."

"Seriously?" Gary asked.

I nodded, then looked up at Rory. "Why don't you tell it."

Rory grinned. "Well, there's not much to this one. Zack and J.D. and I had come into possession of this old riding lawnmower. And we also sort of 'came into possession' of a V8 engine. It took some fiddling, but we put the two together, and we decided to take our first test run at the yearly family picnic."

"She was a beauty," Zack said. "We'd painted flames down the sides—"

"Those were *flames*?" I asked. "I'd always thought they were penises."

"*Flames* down the side," he repeated with a glare, "and we'd installed these awesome spoilers."

"Eye of the beholder, I guess." I shrugged. I hadn't gotten a real good look at the thing, but the glimpse I *had* gotten gave the impression of something that could have auditioned for a horror flick. Or maybe the horror had come from being suddenly near-naked in front of my whole family.

"So we fired her up," Rory said, reclaiming control of his story, "and we roared through that picnic. And, I still, to this day, could not tell you how it happened—"

"It was the spoiler," I muttered. "The spoiler snagged the skirt."

"—but Helly's dress came with us. She was just standing there wearing a purple dress, and then...she wasn't. And it wasn't really a prank. It was an honest-to-God accident."

"I was thirteen, and I've never felt more humiliated in my life," I said.

"And do you know how she got us back?" J.D. asked with a smile.

"I'm guessing she humiliated you," Gary said.

"That she did," Zack said. "This one took a while, though. We were really into paintball at the time, and she figured the way to humiliate us was to beat us at our own game. So she practiced, pretty much non-stop for months—"

"The most concerted effort we'd ever seen her put into anything," J.D. agreed.

"—and she began winning. Not just winning, but winning by a landslide."

"I spanked their asses," I added.

Zack nodded in agreement. "She could tag us, all three of us, without us ever even seeing her. She was incredible. We were proud, but...we couldn't exactly let our friends witness that shit, ya know?"

"So that's where you got your aim," Gary said.

I nodded.

"What with her aim and her tendency to get even," Zack said, "it's a good thing you haven't gotten on her bad side."

I choked a little.

Gary looked over at me with a wry grin. "Wouldn't want her to spank my ass," he agreed.

Zack served the steaks, and I found out they'd baked some potatoes on the grill, too.

I was about halfway through my meal when I remembered the

pie. I squawked, set down my food, and hurried inside.

Suzy appeared in my peripheral vision as I bent to rescue our blueberry creation from the oven. "Helly…" she said.

I set the pie on a rack to cool, glad to see I'd only browned the crust slightly. "What?"

"Gary hasn't taken his eyes off you once all evening," she said.

"So?" We'd been talking. Of course he'd been looking at me.

"He watches you. And he has this look in his eyes when he's doing it. Helly, I think that man really likes you. Like really, really likes you."

I shrugged, not ready to read that much into it. "What about you, out there flirting with my brothers?" I asked. "What the hell is that?"

To my amazement, she blushed. "They were just telling me about hunting the bear. And I hadn't known Zack played hockey for the Alaska Aces until he was injured last season. That was so great of Rory to give him some work. Did you know he's taking classes this fall?"

"Suzy…these are the guys that put a frog down your shirt. The ones that launched your bike onto the highway with a catapult. The ones that—"

"I know, I know," she said, looking flustered. "But that was over ten years ago. It seems like they've changed."

I shook my head. "They really, really haven't."

Suzy didn't look like she believed me, and my suspicions were confirmed when she changed the subject. "How long should we let the pie cool?"

"Let's give it fifteen minutes," I said, and started for the door. I'd given her my standard warning. She was fully capable of making her own decisions, and of learning her own lessons. If she wanted to flirt with my brothers—flirt with mindless mayhem and destruction, more like—that was her problem.

"Oh," said Suzy, "They told me to ask you if you've got any more beer. They're out."

I glanced back at her. "Other than what I hid, that's it." She knew damn well I hid it, and she better not have told.

She nodded, and followed me back out. "No more beer," I heard her report back.

Rory slapped his thigh and stood up. "That's it," he said, and then he headed into my cabin.

"What are you—" But he was already inside. "What is he doing?" I asked Zack.

Zack shrugged, looking morosely at his empty bottle.

Rory came back out holding two metal hangers and a wire snipper. I watched as he unwound and clipped and bent them, until he had two L-shaped pieces.

"What the hell are you—?"

"I'm dousing for beer," he said. And then the idiot grabbed the two pieces by the short ends, holding the longer ones out in front of him, and he started walking slowly across my yard.

Honestly, at first I thought he'd finally lost it. 'Dousing for beer'? Like one 'douses' for a good well site? Fucking ridiculous.

But then he veered toward my generator shack. At the other side of which was some freshly-turned soil. Because I'd dug a hole there. And buried my beer.

I probably didn't give Rory enough credit. I knew he was smart; he just acted like an idiot so much of the time that I tended to forget that. My guess was he'd seen the evidence of the hole-digging, and he'd put two and two together.

Sure enough, his little dousing rods went apeshit right over the site, swinging back and forth. "I think I've found some!" he yelled. He tossed my mutilated hangers aside. "Hurry! Help me dig!"

Zack perked up at this. He looked confused, but he nevertheless hurried over to his brother, and the two began digging for my beer.

"What the hell are they doing?" Gary asked.

"They're digging for beer," I replied.

"Are they always like this?" he asked.

"Yup," I said, casting a glance at Suzy.

I don't know whether it was Suzy, or Gary, or J.D. who was more surprised when they pulled a box of beer out of that hole.

"Ah. Buried it this time," J.D. said.

"Yup." I thought about objecting to them drinking my booze,

but you know what? *Fuck it.* I hadn't actually held any *real* hope that they wouldn't find it. And obviously I did stupid shit when drunk, so…yeah, whatever. The more they drank, the less I would. If they wanted to drink my beer, so be it. They *had* built me a shed.

We had my awesome, limited-edition blueberry pie, and sat around the fire telling stories long into the night. The brothers drank my entire stash, I drove Suzy back to her boat, and by the time I got back, Gary was gone.

# <u>Chapter Nineteen</u>

A ny sounds I might have made were masked by my brothers' snores as I tip-toed across the floor.

Mocha looked up as I passed. If she'd had eyebrows, one of them would have been raised in a long-suffering, but not at all surprised expression. She watched me till I got to the door, and then, with a soft snort, she laid her head back on her paws.

Then I was out the door and traversing my yard in the cool silence of the night. At one in the morning, the sky was a faint greyish-blue, and I didn't need a flashlight to see. Out on the lake, a lone loon drifted, probably wondering what the heck the crazy blonde was up to.

I wasn't going to leave it to chance again. I was taking matters into my own hands.

I switched from a fast walk to a stealthy creep as I crossed his lawn and skirted around the helicopter. I rounded the cabin and looked up at the window I had slipped out of when I'd sabotaged his tools. It was higher than I remembered, and closed.

I stretched up on tiptoe and leaned in, grunting as I strained to push the window up. At first I thought it was locked, but then it gave an inch. Then another. I was sweating and panting by the time I got it raised almost a foot.

Then I gripped the windowsill, and hauled myself up. At least, that's how it went in my head. In reality, I hung there, straining with all my might, grunting with exertion... and barely moved. I struggled this way and that, even scrabbling with my toes against the siding as I tried to pull myself up. Finally, after a full minute of this, I came to the shameful conclusion that I simply didn't have the upper body strength.

Panting, I dropped back to my feet. I looked up at the damn window with frustration. Gary had made this look so damn easy, and he'd been going in the *second story*. Maybe if I got my foot in first...

I kicked my foot up, missed, and banged it pretty loudly against his siding. I winced and stood still a second, waiting to see if I'd woken him.

The cabin was quiet. In the stillness, a half-dozen mosquitos floated around my head, each and every one of them out for blood.

I kicked my foot up again, and managed to hook my heel over the sill. I was practically doing the splits on the side of his house, and I reached for the sill again. Somehow, with what felt like a superhuman effort, I managed to pull myself up until my calf slid over.

I hung there panting, my muscles shaking with exertion, glad there were no witnesses.

A sudden sharp pain stabbed at my ass.

I shrieked and jumped. My window-inserted leg kicked, and I would have fallen butt-first to the ground, but a pair of strong arms caught me.

I looked up into Gary's grin. "Did you... pinch me?"

He shook his head.

"You..." Realization dawned. "...bit me!"

His grin grew just a little wider, and his gaze flicked up at the open window. He looked back at me, seemingly comfortable to just stand there and hold me. "What are you up to?" he asked.

"What does it look like?" I returned, rolling my eyes.

"You didn't wear your skirt, so I'm not sure. Making a ridiculous attempt to trespass, maybe?"

"Ridiculous?" My hackles began to rise.

"Absolutely. I've got a whole wall open around the other side of the house, and the door was unlocked. You could have just walked in, but instead you're...well, there aren't really words for what you were doing. Proving gravity's a bitch, maybe?"

Somehow, his attitude wasn't making me as mad as it had the first days I'd known him. It made me kinda hot, actually, that sardonic curve to his mouth. As I stared at his lips, his strong jaw, his sexy dark stubble, I was struck again by that urge: Smack him or kiss him just as hard.

Before I could do something I'd probably regret, I pulled his mouth down to mine. I kept thinking maybe I'd hallucinated how perfect his mouth felt on mine, but... nope.

I lost myself in our kiss. His fingers tightened on me as I coaxed his tongue into my mouth. I pulled myself tighter against him, practically hooking one knee over his shoulder in my eagerness to get closer. The way his lips curved against mine made my heart sing.

Long moments later, I finally pulled back, found my breath, and spoke. "I wanna do your fantasy."

"Hmm?" He blinked, obviously having difficulty changing gears.

"When you first climbed in my window, you said we'd done my fantasy, 'next time, mine'. I want to do yours."

His eyes started to twinkle. He set me down, and then rubbed a hand over his mouth. "What if it's kinky and utterly depraved?"

I leaned against his chest as excitement rose in me. 'On my wavelength', indeed. "Even better," I said.

"Well..." He smoothed a loose lock of my hair behind my shoulder. "...I've always been a bit of an exhibitionist."

"Okay." My heart started to pound as I thought furiously. We could do things outdoors around here, without any danger of getting caught... But, would that defeat the point?

He might have been having the same thoughts because he glanced toward the lake, and then focused back on me. "Do the Ramseys leave their picnic tables out all the time?"

"Yes..."

"Because when I saw you at that barbecue," he said, his hand drifting downward, his thumb just barely brushing my nipple through my shirt, "all I could think of was throwing you across one of those checkered tablecloths."

I was hanging on his words, my mind going wild with them. In my head, he tossed me across one of the tables, unheeding of the people around us. Food went flying, I got mustard in my hair, and then we *really* shocked Suzy.

I curled my fingers in his shirt, wanting to be there, now, and make it real. But it was fifteen minutes downstream, through the quiet dark, and we'd probably wake people up with our boat motor. Plus, it would be kinda rude to have sex on your friend's parents' picnic table in the middle of the night.

Most importantly, I didn't think I could resist him for a full fifteen minutes.

A mosquito bit my cheek and I slapped it, irked that it had the nerve to try and break the moment.

"Next time," I promised him. "Next time they have a party, let's do something."

"Would this be like a date, then?" he asked. His fingertips were brushing the curve of my waist now, and he had gotten closer without me even really noticing. My back pressed to his dark green siding and his mouth hovered only inches from mine.

"Better than."

"Mmm."

I gasped as his mouth slid on by, and he nuzzled my jaw.

"What about right now?" he asked directly into my ear. He pressed me more firmly back against his cabin. "What do you want to do right now?"

I arched my back so my breasts rubbed his chest. "You."

"Good answer," he murmured into my neck.

I thought so. I dug my nails into him as he scraped his teeth across my skin. One of my legs hitched around his hip of its own accord. When I strained up on tiptoe, I could just get the bulge of his erection where I most needed it.

He grabbed my butt, lifting me. Then he leaned into me harder, pinning me against the cabin. He watched my response as his hips moved, rubbing us together.

I slapped another mosquito, this one on his forehead. It fell into his neckline, and I knew I couldn't continue with a little bug carcass *right there*, so I nabbed it by a skinny leg and dropped it to my right.

"Mosquito," I said at his confused look.

He blinked, then laughed, and brushed one away from my face. I shook another off my right hand.

He leaned back from the wall, taking me with him. "My place or yours?" he asked.

"My brothers are at my place," I said. And then, realization came: *My brothers were there.* And Mr. Exhibitionist wanted to give somebody a show. "My place," I said, giving him a little nudge with my heel as though he were a horse.

He slapped my butt in retribution—and I liked it.

He started walking.

I wiggled on him, not helping him navigate the dark at all as I explored his neck. Each of his steps jounced us together, and when I pulled in close, the friction against my nipples made me desperate.

What the hell had I been thinking, wearing pants? This couple-hundred-foot walk was interminable when he was holding me like this, the hateful barrier of our clothing separating us. I moved on him with growing impatience, rubbing myself up and down his length.

He stumbled, braced us against a tree, and took my mouth again. I could feel him throbbing through the thin material of his sleep pants, and the thrust of his tongue had become demanding. I met his demands with some of my own, pulling myself up until I had the higher ground. The heat between us spiked; if I'd worn glasses, they would have steamed.

He added a new dimension to my pleasure when his hands slid up my thighs until his fingers curved into the dent between. I shuddered as he squeezed my cheeks, opening me to the rub of his fingertips.

I was thinking we wouldn't make it back to my cabin—and *dammit to hell*, the mosquitos could take what they wanted!—when the loon's long, lonely cry pierced the urgent, fumbling quiet. We pulled apart, our breaths shuddering in the same space.

"Go," I whispered.

He made it up the steps from the beach all right, but then tripped and almost slammed me into my front door. Mocha growled from the other side.

Gary pushed it open, still carrying me, whispering, "It's okay. It's me, girl."

Mocha quieted right down, leaving me slightly irked.

Inside, my brothers' symphony of snores was going strong. Everyone looked to be just how I'd left them. I glimpsed Zack's feet sticking out past the end of the couch, and Rory was sleeping sitting up, splayed out across one end. J.D. was probably curled up on the other cushion like a cat.

Gary closed the door, whirled us around until my back was pressed against it, and then let me slide to my feet. Head hanging low, he braced his hands to either side of me. "Take your pants. Off," he ordered, his voice guttural.

I grinned. "Can I hear a 'please'?"

He lifted his head slightly, fixing me with one dark eye. "You can hear a 'now'."

I wanted to smile at his bossy tone, but instead I gave him a dose of my blonde. "But, my brothers...they might catch us," I said breathily. I inched my sleep pants down, trying my damnedest to look demure.

He'd leaned back to watch me, and his breath went ragged as my thighs slid into view in the dim light. My attempt at demure was completely lost on him because he couldn't seem to tear his gaze off my legs.

I let the pants drop, and then hooked my thumbs into the waistband of my underwear—the cutest pair I owned that hadn't been riddled with bullet holes. They slid down and away, and I leaned back against the door, naked from the hips down.

I got caught up once more in just looking at him. The inky hair that was starting to curl against his neck, the breadth of his shoulders... I even liked the man's *ears*. I wanted to nibble on them, test his response when I dipped my tongue inside. Would he growl at me, or moan, or get squeamish?

He touched my mouth. He brushed a single fingertip over the bow in the center, and tripped it over my full lower lip. I let my lips part, but he ignored the invitation, instead tracing slowly further down. Over my chin, and softly below it in a way that made goosebumps ripple. I made a little noise as my hands curled into fists against the cool metal of my door.

I swallowed as he traced down my throat. My heaving breaths became painfully obvious when each one pressed my breastbone against his fingers. My breasts were already tingling, and I wished like hell he'd deviate to the left or right just a few inches.

But he didn't. Instead, he produced more goosebumps as he drifted down my belly through the shirt.

I pushed up on my toes in an effort to get him to his goal faster. I was shaking with anticipation, and I was so worried he was going to hesitate at the last moment, to tease me, that when he actually touched me, I gasped. I grabbed for his shoulders, needing something to hold onto as his fingers slid deep between my legs.

A moan wrenched from my lips. His fingers made me throb as they smoothed past my clit and dipped into me. I widened my stance, giving him more room, wanting as much of him as I could get.

He gave it to me. I shuddered as he pushed two fingers into my aching center. He moved them in long, sure strokes as the heel of his hand pressed against me.

I tilted my chin up, staring into his eyes, breathing his breath. The moment stretched as the fire he was stroking into me spread to my limbs. I tilted my head back further as the tide of pleasure swept me along on its rhythmic, rising swell.

"I love watching you," he rasped. "You're so damn sexy when you—"

I moaned, my lids fluttering as it felt like he added another finger. He was stretching me just to the sweet edge of pain.

"Yes, when you do that." His free hand brushed across my overheated cheek. "The pink color of your blush, the way you forget how to talk." He was smiling down at me, but he still had three fingers wedged into my sopping pussy.

My brain didn't even try to handle all the inputs. I just locked my knees and tried to keep my eyes open.

Sweet Jesus—it was his thumb now, circling my clit. Not quite touching, just nudging me ever upward. The pleasure was becoming a riptide, increasing in pace, dragging me toward the end of the line. I could feel the heat rising, my muscles trembling.

I harnessed enough brain cells to spit out a word. "Wait." I pushed at his hand. "You. I want you. Inside me when I cum. Please."

When he stepped back, his breaths heaved. "Take your shirt off," he said. Then he reached into his pocket, retrieved a condom, and shoved down his pants.

I fairly ripped off my shirt, but even so, he was bearing me back against the door before I flung it away. I didn't know where it went, but I didn't give a fuck. I was busy sucking Gary's tongue into my mouth.

He was just this side of rough. He lifted me up, pinned me to the door, and pushed into me. We both groaned, and then it was a frenzied race to the finish line. The door thumped in its frame with each of his powerful thrusts. I felt each thick, wonderful inch of him as it pounded into me.

The feeling quickly blended into a crazed crescendo of pleasure. I screamed into Gary's neck, dimly aware my brothers were still just a few feet away. Mocha growled again, and if I'd been paying any attention at all I might have been gratified she was worried that Gary was killing me.

But my body currently had selective hearing. I could 'hear' Gary's thick cock buried in me to the root, his hard chest flattening my tingling breasts, his firm hands on my thighs and buttocks. I could smell the sweat on his skin and hear his deep groan as he followed me into the roiling abyss.

Minutes passed where I was just a trembling mess, and it was all I could do to breathe, once I recalled how. Luckily my heart kept doing its thing, and my vision did eventually come back, so that was good.

Gary set me down before I was entirely ready. He steadied me, laughing as I wobbled. "I was the one holding us both up," he pointed out.

I grunted; post-coital conversation was not my forte. I leaned back against the door, still trying to recover.

Gary scooped up his clothes and walked into the bathroom. I heard water running, and when he came back out, he was dressed, and looking as scrumptious as ever.

I winced as his foot glanced an empty beer bottle. It fell with a rattle, then rolled and clanged against a chair leg.

Gary glanced at the brothers. They hadn't even stirred. "Wow," he said. "They are really out. I thought with some of the noises you were making we'd be caught for sure, but..."

I started to put my shirt on like pants, but got myself straightened out before anyone noticed. I yanked my sleep pants up my legs. I had no idea where my underwear had gone, but I'd find them later, I was sure.

I crossed to Gary, and observed my troublemaking siblings. In sleep, they should have looked innocent, but mostly they just looked sloppy. Zack was sprawled on the floor, naked except for a pair of boxers, his mouth gaping open like a dead person's. Rory's neck was bent at an angle I was sure he'd feel in the morning. His feet were on Zack's legs, and his shirt had ridden up to reveal a hairy belly. J.D. was curled up on the next cushion. He'd retained his clothes, but not his dignity; his thumb was trying to find its way into his mouth.

"They drank *a lot* last night," I said.

Gary slanted a look at me. "Do you think they were maybe couldn't-even-remember-what-happened-last-night drunk?"

I started nodding, and then my gaze locked with his.

He rubbed his chin. "Didn't they... lose your boat?"

"They did," I said. "They also cellophaned my toilet, and drank my beer. And they stink," I added, noting the lingering bouquet of ass.

Gary's grin widened as his eyebrows climbed. 'Well? What should we do to them?' his dancing eyes asked.

"We could draw penises on their faces," I suggested. "I have a magic marker around here somewhere."

"Classic and funny," Gary said, "but..."

"Yes?" I'd taken a couple steps toward the markers, but was arrested by his naughty expression.

"...would you like to *really* humiliate them, and possibly cause permanent mental scarring?"

I sat at the table, leaned back, and crossed my legs. "I'm listening."

He sat across from me, his grin infectious. "How about we position them to make it look like they had sex? Strip them, arrange them so they're spooning, leave a bottle of anal lube lying nearby. Take some pictures..."

"I do like that idea," I said. "But. Problems. One: I get the feeling if my brothers were to wake up spooning, the one in the back would just give the other a squeeze and whisper softly in his ear, 'Good morning, sweetheart'."

Gary pursed his lips. "So we make it worse than spooning. And even if they play it cool, we will have at least created a niggling doubt, I guarantee it."

"We? That was my next question. Are they out enough for us to do this, and were you going to help? 'Cuz I can't lift even half of the bigger ones."

"Of course I'll help," he said, pushing to his feet. "Sounds like fun." He crossed to the couch and picked up Rory's arm. When he dropped it, it flopped heavily back to the top of the couch. Rory didn't stir. He pushed Zack's feet with one of his own, sliding them unresistingly across the floor. Then he picked his way around to J.D.

"I'd be careful with that one," I said. "He tends to come up swinging."

Gary leaned over and did something to my youngest brother, and then grinned. "Yup. They're out."

"Okay. Lastly: Anal lube?"

"I can come up with something," Gary said, coming back toward me.

"Can you now?"

He dropped into the seat across from me again and met my gaze.

I felt myself getting flustered, imagining Gary coming at me with a bottle of anal lube in his hand. It was another thing I'd researched and written, but had never actually done. But I'd do it with Gary. Maybe I could write it, and he'd act it out just exactly as he had climbing through my window.

My mind went to work, fleshing out that scene. For the first time, I'd like privacy and a bed, but then we could get crazy. The dock. The canoe. My fingers itched for my keyboard.

Gary snapped his fingers. "I lost you for a minute there," he said.

I cleared my throat, shifting on my chair. "We'll talk about this later," I suggested.

"I was kinda hoping we'd do more than talk."

Just like that, the air between us began to feel charged. I'd had him just a few minutes ago, but I wanted him again. For this helicopter pilot that'd burned my blueberries, apparently I was insatiable.

He was watching me with that intent look, like he was reading each thought as I had it.

I jumped to my feet. "Let's do this."

He looked up at me, his muscles tensed to move.

"The brothers," I added hastily. "Let's do them." I winced. "Arrange them, I mean."

And we did. It took about a half hour of heavy lifting and laughter until we had them arranged to our satisfaction.

"You know," I told Gary as I straightened up for what I hoped was the last time, "this would be a lot more convincing if you wanted to strip down and be sandwiched between them. That way, when they wake up, you could say something like, 'Wow, you guys were great, thank you'."

Gary snorted. "It's a good idea, but yeah, no, I'll pass."

I put my hands on my hips, surveying our work. We'd left Zack on his back on the floor, though had stolen his shorts. We'd put Rory on top of his legs in a folded-down reverse cowgirl, also minus his clothes. J.D., we'd curled around Zack's head so Zack would wake up with a face full of crotch and a really bad feeling.

Gary had run over to his place and come back with a bottle

proudly labeled, 'Anal Lube'. It was cherry flavored, and that kind of scared me—but I was sure I'd live. We'd drizzled it over the appropriate areas so the whole scene was more convincing, and then left it, uncapped, lying next to them.

"They're not the one I'd like to enjoy," Gary added.

I glanced over at him.

"I have another fantasy, if you're interested."

It was after two in the morning, but of course I was freaking interested. I could sleep when I was dead. "I'm listening," I said, trying to play it cool.

He walked a little closer, so he was standing just inches away, looking down at me like he had the day he'd emptied a glass of water on me. This time, I held my ground.

"I want to dominate you," he said.

I *never* would have guessed. "Yeah?" Despite my mental sarcasm, my voice came out breathy. If I was being completely honest with myself, I wanted that too.

"Yes. I want you to surrender to me. Completely," he whispered in my ear. His knuckles brushed the side of my unbound breast through my shirt, making me tremble.

I stepped back to get enough room to think. *Complete surrender.* I didn't know what that involved, but I did like it when he held me down. So… what? He wanted to restrain me, tell me what to do? I had problems following orders, but maybe just this once I could manage. He wanted to be rough? Sweet. I'd actually liked it when he smacked my butt, so I had no real fear there.

Who was I kidding? With him looking at me like that, I'd do whatever he wanted.

"Okay," I said.

His face was serious, but his eyes danced. "Get upstairs."

Quashing my instant impulse to do the opposite, I turned and walked stiffly to the ladder.

"And keep your clothes on until I get up there," he said. "I want to watch you take them off."

My shoulders tightened. "But you just saw me take them off," I pointed out, turning my head to look at him.

"Are you arguing with me?" he asked, his voice dangerously soft.

My skin prickled. *Yes! Yes I am!* "No," I squeezed out.

He chuckled.

This was going to be hard, I could already tell.

# __Chapter Twenty__

"S hirt first," he said. "Slowly."

We'd climbed the ladder, and he was facing me at the end of the bed.

I fingered my shirt's hem, intent on giving him *exactly* what he wanted. I inched it over my waist, revealing my pale skin in the moonlight. His expression went hungry when I revealed the milky curves of my breasts. I languidly pulled the shirt up over my head and let it float to the floor.

"And the pants," he instructed. He was already tenting his. It softened me just a little to his demands, knowing what I did to him.

I eased my sleep pants down, letting them slide the last little bit. I stepped out of them, completely naked, loving the way he looked at me. My body wasn't perfect—whose was, really?—but he was looking at me like I was devastating. My breath came just a little harder, my nipples pebbling in the cool air.

"Now take off mine," he said.

I stepped toward him. Reached out—

"With your teeth," he said, his lips twitching as he caught my expression.

*Really?* I sighed as I looked up into his face. Apparently, he was going to push me.

But, just this once, I allowed my spine to bend. I leaned down and lipped at the hem of his shirt. I was down near his straining erection, so I took the opportunity to blow a long, hot breath on him. *See what you're missing?*

He groaned quietly, and then I got his shirt in my teeth and dragged it upward. He met my eyes when I got up to pec level. "Good girl," he said.

I prickled again. Maybe when he was inside me, I'd let him get away with shit like that...

*This is his fantasy, Helly!* I berated myself. *It's just this once, and if you don't like it, you don't have to do it again.* Even if I was having mental doubts about this, my body was 100% on board. I was wet, soaked through, warm and tingly pretty much all over.

He eased the cloth from between my teeth, and took the shirt the rest of the way off. "And the pants," he murmured.

I looked down, contemplating. Then, feeling flippant, I dropped to my knees before him.

He made an appreciative little sound, and I looked up at him as I slowly leaned in. *Oh, he really likes this.* I slowed down even more, letting him feel my breath. I traced the tip of my tongue up his shaft through the material, and finally took his waistband in my teeth. I pulled the elastic waistband down over his cock, my whole body clenching as he sprang free and brushed against my cheek.

I wanted his cock in my mouth, and was pretty sure he wanted the same. Just as soon as I got these damn pants down, he'd order me to suck him off. Then I could have him. He'd melt before me, and it would be *great.* I dragged his pants down, and then reached for him.

He stepped back, stymying me.

"But..."

He tossed a grin over his shoulder as he walked away with my new favorite toy. He shoved my blankets back and lay down on the bed, propped up on the pillows, his arms behind his head.

Okay, he wanted a lazy blowjob. Not bothering to stand, I crept across the mattress toward him.

"I want you to lick your way down my chest," he said.

Okay, he wanted foreplay with that lazy blowjob. I crawled up next to him.

And then... I got to do that which I'd been longing to for weeks. I put my mouth on that smooth golden-tan skin. With my hair trailing after, I worked my way from his collarbones across his really nice pecs. I'd always thought men's nipples were funny, but neither of us were laughing as my tongue flirted with his.

Then, and only then, did I allow myself to follow his happy trail. I took the scenic route, tracing the dents between each pair of abs as I worked my way down.

Anticipation had me in its hold. I wanted to wrap my hand around him, feel the heated steel of his shaft. Taste him, see if the rubber condom flavor lingered, or the salty flavor of his cum. I wanted to tease him mercilessly, and watch his handsome face darken with need.

I locked gazes with him as I moved downward, licking my lips, letting him see my intention. My eagerness.

"Don't touch my dick," he said.

I froze. "What? Why?" I sputtered.

"Because you look like you want to," he said. "Kiss anything but. My thighs, my knees. My feet have always been pretty sensitive."

Stunned, I sat straight up. "You want me. To kiss. Your *feet*?" I shook my head. "Because I want to lick your cock?" I'd never heard anything so silly in my life. His attempt at domination was to rob himself of my mouth on his cock? It was the most bass-ackwards thing I'd ever heard. Downright dumb, in fact.

It was insanity, and I didn't have to put up with it. He should be *begging* me for the attentions of my mouth, not finally —*maybe*— allowing me to blow him. This right here, *this*, was why women had vibrators.

He grasped my arms, not letting me pull away, and rolled his eyes. "Oh, fine. You want the traditional approach?"

I was about to start cussing when he pushed me belly-down onto the mattress, and rolled on top of me. He had me pinned in under a second, his hands on my wrists, his legs and hips over mine, his chest giving me just enough room to breathe. The move was sudden, and incredibly masterful, and it ground his bare cock against the crack of my ass.

A sudden, insane, absolutely irresistible rush of arousal hit me like a drug. I moaned, pushing my butt back against him.

"Huh," he murmured, his breath hot against my ear. "You like this approach better."

One of his hands left my wrists, and he dragged his fingernails down my side in a long scrape that sent a white-hot billow of sensation through me. Then he squeezed my hip in a way that made me whimper with need.

His weight shifted, followed by the faint sound of my nightstand drawer. I heard a condom packet tear. The sound was loud in the silence, and sent a wave of delight from my ears down to my toes. I knew what came next. My hand fisted in the sheets while my body tightened in anticipation. He slid to the side, probably putting it on.

Without warning, his hand cracked against my ass. I gasped, throbbing as the feeling ricocheted up my spine.

"That's for being difficult," he muttered. Then he rolled back over me. He dragged my hips up until I was angled to receive him, and his sheathed cock began to press into me. It was large and blunt, the feel of it galvanizing. I bucked up against him, trying to get more, faster. He held me down.

I turned my head and bit the pillow as he pushed into me. The feeling was magnificent. He was thick, and with my legs closed he felt almost too large. I started to spread them to ease the ache, but he pushed them back together.

He completed his invasion on a hard thrust, one that made me feel like crawling up the walls. His hips pressed flush to my still-stinging ass, and the thick root of him split me wide. He did his crazy hip-roll, and I swear I felt him all the way up in my belly. The feeling was raw, and I loved it.

He grasped my chin, pulling me so I was looking almost over my shoulder. He leaned in—a move accompanied by him pressing so high and deep I gasped—and kissed me. The combination of his tongue thrusting in my mouth and his cock lodged deep in my body made me feel claimed. Used. It was awesome.

I lay there and I let him use me, felt the spot where he pushed into me become slicker, even more welcoming. I let him force my mouth open, let him kiss my breath away.

He groaned, his thrusts becoming more forceful, his hips pressing mine into the mattress. Our breathing quickened, and I was lost in that place where there was only sensation.

That's why I was very confused when he suddenly shifted. He moved back slightly and dragged me up onto my knees. He pushed his way inside my legs, and I almost cried out when he leaned over me. He was in me so deep, it was bordering on uncomfortable. He pushed my upper body down. I resisted at first, but he used firm and steady pressure until I let my elbows fold.

I gripped my pillow, pressing my forehead into it. My ass was in the air, and he was between my legs, his hands firm on my hips. My body tightened, anticipating him plunging into me like a stallion covering a mare.

It felt a lot like submission. Surrender.

But before I could get bent out of shape, I became aware of his hands moving. They stroked over my hips, my lower back, down my thighs. Gentling me. I felt his cock throbbing, but he held almost entirely still.

I resisted at first. I didn't like the loss of control. He could do whatever he wanted to me in this position. He could hurt me.

But I knew he wouldn't. I knew he'd only bring me pleasure. What he was doing already felt amazing, and he wasn't hardly doing anything. I could put up a fight—or I could let him pleasure me.

With a sigh, I let the tension drain out of my body, and I put myself in his hands. I surrendered.

"Good girl," he whispered.

I grumbled, but the sound cut off on a gasp as he *moved*. He plunged into me, smooth, long, slick strokes, each one balls-deep. My thighs trembled around his with the effort of staying wide and open for him, and with the impact of his strokes.

I clenched the pillow tighter and started to make noises into it. I don't even know how to describe the sounds I made. Whining, mewling kitten sounds some of them. Gasps, whimpers.

This was him telling me he was in charge, and yet...I loved it.

He leaned over me, changing the angle, hitting some deep, pleasurable spot as he pressed into me. His hand slid down my belly, and found my clit. He stroked me lightly, just barely flicking his fingertips across my sensitive bud. Each stroke, inside and out, was a chord that seemed to echo through to my very soul. Each thrust was the drum beat, the tickle across my clit the thrumming bass. I throbbed for him, my whole body in harmony.

His pace quickened. Deepened. My face rocked into the pillow with each one of his punishing thrusts. My breaths came almost in sobs. My body was rioting, and my emotions were climaxing right along with it.

He started to do that thing I loved, where he pressed in as hard and deep as he could go, his hips rotating against me. I gasped. And that's all it took.

I came, my body clamping down around his. I jerked, but he held me still.

He picked the pace back up, plunging into my quivering body, still stroking my clit. He moved harder and harder, until it felt like he was spanking me with each thrust. My butt burned, the depth was intense, and my orgasm refused to end.

I got loud—probably even sounded like a dying baby animal. But he didn't quit stroking me. I moved a hand back to stop him and he grabbed my wrist, holding it, using it to control me.

My clit felt like it was on fire. The feeling ran through my whole pussy, escalating with each violent squeeze of my muscles around him. It went on, and on. I was shuddering, my body turning to jelly. If he hadn't been holding me, I would have slid down into a puddle on the sheets.

And I knew, this was me surrendering even more than before. He gave me pleasure when and how he wanted to, as much as he wanted to, and my only choice was to accept it. That's what he was telling me, covering me from behind, his weight pressing down on me, with his hand firm on my wrist and his cock making a place inside me. And there was absolutely no hiding that I loved it; he was soaked in the evidence of my enjoyment.

I concentrated on breathing, knowing I couldn't take much more. He was pushing me to the edge of sanity. I'd been cumming for what seemed like a millennia now, and I felt like I was going to explode, or perish, or in some other dramatic way spin out of control. Maybe that's what he wanted.

Because he didn't stop. He continued, thrusting, stroking. The area between us was a wet mess, and the sounds we made were graphic.

And I came again. And again. Until my womb cramped and I felt completely broken, yet free. Until I was barely clinging to consciousness, and I was drooling on my pillow. Until I was ready to acknowledge him as my master.

Then, and only then, did he allow himself his own climax. It came with a roar that filled the darkened interior of my cabin. His hands clenched, and he yanked me firmly back as he poured himself into me.

I felt a vague sense of relief, but much, much bigger than that was a burgeoning joy. The feeling was warm and fuzzy, and it evoked hearts and puppies. That imagery worried me slightly, but it was a worry I couldn't sustain. It was almost three in the morning, and the man behind me had worn me the hell out. I couldn't seem to keep my eyelids open, let alone hold onto a thought.

Gary pulled my knees out from under me, and pressed me belly-first onto the bed. Our sweat-slicked skin formed a heated weld, and his heart thumped against my back, racing just as hard as mine.

He kissed my cheek, and then rolled us onto our sides. I was completely boneless. All I wanted to do—all I *could* do—was lie there in his arms. We seemed to be on the same page, because he tucked me against him and pulled the blanket over both of us.

# Chapter Twenty-One

I was initially awoken by a scream. I started to get alarmed. But then I remembered what we'd done to my brothers, which they were probably just then discovering.

I smiled, and drifted back to sleep.

This is what woke me up the second time:

"They're fucking!"

My eyes flipped open to find Rory standing over my bed. Staring at me.

Staring at *us*, I realized. There was still an arm over my waist, a warm body curved against my back. *Shit*. He hadn't left.

"What?" The groggy voice came from downstairs.

"Helly and Gary are fucking!" Rory repeated. His bloodshot eyes had lost some of their wide-open shock, and were now starting to twinkle.

I waved at him, trying to get him to go away. I'd have hit him with a big fucking hammer if I had one, and if he was close enough. I didn't, and he wasn't. And if I lunged up out of the covers at him, he'd see boob.

"What, right now?" asked a disbelieving Zack.

Downstairs, somebody farted. Loudly.

I fell back against Gary with a groan, wishing I could disappear. He pressed his smiling mouth against my neck, unperturbed by my crazy family, and not caring that Rory still stood over us like a creeper.

"Good morning," Gary said, kissing the sensitive spot under my ear.

*Fuck it.* I leaned back and kissed him with lots of tongue, hoping to disgust my brother. He didn't seem disgust-able. He just watched.

"Dammit, Ror," I finally said. "What did I say about my personal space?"

He didn't look like he was gonna move, so I leaned out of bed, grabbed a shoe, and threw it at him. He dodged, and it sailed over the railing.

I winced as it landed on something in my kitchen with a crash.

Laughing, Rory finally slid down my ladder and out of sight.

I was still cussing when Gary turned my chin back around and kissed me again. By the time we broke apart, I'd hiked a thigh up over his hip, my fingers were dug into his hair, and I was panting.

I looked into his eyes, so close to my own. They were a beautiful green, shadowed by thick black lashes. "You stayed the night."

"Oops," he said. He didn't seem the least bit abashed about waking up in the same bed as me. His hand had come to rest on my knee, his thumb stroking little circles on my skin.

I lifted my head, peering out my window. The sun was up, the morning well-advanced. "So is this the key to getting you to let me sleep in?" I asked.

His mouth had moved up to nuzzle my hairline, and I heard him breathe in the scent of my mussed hair. "This?" he asked.

"Tiring you out. Wrapping myself around you, and not letting you escape." I remember I'd once thought about swaddling him in duct tape to get him to be silent. Hardly anything worked better than duct tape, but it appeared that I just might.

He laughed softly, making me very aware of the way my nipples pressed into his warm, broad chest. "Maybe."

"Gary! Come on down here, buddy. We wanna talk to ya." That sounded like Zack.

Gary raised his brows.

I shrugged. "They like to chase my boyfriends off."

His eyes were dancing. "Am I your boyfriend?"

"If I'm not just the flavor of the week, that might be okay," I quipped. I climbed out of bed, not wanting him to see how badly I didn't want to be just some fling for him.

"The flavor of week?" he asked.

"You know, the screamer the second night you were here, the Barbie doll in your shirt. 'Ga-ry'," I said, mimicking her shudder-inducing tones as I stuck my legs into a pair of pants.

He laughed. I liked that sound way, way too much.

"Just out of curiosity, was the first a blonde, too?"

He finally flung the sheet aside and rolled out of bed. "No."

I would have liked to have some witty reply, but the sight of the long, muscular length of him, and that bare ass, arrested my brain as well as my tongue. The rear view was downright spectacular.

We finally made it down the ladder, but it was dicey for a few minutes after he found me standing there topless, staring at him.

My brothers were gathered around the kitchen table. I looked back and forth between them, and then over toward the living area. The bottle of lube was missing.

*Ah, I see.* They were going to pretend nothing had happened. Hopefully that niggling doubt Gary spoke of had been well-planted, because I'd forgotten to take pictures.

Zack tossed my panties onto the table. "Have a seat," he said to Gary.

Gary looked at my brothers, and then at me, and I saw him do a mental *oh-what-the-hell.* He sat.

Zack loomed on the other side of the table like a hungover thug, with his arms crossed and his 'game face' on. Rory was making a pitiful attempt to match his brother's stern expression. And J.D.? Entertained, as usual.

"What are your intentions toward our sister?" Zack asked.

Gary looked at me, hesitating, and suddenly I didn't want to hear his answer. I was only all-too-aware he hadn't answered the flavor-of-the-week question.

"I'm gonna go start the generator," I muttered.

Either they'd come to an understanding, or they'd beat each other up. And I was beginning to think Gary could hold his own with my brothers, so I left him in there with them. After swiping my panties off the table, of course.

The air was warm outside, and smelled green. The sunshine pouring across my yard had chased all the mosquitos away. A thin tendril of smoke curled up from last night's fire pit, and the camp chairs sat around it just as we'd left them.

Dozens of beer bottles lay strewn about. I put my hands on my hips as I took in the wreckage, and added littering to my payback tally.

Then I found out the generator wouldn't start. I'd pre-warmed it, I did everything I was supposed to do, but got no turnover, not even a click. I tried all my usual tricks—tapping this, wiggling that, checking that it had fuel—but nothing worked.

Throwing my hands into the air, I stomped back to the cabin. "The generator won't start," I announced, noticing no one was bleeding.

They all looked at me like, 'And how is this *our* problem?'

"The generator charges the batteries, and the batteries are where we get electricity," I explained, slowly. "If I can't get that generator running, there'll be no showers, no video games. No internet," I said, using the only threat I knew would work.

J.D. practically ran out the door, quickly followed by Rory. To my surprise, Zack and Gary followed. I peeked my head out after them to make sure it wasn't so Zack could break his nose without getting blood on my rug, but all four of them were quickly engrossed in the generator. *Huh.*

I knew I wasn't going to be any help, and I figured if they were going to fix my generator, the least I could do was make breakfast. So I scrambled some eggs, burnt some toast, and headed back out to check on them.

As I was walking up, the generator coughed, backfired, and then roared to life. Gary was kneeling next to it, and as I approached, he looked up with a grin of triumph.

His expression morphed slightly as he saw me, his amusement coming through loud and clear. "Uh-oh," he said. "I'm in trouble now, aren't I?"

I was at a loss for a moment, and then I remembered my comment to Ed about using him for his mechanical skills.

The generator backfired again, and we all frowned at it. Then we realized it wasn't the generator.

It was gunshots.

# <u>Chapter Twenty-Two</u>

T here were gunshots coming from next door.

"What the heck?" I said. As you've probably gathered, gunshots were a pretty darn common sound in the bush, but these ones were coming from Gary's cabin, and Gary was standing right in front of me. It sounded like they were shooting something metal.

Gary was at the corner of my cabin and peering around so fast I didn't see him move. I looked over his shoulder, and saw several men with guns crawling over his property. One stood to the side with a shotgun, methodically blowing holes in Gary's helicopter.

*What. The ever-loving. Hell?* Were these the men that had been breaking into cabins?

Gary turned around and started herding me back toward my door. "Into the cabin," he ordered. "All of you. Now. And get your guns."

"My guns?" I hesitated for a moment, feeling a bit in shock. I talked big, and I waved my shotgun around, but I'd never thought I'd have to use them. Against *people*?

My brothers beat me to my gun cabinet. Zack put the Glock in my hands, and I stared at it like I'd never seen it before.

"I'll take the Remington 700," Gary said. It was the rifle with the scope, the one my brothers had been making neat little groupings with at a hundred yards away.

"But—" Rory started.

"I was a sniper in the marines," Gary said. Yeah, this was a surprise to me too.

Wordlessly, Rory handed him the gun.

Quickly and efficiently, Gary checked that it was loaded, safety off. He accepted a mostly-empty box of extra rounds from Rory. Then he lifted the rifle up to his shoulder, and looked through the scope and my window at the men on his property. I scooped up my binoculars and looked with him.

The door to Gary's cabin was open, and I could see them spilling back out into the yard, shaking their heads. They consulted with a man standing stationary in the chaos, a guy whose fashion sense seemed much in line with those thugs from the other day. He gestured toward my cabin. A pair of them started down the lawn toward us, guns in hand.

"Fuck," Gary said. He lowered the scope and turned to look at us. "These men are after me. They want me dead. I'm going to have to take them out, but I'm going to aim to disable. Use your guns as self-defense only, try not to shoot anybody unless you absolutely have to. I don't want you tangled up in this mess."

My brothers looked amped-up and eager to shoot something, but they nodded. I felt rooted to the floor, watching the men with guns jog along the beach, getting ever closer to my residence, my quiet, peaceful cabin, my favorite place in the whole wide world.

Looking at Gary didn't help—I didn't know this Gary, the one who looked calm and predatory when men with guns were coming for him. Who *was* he? And why did these men want him?

"We're sitting ducks in the cabin," he said. "Team up, go into the woods. I'm gonna start picking them off." Gary met my gaze, and the look he gave me seemed apologetic.

"Why don't you come with us?" I asked. I didn't want him hurt, that I knew. "They'll never find us in these woods, we can get to the river, take my boat—"

Gary shook his head. "I'm done running. I want to end this."

J.D. grasped my elbow. "C'mon Hel, you're with me."

I followed him out of my cabin, still feeling dazed.

Then the shooting began. They were loud shots, one and then

two. I turned in time to see the second guy topple to the ground before he reached the stairs up from my beach. I heard yelling, and through the trees I got glimpses of men pouring down from Gary's lawn. They were headed to my place en masse. A couple more gunshots rang out.

Then J.D. was dragging me into the woods. I winced and finally got my head in the game when a burning lash of devil's club whipped across my leg.

At about fifty feet in, I heard the rat-a-tat of a fully automatic weapon. I winced when I heard glass break. There was another loud rifle shot, and the other gun went silent.

After another several long strides, we hunkered behind an old stump, the currants and wild roses and clumps of grasses growing out of the top offering ample cover. I leaned to the side to peer toward my place.

Gary came out the door, hitting the ground in a single stride. He crouched down at the corner of my cabin, and started firing again. I watched him in awe. He'd shot for shit with the rifles earlier, but it was becoming obvious he'd been fudging it on purpose. Each of his shots was followed by a pained cry.

Branches snapped as a few of the men ducked into the trees at a spot level with my burnt blueberry patch. I heard a shot and then grunts, so I was guessing Zack and Rory had engaged.

A few more reached the stairs up from the beach.

Gary fell back to my generator shack, and then dropped another man on my lawn.

I saw movement from the corner of my eye. One of the men was creeping along the edge of the woods. Just twenty feet ahead of our hiding spot, he stopped and peered around a tree. He brought his gun up, waiting for Gary to stick his head back out.

My gun hand twitched upward. He'd said try not to shoot anybody, but I wasn't going to let Gary get shot. Even if he had told me some half-truths about his past.

"Stay here," J.D. whispered. He dashed out from behind our cover. He crossed the distance without seeming to touch the earth, and slammed a hard kick into the man's side before he had even turned. He struck his gun arm, the gun went flying, and then the other guy was just completely screwed. I winced as my brother ruthlessly pounded the man to the ground.

When I glanced toward Gary again, I saw he was fighting someone hand-to-hand next to my generator shack. The two seemed evenly matched, and the punches and kicks being thrown were brutal.

Movement on the lawn drew my attention to one of the men he'd felled. He was crawling toward his gun. And Gary was standing in the open, completely exposed.

I didn't even hesitate. I shed my cover and flew through the woods, disregarding devil's club and any bullets that might be flying my way. I sprinted out and kicked the gun out of the thug's hand just as his fingers started to curl around it. Then I stood over him, breathing hard, my gun aimed at his forehead.

I almost shot him when somebody grabbed me from behind. A hard arm wrapped around my throat, threatening to cut off my air, and a cold muzzle pressed to my temple.

"Drop your gun," a voice growled in my ear.

I dropped it, and the man dragged me along so that our backs were against my new shed. I could feel his knees pressing against the backs of my legs as he hunkered down, using me as cover.

When I looked up, I saw that the man Gary had been fighting was on the ground, and Gary had popped back out of sight.

"Gary, I've got your girlfriend!" the man yelled. Was this one of those situations where I was the last to know? "Drop your weapon and come out here," the man ordered. When I struggled against him, he dug the tip of that gun into my head, so I wised up and quit.

Gary peered around the building, and then stepped out, tossing the rifle away. The man holding me made a sound of satisfaction.

On our right, Rory stumbled up the steps from the beach. A huge guy came up after him, his gun pressed to my brother's back.

"I know she's got three brothers, and I wanna see all of you, hands up, or I shoot her," the man yelled.

"How do you know that?" I asked, tugging at his arm, trying to give myself some breathing room. I looked over at Gary, worried about him. He was watching me with a look that easily transcended 'worried'. Maybe I *was* his girlfriend.

"Gentleman by the name of Brett," my captor said. "He was actually pretty eager to sell you out."

I growled as J.D. and Zack stepped out of the trees and tossed their guns onto the ground.

"Let them go," Gary said. "It's me you want. I'm the one who shot your men."

Seeing them all so vulnerable, weaponless in the face of armed thugs, was making me angry. I tugged on the arm around my neck again. "Why are you doing this?" I asked, trying to buy them some time. My blonde hair had fallen loose, and I hoped I looked like a complete ditz. I needed them to underestimate me.

"Oh, you didn't tell your girlfriend what you did for a living, how you were able to afford that helicopter?" the man said, caressing my temple with that damn gun. His foul breath was against my cheek as he said, "He killed people for us."

"Who is us?" I asked, making sure my voice came out high and fearful. It wasn't much of a stretch.

"They're criminals. A drug cartel operating out of New Orleans," Gary said.

I stared at him. He wasn't denying it. He just stood there, looking wonderful, and he wasn't denying it. Damn me for always falling for the wrong ones.

"Gary betrayed us," the man hissed from behind me. "He botched a job, he got caught, and he rolled over on us."

I glanced at my brothers. J.D. was eyeing the guy holding Rory, and Rory was eyeing J.D. They both glanced over toward me as the man holding me began to rant about what a traitor Gary was.

Mocha chose that moment to make her entrance. She darted in from around the shed, and sank her teeth into my captor's calf. Snarling, she yanked his leg right out from under him.

He shouted, his gun hand flying out as he tried to catch his balance. We stumbled sideways, and his grip loosened.

I took my opportunity. In one swift movement, I stepped to his side, thrust my knee in behind his, and reach up over his back and around his face. I dug my fingers into his fucking eyes and yanked him over backward, slipping his hold.

Gary surged forward, knocking my captor to the ground almost before I was done with him. The man's gun flew out of his hand, Gary got his hands around his throat, and they started grappling.

"Run!" Gary growled.

I hesitated. I heard a shot, and turned to see that Rory and J.D. were fighting the man who'd been holding a gun on him. He was so frickin' big, J.D.'s blows weren't doing much. A few feet away, Zack was on the ground holding his side.

The blood leaking from between his fingers crystallized things for me. In a millisecond, my fear morphed straight to anger. Like hell I was gonna run. Nobody hurt my brothers. Nobody but me.

I scooped a gun off the ground.

Behind them, another man limped up from the beach, his eyes trained on them, his gun lifting.

I shot the bastard. He toppled back off the stairs.

I heard a branch snap, and whirled to shoot another one approaching through the woods. This one went down with a yelp, rustling brush as he fell.

I swung around, training my gun on the giant my brothers were wrestling with. They were moving fast, but the man who'd shot Zack was a pretty damn big target. I waited for my opening, and then I shot him, too. J.D. and Rory rode him to the ground.

Gary was on top of the guy who'd held me, pummeling him with angry fists. That fight was all but won, so I turned my attention to Zack.

Keeping my gun ready in one hand, I hurried over to my bleeding brother and knelt next to him.

"I'm okay," Zack croaked, when he clearly wasn't. He was kinda pale, and it wasn't a lot of blood, but the bullet hole was in his abdomen, and that couldn't possibly be good. I bunched his shirt over it and helped him apply pressure.

J.D. and Rory had restrained their guy, and I glanced over at Gary, wanting to help him, but saw that I didn't need to. The man who'd seemed to be their leader was barely fighting anymore, his punches weak pushes and bats to Gary's shoulders and sides. His face was a bloody mess.

Gary leaned back slightly — and then he snapped the guy's neck.

I looked on silently with all three of my brothers as he climbed off the guy he'd just killed. Gary was breathing hard, his fists bloody.

His eyes went immediately to me. "Are you okay?" he asked.

I nodded dumbly. I had no idea how I felt about all this. My brother was bleeding on my lawn. My newly minted boyfriend was some sort of hitman. I'd just shot three people. And I had a dozen dead and injured men on my property.

His gaze fell to Zack. "We need to call EMS."

What followed was a flurry of activity. The State Troopers came in their helicopter first, securing the scene. Then the air ambulance landed. They bundled Zack and two others onto gurneys, and left. The Troopers swarmed over my property, taking pictures and gathering evidence.

They took the five of us to Anchorage, where they took our statements. Rory, J.D. and I were released that evening, after it became a pretty clear case of self-defense.

Zack had had a bullet extracted from his gut, and was making jokes by the time the three of us showed up at his bedside. I sat with him in the hospital overnight, but it was obvious he was going to be fine. So the next day, I caught a flight home.

The Troopers were still doing their thing in my yard, but they let me into my cabin. I fed the dog, and then I sat down at my writing desk. I looked out my big picture window at my lover's cabin, and the bullet-peppered helicopter sitting out front. It was pretty out, not much different from the day he'd flown into my life.

A long crack in the glass obscured my view. I followed it up to a bullet hole in the upper corner of the window, which I could just imagine letting in mosquitos. There were some things I couldn't fix, but this...

I went and got my duct tape.

They didn't let Gary go for two more days.

In the meantime, I'd cleaned up after our little cookout. My brothers weren't coming back out, so I'd packed up their things and sent them to town.

I'd laced their clean underwear with itching powder. I *had* hesitated momentarily on Zack's, because he'd been shot and was in the hospital and all. Then I remembered a thirteen-year-old girl, near-naked in front of her entire family, her dress ripped from her by a flaming penis-mobile. Of course I spiked his, too.

Thursday afternoon, Gary stepped out of a float plane onto his dock. I had been trying to limp along, pretending it was life as usual, and that I didn't care, but the worry that they might not release him at all had been consuming my thoughts. It was painful, not knowing if I'd ever see him again.

So it was with a crushing kind of relief that I saw him step out of that plane. I'd gone out on the deck as the plane landed, and it was from there that I watched him approach.

He held my gaze as he climbed the steps up from the beach. He disappeared past the corner of the cabin, and a moment later, I heard the latch click as he let himself in.

"I thought we talked about trespassing," I called, turning to watch him through the open sliding door.

He paused as he noticed the ugly strip of grey tape across my window, and he must have been realizing it was covering a crack that had been caused by a bullet. From his shootout. "I'm sorry," he said. "I'll pay to have it fixed."

"There's a couple bullet holes in my siding as well. And one in my freezer," I added, even though we both knew the freezer had already been fucked. It'd been funny to watch the Trooper take a whole frozen roast with a slug buried in it. Even funnier, all of the Troopers had been really impressed with the gigantic pike on top of it.

"All of it," Gary said, watching me carefully. "I'll fix all of it."

"Don't bother with the siding," I said. An Alaskan cabin hadn't really 'arrived' until it sported a few bullet holes.

I liked that uncertain, squirmy look on him. The hitman looked uncertain. It was priceless, really.

"I'm sorry," he said again. "Can I explain?"

"Please do," I said, cool as a cucumber.

He stepped out into the light on my deck. "I was a sniper in the marines," he said. "I did that for the last seven of my nine years, and...I was ready to try something else. Maybe something where I wasn't killing people. So I got out. I was living with my friend down in New Orleans, and I was doing minimum-wage type carpentry jobs. I'd been looking into going to helicopter school, because I'd always loved to fly, but it turned out the GI bill didn't cover the initial Private Pilot, and only paid for parts of the Commercial rating. So I was trying to save up money, but I wasn't making enough to save. I went on like that for several months.

"And then one day, my friend came up to me, and he said he had this job for me. He showed me a picture of a drug dealer, and he said someone was willing to pay forty thousand dollars to have that man killed. He told me about some of the things this guy had done. The assaults, the murders...he was a really bad guy. Probably much, much worse than the people I'd killed when endorsed by the military. They were offering forty thousand dollars for me to wipe this scum off the face of the earth. That was most of my helicopter school right there. I said I'd do it. And I did.

"Well, a month later, here comes my friend again with another job. Another low-life, another forty thousand dollars. I was working my way through helicopter school at that point, and I'd found out it's hard to get the hours of flight time that you need for people to employ you as a commercial helicopter pilot. One of the best ways, it looked like, was for me to buy my own helicopter. And the way I figured it, a few more of these jobs, and I'd have it. So I did it. And I did another. And another. Pretty soon the organization started to trust me a bit, I suppose. They came to me directly, and I started to learn things about them. Things I wished I hadn't known."

Gary took a deep breath. "I got the helicopter. And I got some money put away beyond that—in stocks," he said with a wry little half-grin. "I was just thinking about telling them the next hit would be my last, when I got caught."

"If you got caught," I asked, "why aren't you in jail?"

"The DEA offered me a deal. If I testified against my employer, the drug cartel I was working for, they'd grant me immunity. I could go free. They even offered me witness protection, if I testified." He shook his head. "I think they only knew about the one attempted hit of mine; they were never able to pin the others on me.

"So yeah, of course I testified. These were criminals; I owed them nothing. I put the boss away, and a half dozen of his higher-ups. The man that was here, the one holding you, was his second-in-command and one of the only ones that got off. The cartel broke up with so many key players gone. So he was out of a job, and he was pissed.

"Like I said, they offered me witness protection, but I declined. I didn't want to live in hiding, or have a US Marshal keep me company for the rest of my life. So I took my commercial license, and my helicopter, and I moved up here. I'd always wanted to come to Alaska. I figured there'd be work, and they'd have trouble finding me if they tried."

"So, they're not pressing charges at all, for," I waved my hand at my bullet-ridden yard, "this."

He shook his head. "Self-defense. And actually, I think the DEA'd been hoping they'd try something."

I looked at him a long moment. He and I both knew he hadn't needed to snap that last guy's neck. The man had been defeated. Gary'd basically killed him in cold blood.

"Why did you kill the one holding me?" I asked.

Gary held my gaze. "He would have kept coming back," he said. "I never would have been safe. *You* never would have been safe. It was actually one of the easier kills I've ever made."

"And what about the three thugs on the riverbank?"

He winced and looked guilty as fuck.

"That really was their boat we saw when we were looking for mine, wasn't it?"

"Yeah," he admitted. "It was. I knew if I let them go, they'd lead the others right back to me."

I didn't ask him what he'd done with their bodies, but I had a pretty good idea. That river had a way of making things disappear.

"So you're a killer," I said. I suppose it should have been disturbing to me, but I'd been coming to terms with it these past couple days.

Life was tenuous in the Alaskan bush. Things died because people killed them. I killed fish daily. Just last week, my brothers had killed a bear. It was a bit of a leap from fish to bears, from bears to people, but it wasn't that big. That bear had threatened me, could have killed me, so we'd killed it. Those men had threatened us, and Gary had dealt with the threat.

I'd spent the last couple weeks with this man. He was loud, yeah. But he wasn't evil.

"Hitman is the official term," he said. "But I'm trying to quit. Trying to change. Like I told you, I just want peace and quiet, and to fly my helicopter for a living."

I scoffed. "Peace? Quiet? Bullshit. What about that huge party you had? If you'd just moved up, where did you even get all those friends?"

"I'd stayed in town for a couple months, long enough to realize I didn't want to live there." He shrugged. "What can I say? I make friends fast. People seem drawn to a handsome, single guy with a helicopter. As to the party: It was the Fourth of July."

I grunted.

He stepped a little closer, and his expression softened. "Will you forgive me?" he asked. "I know you didn't hear it, but what I told your brothers is true. I think you're amazing, and I want you in my life."

"Hard to stay out of it when I live right next door," I grumbled.

His gaze was discerning. "You're not really mad right now," he said. "I've seen you mad. But something's bothering you. Tell me what it is."

I sighed. "They took my guns," I admitted. 'Evidence', the State Troopers had said.

"Oh." He held out his hand. "Come with me."

"If I want to live?"

He grinned. "I'm not gonna hear the end of this, am I?"

"Nuh-uh."

He snagged my hand, and pulled me from my cabin. I trailed behind him across my lawn and down the steps to the beach, very aware of his warm hand wrapped around mine. He'd touched most parts of me, but he hadn't ever held my hand. It felt...really good.

As we walked over to his place, I noticed that we were wearing in a trail between our two cabins.

He led me up his lawn, past his maimed helicopter, and into his cabin. He tugged me into his bedroom, and for a moment I thought he was just gonna toss me on the bed and have his way with me.

But instead, he slid the closet door aside, and revealed a gun safe. And then he opened the safe door, to reveal...guns. Dozens of guns.

Drawn like a moth to a flame, I stepped closer.

"You can have anything here," he said. "Hell, you can have them all if you want."

I finally tore my gaze away from the forest of blue steel beauties, and I looked up at him. He had a look in his eyes, one that said he'd give me the world if I wanted it.

"What if I just want you?" I asked.

He stepped in close, his hand sliding warm and gentle against my face. "You can have that too."

# Epilogue
## *One Month Later*

"**Y**ou remember the first day we met, how I burned your blueberries?"

"Of course I remember." How could I forget? Because of him, there'd be no more blueberry pies. I was still a little sore about that. I understood Gary had to enter my life with a bang, because that was just the way he did things...but I wish he'd 'banged' something other than my blueberry patch.

We were a couple thousand feet up, high above the treetops in his helicopter. It was the end of August, getting on toward fall, and the landscape below us was taking on tints of yellow and orange.

It was my first day off in a week-long run of guiding, and Gary had scooped me into his helicopter immediately after he made me breakfast—pancakes with maple syrup and cheesy broccoli quiche. Yeah, I was a lucky woman.

"Did I ever say I was sorry?" he asked.

"No, you didn't." He'd reminded me I had yet to burn something of his in retribution.

"Well, I'm sorry," he said.

I nodded, but I was still planning arson. "Where are we going again?"

He smiled over at me, and I noted he hadn't gotten any less handsome now that we were getting along. "It's a surprise."

We were flying toward a low, rounded ridge that by Lower 48 standards probably counted as a mountain, but by mine it was a tall hill. The trees ended before the top, giving way to low shrubbery and then ground plants interspersed with rock.

The helicopter was losing altitude, so I figured that was our destination. I had seen Gary load up a blanket and a five gallon bucket with food—because we're classy like that—so I guessed he was taking me for a picnic. Of course, there was also a small pile of something back there he'd been careful to throw the blanket *over*.

I'd been out and about with him in his helicopter almost daily since he'd gotten it repaired after the shootout. Actually, we'd been thick as thieves since he finally told me the truth. I even went riding with him on his stupid jet ski—also after he'd gotten it repaired—and guess what? It actually was pretty entertaining, even if we were just roaring around in really big circles.

His construction was going well. He'd extended his living room six feet and put in a wall of windows. It wasn't entirely finished, but it was sealed up, so he'd been able to unhook the mosquito netting from over his bed. I knew this because we'd been sleeping together every night, either at my place or his. And lately, I'd been leaning toward his. Did I mention he had installed a Jacuzzi tub in his bathroom? I love my cabin to death, but it doesn't have a Jacuzzi tub.

Best of all, though, he's been respecting my sleep-in hours. If I'm at work, he starts hammering almost immediately after I leave—I know because sometimes I hear him even before I fire up my four-wheeler—but if I'm home, he waits until I've woken up. He also got me a pair of noise-canceling headphones for when I *am* home, and don't want to hear his noise. It's real sweet of him, and I try to say thank you in the best way I know how... Let's just say that in the past few weeks, I've gotten plenty of new material for my stories.

The massive pike in my freezer emerged unscathed by both bear and bullets. True to his word, Gary had sent it to be taxidermied. And because he thought I'd enjoy it more, he was going to let me hang it in my cabin. I was planning on putting it right next to the thugs' drone, which I'd dredged off the lake bottom and mounted high on my wall.

And Brett? The law hadn't come down on him like it should have, so Gary and I did instead. We paid him a visit, and Gary made him cry. It was beautiful, and even better: I haven't seen Brett since. And no, we didn't kill him.

Gary set the helicopter down on a bed of lichen and killed the engine. I climbed out, breathing in the clean, tall-hill air as I looked out over the rolling landscape. I could see everything from here, forest dotted with marshland, lakes and ponds, and cut through with winding rivers all the way out to the next mountain range. It still amazed me that a man who had all this available to him, who could go anywhere, had chosen the cabin next door to mine. I mean, my little lake is pretty amazing, but...

"I wanted to show you something," he said. He started down the hillside.

Now he really had my curiosity piqued. Who knew what he had out there. Maybe a jade boulder? I'd heard of people finding ones the size of Volkswagens. Or an albino moose? But how would you keep one of those in one spot? *Ooo*, a hidden cave or waterfall would be cool.

He stopped on a gentle slope dotted with knee-high greenery, and I almost bumped into his back. "We're here," he said.

"We're here?" I looked around. There was nothing special about this spot. Nothing special except—my vision snagged on a round shape, about the size of the tip of my pinkie, peeking out from behind a leaf. It was blue, and when I focused on it, I realized it was part of a clump of these round shapes, and the bush it was on had several clumps, and—*fuck me*—I was surrounded by these bushes.

"Blueberries," I uttered, feeling like the wind had been knocked out of my lungs.

"Yep." He had been watching my face, and now he started to smile.

Gary had taken me to blueberries. This was better than water in the desert. Better than breakfast in bed. Better, even, than sparkly things.

"How?" I asked. I knelt down and pulled gently at a clump. They were perfectly ripe, plump for Alaskan berries, and a whole handful came away in my hand.

"Well...I didn't know what blueberries looked like even after burning yours, and I didn't know where to look, so I enlisted your friend. Suzy and I went scouting, and we were able to find this patch one morning while you were at work."

I stood and emptied a couple blueberries into his hand. "Try," I said.

He popped them into his mouth and made the tart face. "Flavorful," he said.

I ate my own more slowly, looking at him contemplatively. He'd blown me away. This was the best present ever, and it wasn't even my birthday. Or Christmas. Maybe I wouldn't have to burn anything of his after all.

I stepped up to him and looped my hands around his neck. His hands came up to my waist, and I knew I had his complete attention as I said, "Thank you."

"You're welcome."

And then, right there on that puny mountainside, we shared a blueberry-flavored kiss. And another. And then one thing led to another, and that blanket got drafted for something besides picnic duty. Namely, cushioning my bare ass.

And that's when it started to rain. There was one damn cloud — barely a wisp, really — directly overhead, and it opened up and sprinkled on us. It was sunny, and yet it was sprinkling, so yeah, just another beautiful day in Alaska.

I laughed as water dripped from Gary's hair down onto my face. The man was forever getting me wet.

## THE END

# About the Author

Shaye Marlow is an Alaskan weirdo with a love of humor and sexy times. She is happily married, but does not have little people, a white picket fence, or a menagerie. She'd like to run on at length about her awards here, but she hasn't won any yet. Her hobbies include mass consumption of romance novels, breathing life into junker (not classic; junker) cars, hybridizing African Violets, crochet, baking, and woodworking.

Shaye has a website, shayemarlow.com. If you're into more interactive stalking, she's also on Facebook and Twitter, facebook.com/shaye.marlow and @shaye_marlow, where she enjoys chatting with her fans.

# Excerpt from
# *Two Captains, One Chair*
the second book in the Alaskan Romance series

Available Now, and Free with Kindle Unlimited!

A fter all that screwing around, I didn't have long to wait.

Ed's eyes fluttered open. He looked dazed. Disoriented.

I waited until some semblance of sense had started to seep into them. He looked around, and it appeared he was recognizing my cabin. Then his shoulders bulged as he tugged at his arms, and realized they were tied.

His gaze shot to me.

I smiled, uncrossed my legs in an extremely indecent way, and stood up.

He looked stunned, but it was no longer just from the tranq dart. He was taking in my attire. I saw his Adam's apple bob as he dragged his gaze from my face, past the tiny scrap of sheer satin and lace I was wearing, all the way down to the peep-toe that revealed my toenails were electric purple today. And sparkly.

"So. Ed," I said. I really, really wanted to maintain my poker face, but my smile couldn't be contained. I had him just freaking exactly where I wanted him, and neither of us would be running away. Not this time.

He swallowed again, his eyes stuck to the spot where my negligee in no way concealed the outline of my nipples. "Yeah?" he rasped.

"I was wondering if you could help me with something," I said. I twirled a strand of hair around my finger, going for mockingly guileless.

His gaze met mine. "Sure," he said. He did it in his innocent nice-Ed voice, as though I was soon going to forget that he'd threatened me with a sandwich.

I stepped closer, just between his knees. Gary had decided tying his ankles to the chair would be wise. Personally, I'd laughed at the idea of Ed trying to squeeze the life out of me with his legs, like that Russian James Bond lady... but I deferred to Gary's superior people skills. Ed was an unknown, he outweighed me by a hundred pounds, and we didn't have a chaperone, so I couldn't be too safe.

I reached toward Ed, and fingered the first button of his shirt. "You see," I said, "I've got this mystery I'm trying to solve. A couple mysteries, actually."

"The gold nugget," Ed said, swallowing again when the back of my knuckles brushed his neck. His first button slipped free, revealing an inch or two of his undershirt. Like I said, way too damn many clothes.

"Yes..." I brushed my fingertips along his skin just above his neckline for a moment, smiling when I felt his shiver. Ed was lots of things, but unaffected was not one of them. Inwardly, I rubbed my hands together in anticipatory glee. "...and the other one, the one I'm focusing on right now, is that of the dual-personalitied Ed and his merry band of kidnapping fishing guides."

"Mmm," he said. He seemed very distracted by what I was doing to his buttons, and his eyes were super-glued to my chest.

But he was still nice-Ed, and I wanted to see bad-Ed again. I wanted to see the one that had gazed up at me with those dark, promise-filled eyes, the one that'd loomed over me, trying to scare me off.

I yanked his shirt the rest of the way open, making buttons fly.

His chest tensed up, his pecs making an impression on the thin white cotton stretched over them. I licked my lips, looking over my newest obstacle. I could push that shirt up, but it would only go to his armpits.

I'd rather just have it out of the way. Giving him a little smile full of promise, I crossed to my knife drawer, and pulled out my kitchen shears.

*Now* I had his attention, as I moved back in front of him holding the big pair of scissors. I flexed my fingers a few times, watching his expression become just a little apprehensive. *That's right,* I thought. Scissors cut sandwich.

I lowered my shears to within a bare inch of his crotch, and could have heard a pin drop in the resulting silence.

"Sure you don't have anything to tell me?" I asked.

He shook his head. He wasn't even breathing, his eyes following those scissors as closely as if they were a poisonous snake.

I made the first snip up through the center of his shirt, revealing a couple inches of his tensed-up abs. I made the next, and the next, watching his face, his eyes, enjoying unsettling him.

If nice Ed were just a two-dimensional Nice Ed, I might feel bad about this. It'd be taking advantage, torturing him, stepping up to a point where he couldn't meet me. But I'd seen the other Ed; I knew he could handle it, and I honestly doubted he'd snap.

Only one way to find out for sure.

I tossed the scissors aside and spread the halves of his shirt apart. As I'd noticed before, Ed was built. He had a wiry strength, spare and perfectly proportioned. His pecs weren't overly bulky; they were firm and well defined, and he had a double row of abs marching down either side of his flat abdomen.

He had a damn cute belly button, I noted. I wanted to dip my tongue into it.

I looked into his eyes, which had narrowed somewhat on me. *There he is.*

I smiled lazily at him. I put a single fingertip in the dent between his collarbones, and started to trail it down his chest. "So. You're going to tell me," I said, "just exactly what you're hiding from me."

"You think you can get me to talk?" he asked. He seemed amused.

I leaned in further, until my mouth was a whisper away from his. "I can get *anyone* to talk."

He searched my eyes. "I believe that," he said, as his muscles jumped under my touch.

For someone with so much beard, he had surprisingly little hair on his body. I'd expected him to have a pelt under all those clothes, but he didn't. His skin was soft, just a shade or two darker than mine, and it stretched in the most glorious way over a whole lot of firm man.

"So we can do this the easy way," I suggested, as I smoothed my fingertips over the abs I'd been admiring. "Or—"

"Or we can do it the *hard* way?" Ed asked, a wry twist to his lips.

"Yes." I slid my hand into his lap, and squeezed him through his jeans. He was already hard, and way more than a handful. I started to breathe a little faster, a heady cocktail of excitement brewing inside me. I swayed toward him in a momentary lapse of self-control.

He shifted under my touch, and from his expression, I could tell that Bad Ed was in the house. "I think I prefer the hard way," he said.

That look on his face was pure challenge, and it made me burn.

I went for his fly, and his abs rippled as I slid my hand under the waistband of his underwear. He sucked in a breath as I wrapped my hand around him. Meeting his eyes, I held him, feeling his hardness, his size, and watched his cheeks flood with heat.

I pulled his waistband aside, and transferred my gaze. His cock was circumcised, and smooth, and rose several inches from his lap. In my few fumbling experiences with sex with clothes on, there hadn't been much left sticking out to work with. But, that didn't seem like it would be a problem here.

"I'm kinda small," I said, trying and failing to wrap my hand around him.

His mouth worked, and finally he was able to push out words. "You don't say," he said. His eyes fluttered closed as I rubbed the sensitive spot at the base of the head.

"Yes. It's gonna be a tight squeeze," I said in my innocent voice, watching his face. I squeezed him, then paused. "You sure you don't wanna tell me what I want to know?"

"Jesus, if it's going to make you stop, I would never." His chest heaved, and his hips moved subtly, pushing him into my hold.

"What if…" I slipped my hand away. "…I'll only continue if you give me something."

His lids lifted and he looked at me from beneath his lashes. "You are very cruel."

I licked my lips. "C'mon, tell me what you're up to," I coaxed. "Gimme some little tidbit. Some unimportant detail." I cupped my breasts, rubbing my hardened nipples through the silken material. I moaned as tremors of sensation ricocheted through me, and the covetous look in his eyes drove me higher.

Hell, maybe I should just go get one of my vibrators...

"Okay, okay," he said. "Just put your hand back on me. Please."

I did, and he shuddered. "Well?"

"I have a secret," he admitted.

I rolled my eyes. "More," I said. I pushed my hand back into his underwear, cupping his balls. I rubbed the warm skin with my thumb, feeling it shift and tighten in my hold.

His head rocked back, and he seemed to be hanging from my touch, breathing in rhythm with my strokes. His breath caught when I tugged lightly.

"More," I urged.

He groaned, and his eyes opened, focusing on me. "It has to do with gambling," he said.

"Gambling?" That was one of the last things I'd expected to hear. "Please tell me I'm not torturing you so you'll fess up to some private salmon derby."

"Torturing?" He laughed.

I shifted my hands back up to his shaft and squeezed him again, making his laughter cut off.

"No, no salmon derby. Please, continue your torture."

I slid my hand into my bodice and retrieved one of my breasts. He went quiet as my pink nipple came into view. It was about at his eye level, and fit perfectly into my small hand, and he wasn't looking at anything else as I rubbed and teased and squeezed the soft white flesh. My nipple was pouting at him, and he'd started to lean forward, doing a very good impression of me when I'd tried to kiss him earlier.

"You want a taste?" I asked.

"Oh yes. Please," he said, his voice deepened and raspy. I loved how free he was with that word. Every time he used it, I felt a giddy heat expand through me, softening me to his demands.

I had to be careful here, and remember who was tied up. And who was in charge.

I crowded between his knees, and leaned forward slowly, offering it to him.

I gasped as he captured my nipple—and most of my breast, really—in his mouth. I imagine he would have grabbed me and yanked me against him, but I fell almost into his lap. The effect was the same.

I braced my hands on his shoulders, seeing stars as he did wicked things with his tongue. "Oh…" I was panting, trying to figure out if I should be doing something, yet capable only of looking down at his thick dark hair, seeing my pale flesh disappear into his mouth, feel the tug as he sucked.

I groaned, my nails digging into him. I wanted to give him the other breast. I wanted to untie him and see what he could do with his hands. I wanted him to take me right here on my kitchen floor, just toss up my little pink skirt and push that thick cock deep into the pinkest parts of me.

But I *couldn't. Because I need info*, I told my desperately horny self.

Pulling away from him was one of the hardest things I'd ever done.

He groaned a protest, and looked up into my eyes, and we were totally on the same page. The same paragraph, even. Maybe even the same word.

"More," I said.

"That's what I'd like to give you," he growled. "If you'd just come back here." Nice Ed had been thoroughly banished, and this one squeezed his knees around my thighs, trying to tug me closer.

"Details," I elaborated. "Give."

"Fuck," he said, looking hot and bothered and frustrated because I'd tied him up, and he couldn't do a damn thing about me withholding my nipple.

Why did I like it so much when he cussed?

"Suzy," he panted. "Baby. I can't tell you. I simply can't do it. You're a gossip. You have a loose tongue. You'd be a liability to the business. You'd get us caught, and then we'd be shut down. Not to mention 'prosecuted to the fullest extent of the law'. But if you just bring that beautiful breast of yours back over here, I promise, I will pleasure you to the fullest extent of—"

I grabbed his head, and looked straight into his eyes. "You listen to me," I said. "I can keep a secret. Hell, Gary's gonna ask Helly to marry him on the Fourth of July, but have I told anyone? No."

"You just told me," he pointed out, as the corners of his mouth crept upward.

"Yeah, but you won't blab."

"Like hell I won't. If you don't untie me, I'm gonna tell everyone."

I frowned at him. "I've got you tied up. You're supposed to be trying to convince me to let you go. Don't you think what you're saying is counterproductive?" I asked, throwing his own words back at him.

I was sure underneath that beard was a moue of disgust. "You suck," he said.

"I could," I replied.

He swallowed hard.

"So it's a business, huh? A gambling business. Tell me more," I said.

Then I dropped to my knees.

"Oh holy fuck," was what he told me. He wiggled on the chair, straining against the ropes.

I smiled because cussing was good. Cussing meant he didn't have this situation under control. Cussing meant he was worried.

I kissed his knee. Then the other. Then I smoothed my hands up his thighs and moved between them. My bare breast rubbed against the rough material of his pants as I leaned in.

I caught him in my hands again, noticing he was even bigger, even harder than the last time I'd touched him. A bead of precum welled at his tip, making my mouth water. But this was my trump card, and I had to be careful how I played it.

"What else do you want to tell me?" I asked him.

"You're beautiful," he said.

I smiled. He was definitely worried, throwing out things he hoped would divert and distract me. But, at this point, I had what some would probably call a single-minded focus.

I flicked out my tongue, and licked around the crown of his cock.

"Jesus God! Fuck!"

"You want more?" I wanted to give him more, so at this point I supposed it didn't really matter what he wanted. Though I suppose, if he started screaming rape, I'd have to let him go.

But he didn't cry 'rape'.

Instead, he said "Please!" and nudged his hips toward me.

"Spill," I said. The feel of his cock was making me wet, the soft skin that moved slightly over his rigid hardness as I rubbed him. He throbbed in my hands.

I wanted him inside me. One way or another.

He gazed at me through slitted eyes. "You're a hard woman."

"And you're a closet thug," I said. "Now tell me what I want to know, and I'll give you what you want." I rubbed my lips down his shaft and back up, nuzzling him.

He shook his head, the movement hard, as though he were telling himself 'no' as much as me.

I licked off the bead of precum that'd been teasing me. I licked him a few more times, drawn in by the taste of him, the catch of his breath, the way his thighs tensed under my hands.

"Suzy," he groaned. I loved the sound of it, like it was being dragged from his depths, a ragged, desperate plea.

Looking up into his eyes, I sucked him into my mouth. I slid down on him. Then further, until he was pressing into my throat.

He was watching me as I took him, and I didn't gag, and I think he got my point. His eyes had gone glassy, his cheeks were dark, and his breath heaved. His muscles rippled as he tugged at his restraints, and a fine sweat had sprung up across his chest. He wanted me so badly, I could feel it, like some relentless magnetic pull.

I pulled up, caressing him with my tongue, and then plunged down on him again, taking frickin' all of him.

"Oh, shit. For the love of... Suzy," he moaned. "Suzy, Suzy." He gasped as I slid up again, and squeezed his head between my lips. I reached up and scraped my nails gently down his abdomen.

He jerked, and his shoulders strained, and if it hadn't been a sturdy chair, I would have been screwed. When he opened his eyes again, they were on fire. "On my lap," he barked. "Now."

**Wondering how the hell Ed wound up in that chair?**
**Get *Two Captains, One Chair* to find out!**

Made in the USA
Middletown, DE
02 June 2020